NINE DAYS IN VEGAS

QUINT ADLER BOOK 4

BRIAN O'SULLIVAN

BIG B PUBLISHING

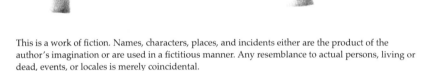

This is a work of fiction. Names, characters, places, and incidents either are the product of the author's imagination or are used in a fictitious manner. Any resemblance to actual persons, living or dead, events, or locales is merely coincidental.

NINE DAYS IN VEGAS

❀ Created with Vellum

This novel is dedicated to all the late bloomers out there!
If you had told me in my twenties and early thirties I was going to be a novelist, I'd
have said you were crazy.
And you would have been.
And yet, here we are!
It's never too late to follow your dreams.

PROLOGUE

More than any other city in the world, Las Vegas seems to divide people along love/hate lines.

It makes sense. There are ample reasons for both.

I love it because of the lights, the hotels, the gambling, and the gorgeous women.

Not to mention there is world-class dining and pre-eminent architecture. The city really does have it all.

And yet, I was currently siding with the people who despise Vegas.

Why?

Well, when it's a hundred degrees in the middle of the desert, you have a shovel in your hand, and you're trying to excavate the body of a twenty-two-year-old woman, you tend to focus on the negative.

Especially when your shovel just struck bone.

PART 1: A MISSING SHOWGIRL

CHAPTER 1

FRIDAY

(Six days earlier)

My ex-girlfriend, who had been my girlfriend only minutes before, left me with a warning:

"Private investigators usually turn into assholes," Cara Hudson said. "Don't become a stereotype, Quint. Be tough when you need to be. And don't give the bad guys any leeway. You've always had a good soul and been fair with people. I don't want you to lose that just because you've become a PI."

That's me. Quint Adler, a crime reporter turned private investigator. Although, I felt more like a punching bag at the moment.

Above all, I was sad.

Cara and I had been together for most of the last decade, with several of these mini-breaks thrown in, though this was undoubtedly the worst. There was some real anger on her end.

Cara was smart, beautiful, and loyal. It was me who had fucked this up. And even though I hadn't physically cheated on her, I'd chosen a case over her, and spent a lot of time with a woman who wasn't her.

Like she'd told me when my recent murder investigation in Hollywood ended, "There's different kinds of cheating."

She wasn't wrong.

When I arrived back at our apartment in Walnut Creek, twenty miles east of San Francisco, we tried to get past it. We had a pleasant month spent largely in bed, where we were always on the same page.

When not engaged in carnal activities, we were cordial, and despite the underlying tension, we got along well enough.

But then I fucked up again.

I'd become restless with no new job opportunity. The Hollywood case had been my first, and to this point, only foray into private investigation. I had been paid handsomely, thanks to an eccentric Hollywood millionaire, but I was now hemorrhaging money and needed a gig.

As we watched T.V. on a random Friday in late May, I broached the subject to catastrophic results.

I told Cara about Abel Peters, a man I'd met in Los Angeles, and the story of his niece, a twenty-two-year-old showgirl who'd gone missing in Las Vegas.

"Then go to Vegas if that's what you want," Cara said, obviously upset.

"I'm a PI now, Cara. If I'm offered a case, I have to take it. If not, we'll end up eating at some soup kitchen."

"That's weird. I watch the news every day, and I know there's crime in the Bay Area. And yet you want to go to Las Vegas."

"You have to be hired, Cara. I don't have a job here. I do have one if I'm willing to travel to Vegas."

"You do remember what we've been fighting over, correct? About you spending too much time with another woman. And now you want to go hang out with a showgirl in Sin City? You must understand why that stings!"

"I'm trying to find a missing showgirl, not spend time with her," I said, trying to plead my case.

"I'm sure you'll spend some time with her twenty-two-year-old friends."

"That's unfair," I said.

"That's only a few years younger than what's her name!"

"I never touched her," I said.

And I knew what was coming next.

"Like I've said ten times, there's different kinds of cheating."

"If you are just going to crucify me every day, what's the point?" I asked.

That was a big mistake.

The conversation continued to deteriorate and she broke up with me a few minutes later.

We were silent for several minutes after.

Finally, in front of Cara, I called Abel Peters and told him I'd take the job.

"You're really going to take this case?" she asked.

"You just broke up with me. And I have exactly one job opportunity."

"Whatever," Cara said, which, coming from her, was as cutting as any swear word.

"When I come back from Vegas, we'll have a longer talk," I said.

She shrugged and I didn't think she was going to say anything.

I was wrong.

"I might be in a new apartment by the time you get back," she said. "Can I be honest, Quint?"

"Of course."

"I still haven't forgiven you for what happened in Hollywood."

"Yeah, I know," I said succinctly.

~

I quickly started packing for Vegas. Cara, meanwhile, was grabbing her own clothes, intentionally getting in the way of what I was doing. Our apartment was a mess, just like the current state of our relationship. Or, former relationship, as it were.

I booked a flight to Vegas, making my trip official, which caused another round of arguments. It was getting exhausting.

"Can we not end it like this?" I finally asked.

Cara looked me over to see if I truly meant it. She then nodded in agreement.

"I'm sorry. I still love you, Quint. I'm just not sure a healthy relationship is possible with a PI who travels for each case."

It stung, because it was true.

"I still love you too," I said. "And eventually, I'll build a business here in the Bay Area. For now, though, I have to take the cases I get offered, because there won't be many of them at the beginning."

For the first time since we'd started arguing, I saw some compassion in Cara's eyes.

"I get where you're coming from, Quint. It's just hard being a woman and knowing you're going to be up and leaving for each new case."

"And I get your concerns, Cara. Let's talk in a few days once we've both settled down."

That's when she looked me in the eyes and warned me about becoming an asshole like so many other PIs.

I took her warning to heart and told her I wasn't going to change. I hoped I was right.

I pulled out my cell phone and looked at the time.

My flight was still over two hours away, but I figured the time would be better spent at the airport than our powder keg of an apartment.

I left ten minutes later and headed to the airport.

There was the briefest of kisses and a half-hearted hug goodbye.

I loved Cara, and she loved me, but there was no love lost at that moment.

~

I took an Uber to the airport. My mind remained on Cara, despite trying not to think about her. If we were going to take a physical break, a mental one might be beneficial as well. We'd both been too high strung lately.

I arrived at Oakland International Airport and checked my duffle bag with the Sky Cap, keeping my backpack with my trusty laptop for myself. I'd never check that in.

Airport security took more than thirty minutes to get through and my flight was a mere hour away when I arrived at the gate.

I tried giving Abel a call, but he didn't answer.

I had some time to kill and started listening to a jazz playlist on Spotify. It's one that had calmed my nerves over the years.

But it didn't work. I was still fired up about how it ended with Cara, at least for now. With our history, I couldn't rule out us getting back together down the line.

Another voice told me that going to Vegas to investigate a missing - and likely dead - showgirl wasn't going to be pleasant. And no amount of Miles Davis or John Coltrane was going to settle that uneasiness.

Forty minutes later, the loudspeaker notified us we were to begin boarding. I called Abel again and this time he answered. I asked him for a more detailed rundown of his niece's disappearance.

"I'll start at the beginning," Abel said. "It'll give you a better understanding of Emmy as a whole."

And he started.

~

Emmy Peters was the daughter, and only child, of Chance Peters and his wife, Liz. Chance was the older brother of Abel. Emmy was an intelligent, and often precocious child, who was the apple of her parents' eyes. They tried to make Emmy a big sister, but Liz's ovaries wouldn't cooperate and despite years of trying, they were never able to have a second child.

After an idyllic childhood growing up in Torrance, just inland from Redondo Beach in Los Angeles, the family moved forty miles north to Bell Canyon, a rich, gated community. Emmy was only fifteen and about to enter her freshman year of high school. It was a tough time for any girl, to be sure, especially one who just moved.

Chance Peters was the Vice President of a dot com company specializing in fitness, and they'd come out with a self-tracking wristband that put the Fitbit to shame. When his stock options kicked in, Chance was an instant multi-millionaire.

So, he decided to move the family into a house that fit his pay grade. Torrance was fine, but it had nothing on Bell Canyon and its beautiful, sprawling views of the mountains. More than a few celebrities called it home as well, which Chance never failed to mention.

Emmy hated it immediately. She was now an hour from her friends in Torrance and considering it was a posh, gated community, it felt more like five hours. Emmy met a few friends, but her parents knew she wasn't happy.

Chance Peters was no dummy, and could sense this was happening, but hoped Emmy would grow into loving Bell Canyon. And for a while, it seemed like she did. Emmy made more friends through her freshman and then sophomore year of high school.

She would still remind her parents that her best friends would always be the ones she grew up with in Torrance, but she had acclimated to Bell Canyon, which was all her parents ever wanted. Liz and Emmy had a very nice mother/daughter relationship, with the occasional fight thrown in, which was seemingly inevitable with a teenage daughter in the house.

Emmy had long been a great dancer. Ballet was her go-to, but she could do it all. She'd been taking classes since she was seven and this continued during high school. Chance and Liz weren't sure if it was just for fun, or a potential career down the line, but Emmy loved it, so they kept paying for the classes.

As her junior year wound down, Emmy started applying to colleges. As her social stature grew - she'd become quite popular - her parents noticed that her grades were suffering. While UCLA, Chance's alma mater, had appeared likely after her freshman and sophomore year, it was now out of the question. This drove Chance nuts, and he would have done or paid anything to get Emmy in, but with the recent scandals of rich parents getting their kids into college, he knew better than to push it.

Emmy was extremely smart so this became a huge point of contention for her parents. They'd tell her that having a 3.4 GPA didn't belie the intelligence she'd been born with. Emmy would tell them her grades suffered because she was always trying to make new friends like the ones she'd left behind in Torrance.

It wasn't a very good excuse, but it still cut deep with her parents.

When her college admissions came back, UCLA had declined her. So had UC Berkeley. And UC Santa Barbara. And UC San Diego. The only UCs that Emmy had gained acceptance into were UC Riverside and UC Irvine.

Her admissions had been very UC centric.

Chance was still holding out hope she'd eventually go to UCLA and advanced the idea of Emmy going to a community college for two years and then transferring in. Emmy said she wouldn't be attending a CC after earning a 3.4 GPA.

Maybe it wasn't good enough for UCLA, but it was far too accomplished to attend a CC.

The two were at a standstill, with Liz Peters supporting whatever her daughter decided. Emmy didn't really want to go to Riverside or Irvine, and Chance didn't much like this idea either. Those two were not considered top-notch UCs. He'd have preferred the Community College route.

Emmy came up with an alternative plan.

She'd applied to a few non-UC schools and one of them, The University of Nevada, Las Vegas, had accepted her.

She proposed going to UNLV for two years, getting good grades, and then transferring to UCLA. While Chance didn't love the idea of his daughter living in Las Vegas, she'd been so adamant that she'd do well and eventually transfer to UCLA that she won him over.

Plus, one of Emmy's favorite relatives, Duncan Hobbes, lived there. A former private detective, Chance hoped Duncan could keep Emmy out of trouble. That was probably a stretch, but it gave Chance some added comfort.

Liz Peters just wanted what was best for her daughter. She, like her husband, wasn't sure Vegas was the ideal spot for a young woman, but Emmy would say how UNLV was an up and coming school and she'd rattle off all its good programs, including nursing and computer science.

Emmy won out in the end, with two stipulations from her parents.

She couldn't work on the Las Vegas Strip. And she had to come back home once a month.

Emmy agreed and signed her letter of admission to UNLV.

At this point in Abel's story, I had begun boarding my flight to Vegas. I told him to pick up the pace.

Emmy started attending UNLV and she excelled immediately. She received two As and two Bs in her first semester. Her second semester was even better. Three As and one B. Her parents were ecstatic.

Chance Peters just knew his daughter would be transferring to UCLA after her second year. But it didn't come to pass.

Emmy grew to love UNLV and Las Vegas itself.

She ended up staying all four years and graduating with honors.

There would always be a part of Chance that regretted her never going to UCLA, but Emmy had graduated from college with great grades. He couldn't really complain.

Chance and Liz were a bit surprised when she decided to stay in Vegas after her graduation. They thought it was the type of city that you'd grow sick of after four years, but that wasn't the case with Emmy.

Chance's company was still thriving and Vegas was a fun city if you had a lot of money, which he did. So while they weren't thrilled she'd stayed in Vegas, Chance loved visiting his daughter every few weeks. He'd fly on private jets and take Emmy to all the best restaurants that Vegas had to offer.

I had entered the airplane, still listening to Abel give me the rundown on Emmy.

"Abel, you've got to be quick. I'm on the plane."

"And then, right after graduation last year, Emmy made an odd decision," Abel said.

"What was it?"

"She decided to become a showgirl."

"That does seem odd. especially after just graduating. Why did she?"

"She'd chosen to enter your old field."

"Journalism?"

"In a way. Emmy decided that she wanted to become an author."

"I wrote, but I wouldn't consider myself an author," I said.

"Close enough," Abel said.

"Then why become a showgirl? Surely her father would have paid for her."

"Without question. But Emmy was stubborn. She wanted to make her own money. She'd remind her father that he was self-made and she wanted to be the same. So, she'd be a showgirl for a year or two, all while writing her first novel. She told her parents it was better than many other jobs a woman could get in Vegas."

"Hard to argue with that," I said.

"And she said it wasn't crazy hours, so she'd have time to work on her novel. She'd also remind her parents that it was they who had paid for all those dance lessons when she was a kid."

"I like how Emmy thinks," I said.

"She is smart, without question, and hard-headed in a good way."

I noticed how Abel kept talking about Emmy as if she was alive, even though he must have had his doubts.

I found my seat, and having signed up for the flight only a few hours in advance, was stuck in the back of the plane.

I was one of the last to be seated and I knew the flight would be taking off soon.

"Have to wrap this up, Abel. At least for now. We can talk when I land."

He started talking rapidly.

"Emmy moved to Summerlin, about twenty minutes outside of Vegas. Chance said he talked to Emmy on January 9th, 11th, and 14th of this year. She had completed her training and was enjoying being a showgirl. She'd even finished the first few chapters of her debut novel. The whole family seemed happy. Chance called Emmy around four p.m. on Friday, January 16th, but Emmy didn't answer. It wasn't like her, so he tried again without a response. His wife called as well, with no luck either. Chance had our relative who lived in Vegas, Duncan Hobbes, go check to see if she made her showgirl gig that night. Emmy had been a no-show and that's when Chance really got scared. He called the police and said he'd be arriving in Vegas the next morning. He asked them to do a welfare check on her apartment, but she wasn't there. They asked her roommate, who had no idea where she'd gone. Emmy hadn't been acting weird, the roommate let the officers know. The officers relayed the information to my brother. Chance was rightfully scared and booked a private jet that flew them to Vegas at five a.m. the next morning," Abel said.

The pilot got on the loudspeaker telling us we had to turn off our phones.

"Abel, we are about to take off. We'll have to continue this when I land in Vegas."

"I'm almost done," he said. "Chance and Liz arrived in Vegas, and there has never been one solid clue in the disappearance of Emmy. No gambling debts. No scary people hanging around. No blood in her apartment or car."

I saw the stewardess approaching me and I knew what was coming.

"Sir, you have to hang up your phone," she said.

"I've got to go, Abel. I'll call you when I get situated."

"She just vanished into thin air, Quint."

The sadness in his voice was crushing.

"I'll do what I can," I said.

"I have faith you'll find something. Talk soon."

On that note, I hung up.

The stewardess was still looking at me, so I put my phone in my pocket.

"Thank you," she said, with more than an air of condescension.

I closed my eyes and thought about the conversation with Abel.

My initial impression was that if Emmy was going to be found, it wouldn't be alive. Over four months had passed. These cases usually didn't end well.

A voice could be heard over the loudspeaker.

"This is Captain Conover. I have the privilege of being your pilot on this beautiful May day. I hope you are all ready for beautiful Las Vegas, or Sin City, as some people like to call it."

Some people around me laughed.

I did not.

I was too busy thinking about Emmy Peters.

And scared to discover what sins had been carried out on her.

CHAPTER 2

The plane landed safely, but not before a bumpy ride coming in. That seemed to be the norm when flying into Vegas. I know it's not God telling you to beware, but it might as well be.

I've been through scores of airports and most of them just blend together. McCarran International Airport is different. I don't know if it was the slot machines, the excitement of the people arriving, the hangovers on the departing faces, or something else. Whatever it was, you always knew when you were at McCarran.

It stood out like a sore thumb, but a fun, wild thumb.

I picked up my checked bag and made my way outside, where I stood in the cab line for nearly forty-five minutes. It was my own fault, flying into Vegas on a Friday night at 6 p.m. It was an amateur hour decision by yours truly. Although, it's not like I had much of a choice. The break-up with Cara had forced my hand.

I could have ordered an Uber, but for some reason, I'd always been old school when it came to airports and inevitably headed towards the cab stand.

Finally, I arrived at the front of the line.

It was at this point that I realized I probably should have just rented a car. I was going to be investigating all over town, after all. I decided I'd waited in the line this long, I might as well just take it. I'd get situated for the night and come back and rent a car the following morning.

I entered the cab.

The driver was quiet and only spoke when I asked him a few questions. Mainly, I asked how the town had changed. Perhaps no city in the world changed quicker than Vegas. And while it had only been two years since I'd visited, that's an eternity in Vegas time. I was sure some new hotels or casinos had popped up and my driver let me know about a few.

I took in all the lights as we made our way to the Strip. That never got old.

I was staying at the Cosmopolitan. Maybe not Vegas royalty, but it wasn't Circus Circus either. Abel Peters had been very generous in agreeing upon The Cosmo, or sometimes just Cosmo, as it was called.

Well, truth be told, Chance Peters was paying for it. I just negotiated with Abel.

The irony that I was being put up in another hotel for a week, just like in Los Angeles, didn't go over my head. I realized just how crazy the last few months of my life had been.

I was given a per diem of $100. I'd usually say that's very generous, but $100 in Vegas lasts about as long as the spin of a Roulette wheel.

Along with the hotel and per diem, Chance Peters had set up a very generous pay scale. It was also tremendously sad.

When I'd landed, Abel had texted me the numbers that Chance had come up with.

For spending a week in Vegas and investigating the case, I was being paid $2,500.

Abel made it clear that I would be handsomely rewarded if Emmy was somehow found alive. With much less fanfare, he said I'd also receive a bonus if my investigation led to Emmy's body or the killer being identified.

I understood why he included it, but man, was that tough to read.

Before I knew it, I was dropped off in front of The Cosmo. I turned down the offer of a bellhop. I could handle a backpack and one rolling duffle bag. I was forty-one years old, not eighty-one.

I checked in and made my way up to my room. It was eight p.m. on a Friday night, and I knew starting the investigation the following morning made a lot of sense. On the other hand, this was Vegas! I wasn't just going to sit on my ass.

When he'd texted me the financial arrangements, Abel also gave me the names of six people who might help me get started on the investigation. Four of them were friends of Emmy's, two of which didn't even live in Vegas anymore.

I would not be calling them. It felt wrong to invite a twenty-something out to the Strip on a Friday night, even if it was just to talk. I was a lot of things, but a creepy old-ish man wasn't one of them.

Truth was, I missed Cara. We'd had several great trips to Vegas over the course of our relationship. And every single one of them included many rounds of great sex. There was something about this city.

I felt myself getting distracted and tried to keep my mind on the case.

The fifth person was the private investigator who also happened to be a relative of the Peters. Duncan Hobbes was his name. Abel had mentioned him in his rundown of Emmy. Although he was a retired private detective, Abel said he'd helped a little bit in the early stages of Emmy's case. He asked me to wait until Saturday morning to contact him. He didn't say why.

The sixth, and final number that Abel had left me was that of Kenneth Croy. Croy worked on the Strip at the Bellagio as a blackjack dealer. Judging by his picture, he was quite a bit older than Emmy.

Apparently, Emmy had been dating him off and on.

I texted him, but didn't hear back.

I could have easily just walked around the Cosmo and gotten my bearings. It was my first night, after all. That's not how I'm wired, as you might have guessed.

I went downstairs and got in the cab line. This time it only took a few minutes.

And I was off to the Bellagio.

Maybe Kenneth Croy hadn't texted back because he was dealing tonight. I could stand for a few hands of blackjack, put that per diem to work.

Kenneth Croy was tall, dark, and handsome, with a mischievous smile to boot. Usually, that wouldn't sway my opinion one way or another, but since he was dating a woman much younger than him, I didn't like the sly smile, and assumed he was a scumbag.

That probably wasn't fair. I started dating Cara when she wasn't much older than Emmy. I had only been thirty, though, while Croy was probably in his mid to late thirties.

I decided to give him the benefit of the doubt, with the very distinct possibility I'd quickly be rescinding it.

I'd always liked the Bellagio, one of the most well known hotels on the Strip. It was a beautiful resort, possibly most famous for the epic fountain sitting on Las Vegas Boulevard. They now had a rotation of songs played, but *Time To Say Goodbye* by Andrea Bocelli had always been the song people thought of when the fountains came to mind.

Croy was easy to recognize from the pictures Abel had sent me. Just to be positive, I looked at his name tag. Sure enough, it said Kenneth.

I'd eventually have to tell Kenneth Croy who I was, but I first wanted to get an impression without him knowing who I was.

He was dealing at a $25 minimum table, another drawback of getting to Vegas on a Friday night. They upped all the table minimums. Also, I was at the Bellagio, not some rinky-dink casino downtown.

I grabbed a hundred dollar bill and reminded myself to behave. I was in Vegas to earn money, not waste it at the tables.

"Changing a hundred," Croy said.

The pit boss gave me a cursory glance only. A hundred dollar bill was like a penny for a place like the Bellagio. If I'd bought in for a thousand dollars, the reaction probably would have been the same. Big gamblers in Vegas were measured in the tens of thousands.

I laid out one of the four $25 chips I was given.

I was dealt a seven and a four for an eleven. The dealer had a seven showing.

There was no question what I had to do.

"Double down," I said.

Kenneth Croy gave me a queen. A twenty-one!

After busting his hand, he pushed the two extra $25 chips in my direction.

"Nice start," Croy said.

"Thanks."

I decided I had to make some small talk if I was going to get anything out of him.

As he dealt the next hand, I asked, "Been in Vegas long?"

"About seven years. Which is like thirty years in any other city."

I thought of Hollywood and how that aged people. I'm sure it was true of Vegas as well.

"I have no doubt. I can usually only handle a weekend."

I had an eighteen and the dealer showed a seven once again.

"I'll stay," I said.

Croy turned over a ten, for a seventeen total, and I won another $25. The other people on the table, two women who looked to be in their seventies, had won also.

"You're good luck," one of them said to me.

"The gambling gods seem to like me."

They smiled.

"Where are you from?" Kenneth Croy asked.

"The Bay Area," I said.

The conversation was boring and I'd already formed my initial impression of the man. Measured. In control. Unflappable. And other similar words.

So I decided, sooner than I probably should have, to amp things up a little bit.

"But it's a friend from Los Angeles who actually brought me here," I said.

It was cryptic and I looked to see if Croy was affected by it. He showed nothing.

"Oh, yeah?" he said. "Two old friends hanging out on the Strip?"

And that's when I stuck the knife in.

"No, he's having me investigate the disappearance of his niece," I said.

His expression quickly changed. Not that I could blame him. His eyes narrowed and I was surprised at what he said next.

"Let me guess, Emmy Peters?" he said, very quietly.

"You got it."

He dealt another hand. I had seventeen and stayed.

He whispered again.

"I like my job. Can we please talk on my break?"

He had a point.

The older women looked on, wondering what was going on. This polite guy who had just sat down seemed to have riled up the dealer.

"Sure. We'll talk later," I said.

He finished the hand and busted. I was now up $100.

I grabbed my chips and subtly placed a business card on the edge of the table.

"I'm staying at The Cosmo. Call me if you'd like to talk."

I turned to go.

And then I flipped him one of the $25 chips.

"Thanks," I said.

He grabbed the chip and hit it twice on the felt, in recognition of the tip.

But there was no smile. Instead, just a pissed off glare.

I hit the cashier, and even with the $25 I'd tipped him, I was still up $75. Not a bad start.

I spent the next half hour walking around the Bellagio, taking in my surroundings. Beautiful women. Sharp dressed men. Expensive dresses. Tailored suits.

I saw a high limit Baccarat section. Their minimum bet was probably something like a grand. It put the $25 of the blackjack table to shame.

At one point, I circled back around towards the blackjack table and I saw Kenneth Croy peering at me. I couldn't blame him. If the roles were reversed, I'd be doing the same.

One minute I'm the new player at the table, winning $50 on my first hand. And the next minute I'm asking him about the case of a missing girl, one in which he might be involved.

It would be odd if he wasn't a little pissed.

After I'd taken in what the Bellagio had to offer, I decided to head back to The Cosmo.

I doubted Kenneth Croy would be calling me.

I was wrong.

CHAPTER 3

I was lying on my bed, a few minutes from midnight, assuming I was in for the night, when he texted me.

"Let's get this over with. I'll meet you at The Cosmo lobby bar in twenty minutes."

"I'll be there," I texted back.

I walked down the hall of the 12th floor and hit the down button on the elevator.

A man and a woman came around the corner. He was firmly in his fifties and she was firmly in her twenties. They were all over each other, and I couldn't help but think that Las Vegas lived up to each and every one of its stereotypes.

"How's it going, boss man?" the man asked.

Before I had a chance to answer, the young woman said, "He's handsome!"

"Just being a boss, looking handsome," I said.

She laughed. He shrugged.

And then he grabbed her closer, letting me know that she was all his.

An awkward elevator ride followed, where no words were exchanged. I was just happy they didn't start making out, which I'm sure the guy wanted.

We went our separate ways as we arrived at the casino floor and I headed towards the lobby bar.

～

Kenneth Croy was waiting at the entrance. He had changed and was now wearing jeans and a too-tight t-shirt. I was in solid, if unspectacular, shape, but I'd have had trouble breathing.

"Thanks for meeting with me," I said.

"Do I have a choice?" he asked.

"Yes, you do," I said honestly. "I'm not the police."

"What are you then?"

"A private investigator. I told you, Emmy's family hired me."

"Well, I'm here. Let's get it over with."

In Vegas lobby bars, you could throw a few bucks in the video machines located at the bar and get your drinks for free. However, we'd be surrounded by people, and that's not what either of us wanted.

So I chose a table in the corner and he followed.

A waitress came over. She was young and cute, speaking with a southern twang. Kenneth Croy oogled her a second too long.

"Jack and Coke," I said.

"I'll have the same," Croy said, "with a shot of Fireball."

I would not be joining him. I wasn't opposed to getting drunk in Vegas if it became necessary. But as of now, I was on the case, and a Jack and Coke was plenty.

"Do you even know Emmy?" Croy asked.

"No. Just friends with her uncle. He hired me."

"Not the asshole father?"

"He bankrolled it, but I'm not dealing with him. Why do you call him an asshole?" I asked.

"Because he accused me of killing his daughter on the first day he met me. Chance. Nice fucking name!"

I let out a slight smile. Chance was a ridiculous name.

I held back from making any terrible Vegas puns. '*A game of Chance*' came to mind.

The drinks arrived. It sure didn't take long in Vegas. They must assume the more liquored up you are, the more gambling you'll partake in. They weren't wrong.

I was already up $75 thanks to the guy next to me. It was unlikely to last, but it was a nice start.

"If word had gotten back to the Bellagio, I would have been fired for sure."

"Why did he suspect you?"

"Probably because Emmy and I went out on a few dates."

"You are quite a bit older than her," I said, quickly remembering the couple on the elevator.

"She was twenty-two-years old. That's legal."

I hoped his faux pas was an accident.

"Was?" I asked.

He realized his mistake.

"Is. Was. I don't know. Let's be honest, she's probably dead."

Croy pounded half his drink in one gulp.

"Why do you say that?"

"She's been missing for several months. Don't you watch any of these cop shows?"

Half the Fireball shot went next. Kenneth Croy was quite thirsty.

"I tend to focus on the ones with happy endings," I said. "When they find the girl in the end."

"Yeah, well there's a lot more that end with grieving families."

"Not too much sympathy, huh, Kenneth?"

I used his first name intentionally, trying to elicit a response.

"I liked Emmy. She was beautiful. Sexy. Free-spirited. But we spent less than ten nights together and now I've got suspicions surrounding me. It hardly seems worth it."

"What do you mean when you say free-spirited?"

"What do you think I mean? She was wild. She was young and living in Las Vegas. And she was a showgirl. You kind of have to be a free spirit to be one."

"Why is that?" I asked.

I was definitely following the old Socratic method. Question after question. Allow him to hang himself. If there was anything he was guilty of, he'd reveal it.

"I don't know. You need balls to stand up there in front of a crowd. Or, at least a free spirit."

It made some sense.

"Did you ever see her perform?"

"No."

"Did she ever try to gamble with you?"

I figured money and gambling was always a possible angle in a Vegas disappearance.

"Hell, no! I told her she couldn't come to the Bellagio. Like I said, I value my job. I make good money."

"Yeah, because people throw you $25 chips."

For the first time, Croy smiled.

"Thanks for that."

"I played three hands and won them all. I should stop while I'm ahead."

"Yes, you should. But, you won't. They never do."

We'd had a brief moment of levity, so I tried to swing the conversation back to Emmy.

"Did Emmy's free spirit ever get her in trouble?" I asked.

"Not that she told me. When she went missing, it took me totally by surprise. She wasn't a prostitute. She wasn't a drug dealer."

"Did she use drugs?" I asked.

"Not that I had seen, but she did talk about doing E together sometime. That's ecstasy."

"I know what E is," I said. "So it never happened?"

"She went missing before we ever picked a day."

"If you had to guess, what would you suspect happened to Emmy?"

"I don't fucking know!" he yelled a bit too loudly as a few people looked in our direction.

"That's why I said guess," I said.

"Ah, we've got a smart guy," he said, but I could tell he was pondering my question. "If I had to guess, I'd say she ended up with the wrong guy one night. And shit happened and he buried her in the desert."

"You guys weren't exclusive?"

"This is Vegas," he said, like that answered the question.

"I know some couples in Vegas. Even a few married ones," I said sarcastically.

"Well, we weren't a couple. And we certainly weren't married. She was twenty-two. We were having fun. That's it."

"Would your friends or family have been ashamed that you were dating someone that young?"

"We weren't technically dating."

"Allow me to rephrase," I said, sounding like a lawyer. "Would your friends or family have been ashamed that you were banging a young showgirl who had just graduated from UNLV?"

He bowed his head.

"They would not have been impressed."

"How old are you, Kenneth?"

"Thirty-seven."

It was time to poke the bear.

"So, Emmy's going missing potentially saved you from a few tough conversations."

"That doesn't even deserve a response. I liked hanging out with Emmy. If you think I wanted her dead, you are sick."

Croy finished the rest of his drink. I took my second sip.

I tried to look at it from his side. Sleeping with a twenty-two-year-old wasn't illegal. And if she was truly as attractive as the pictures I'd seen, which I'm sure she was, there's a great many men who'd have jumped at the opportunity.

"You know I have to ask these questions," I said. "It sounds like you enjoyed your time with Emmy."

I could feel Croy loosen up at my new line of questioning.

"Like I said, she was fun and sexy. We had a great time together. Was it going to last? Who knows? But it almost didn't matter. We were just enjoying it in the moment."

Although I wanted to hate him, Croy did have a likable side. He was being very forthright, which I hadn't expected.

"And then she goes missing and her father accuses you of being her abductor?"

"Exactly. He even tells the police to investigate me. I know that was him. So

I got called in to the station a second time, even though the police knew I had nothing to do with her disappearance."

"How can you be so sure?"

"Emmy went missing on a Friday, they think somewhere between four and eight p.m. And I worked from three to midnight that day."

"How did they know what time she went missing? Not to cast dispersion on you, but why couldn't she have just walked around the strip until midnight and then found you?"

"I heard through the grapevine that Emmy's phone was turned off at six p.m. that night, and was never turned back on. If you knew Emmy, she'd never turn her phone off. But not for the reasons you're thinking. Not Instagram or Tik-Tok or those things. She loved googling stuff. Reading Wikipedia. Learning things. She was very mature for her age. So trust me, if her phone went off at six, it's because that's when she was accosted. Or kidnapped. Or whatever the hell happened."

I hated the visual of Emmy being abducted.

"And they never found the phone?"

"No," he said. "Haven't you talked to that other PI? Duncan Hobbes. The one who tailed me for like a week. He was shitty at his job if we're being honest."

I hoped to meet up with Duncan Hobbes the following morning.

"Why was he so bad?"

Our waitress came by again. Croy ordered another Jack and Coke, but didn't include the Fireball shot this time. I passed, but did take a sip of the drink I still had in front of me.

When the waitress walked away, he spoke again.

"There was a stretch right after Emmy disappeared where I worked like four straight days. And every day I left the Bellagio, this same old-ass white Cadillac was following me. I mean, who follows people in a freaking caddy? And a white one? It's like wearing a sign saying *HERE I AM!*"

I couldn't argue with him. You try to be inconspicuous in my line of work. And I know I was a newbie, but that was lesson number one. I was interested in meeting this Duncan Hobbes character. Maybe time had passed him by.

"A white Caddie? What is this, *GoodFellas*?" I asked.

Kenneth Croy dropped his guard a second time and started laughing.

"Seriously. And who knows? Maybe this town was filled with caddies back in the day, but now you just stand out as some old guy."

"Duncan Hobbes is old?" I asked.

"Does a one-legged duck swim in circles?"

It was my turn to laugh, imagining the funny visual.

"Point taken."

I hated to admit it, but I was starting to warm up to Kenneth Croy. He might have had some questionable morals, but that didn't make him a murderer.

I needed to get back to discussing Emmy.

"What happened to you the night Emmy went missing?"

"Well, nothing that first night. Like I said, I was working. But the next morning, Saturday, the cops came by my apartment. I assumed one of Emmy's friends had told them about us. They asked if I knew where she was. At that point, she wasn't even officially missing. I answered them honestly and told them I'd talked to her on Friday, right before work, and nothing seemed odd. They seemed to believe me and left my apartment. Obviously, I was really scared for Emmy. And then her crazy father comes to Vegas later that day and the cops call me back and want me to come to the station the following morning, which would have been Sunday. I know it was because of Chance Peters. At least the cops didn't show up at my work. That probably would have gotten me canned."

Kenneth Croy was spilling his guts out to me.

"Can you really blame Chance Peters?"

"I guess not," he said. "But it's like he wanted me to be the guy who did it. I don't know why."

"I do," I said. "You're a good-looking guy who's too old and possibly corrupting his daughter. Or, at least, that's how he sees it."

Croy shrugged.

"I guess."

"What happened the second time you talked to the cops?"

"We basically just went over the same things as the previous morning. I still had an alibi. And if they'd known at this point that Emmy's phone was turned off at six, they probably knew I was innocent. Even if her father was hoping they'd pin it on me."

"And when did Duncan Hobbes start following you?"

"That second day I left the police station a white caddie was behind me, but I didn't think anything of it. When it also followed me home that night after work, I knew it was no coincidence."

If Abel Peters thought Duncan Hobbes was a great PI, what did that say about his endorsement of me? I tried not to think about it.

We were off track. I hadn't come to talk to Croy about Duncan Hobbes.

"Did you know Emmy's friends well?" I asked.

"No. I mean, if we're being honest, I didn't even know Emmy all that well. I did meet like five of her friends a week before she went missing, but it was awkward. They wanted to hit a club, and I told Emmy I didn't feel comfortable doing that with all of them. While we weren't at the Bellagio, it's still something that someone might see."

"It's not illegal," I said.

"I know. But because of the age gap, it wouldn't look good if it ever got back to the Bellagio."

It was the third time he'd mentioned potentially losing his job. It didn't necessarily mean anything, but I still took notice of it.

"So, what happened?"

"Emmy went with her friends to the club, but then texted me about two hours later, wanting to come over."

"Do you live close to the strip?"

"Henderson. It's about twenty-five minutes."

"When you and Emmy needed alone time, is that where you'd take her?"

"Mostly. I went to her house a few times. But she had a roommate. It was awkward."

"It would hit home how young she was."

"Something like that," he admitted. "Even though, like I said, she was actually quite mature for her age, and very, very smart."

I kept wanting to hate Kenneth Croy, but I just couldn't. He had bad judgement in women he dated, but Emmy Peters was of legal age, after all. And he'd been much more candid with me than I'd expected.

"Is there anything else you find suspicious? Or interesting? Or something that has been nagging at you?"

"Just Emmy's final day. She'd left her apartment and then just went missing. Where was she going? And what the hell happened?"

"Did she ever surprise you at work?"

Croy nodded.

"One time. She knew I was working and just started passing the blackjack table every half hour or so. I knew she was just trying to mind fuck me."

"Maybe she was on her way to the strip when she went missing?" I said.

"It's possible. Makes as much sense as anything else."

I felt like I'd gotten all I could have out of Kenneth Croy.

"Thanks for your time," I said. "You have my card. Please call me if you think of anything. And I do mean anything. Even the smallest tidbit might help."

"Thanks, Quint," he said, using my name for the first time. "You seem fair."

"That's only because I believe you. I'll be a son-of-a-bitch if I start doubting your story."

He smiled meekly.

And with that, I took the last sip of my drink, shook hands with Kenneth Croy, and walked down the four tiny steps of the lobby bar.

CHAPTER 4

SATURDAY

Duncan Hobbes was old.

Not old for a private detective, old in general. He had to be approaching eighty.

For the life of me, I couldn't figure out why this is the guy that Chance Peters would have hired. I don't care if he was a relative. When you're talking about a missing loved one, you hire the best, not some dinosaur in the twilight of his life.

I'd called Duncan that morning and he'd agreed to meet me in an hour.

I had some time to kill, so I went to a local Enterprise Rent-A-Car. The employee asked me what I wanted and I told him "something that blends in." Considering the city we were in, he must have thought I was up to no good.

"Something that blends in" ended up being a gray 2018 Subaru Legacy. It would do just fine.

After prepaying for a week of the car, I headed towards Duncan Hobbes's home.

He lived in the suburbs of Las Vegas in a huge, light blue home. It was the biggest house on the block and the most colorful. Most homes in Vegas seemed to be tan, white, or a pale yellow. Likely that had something to do with keeping the temperature down.

It was only ten a.m., but the Vegas sun was already beating down on me as I waited for him to answer the door.

"Hello, you must be Quint," he said.

That's when I realized I was dealing with a potential octogenarian. Duncan Hobbes was long in the tooth, wrinkled, and had a good twenty extra pounds padding his midsection and hair that had gone completely white. That being said, he seemed very vibrant for a man his age and his voice had an authority to it. He wasn't some pushover.

"I am. Nice to meet you, Mr. Hobbes."

"Mr. Hobbes was my father. Call me Duncan."

I almost laughed out loud. Usually, when someone uses that phrase, it's because they are forty or fifty and their father is eighty. It's not the eighty-year-old saying it.

"Duncan it is," I said. "Nice to meet you."

"Why don't you come in?"

"Thanks," I said.

I walked into his home which was pristine as could be. Every picture on the wall was framed impeccably. I peaked at several of them. They were mostly awards or recognition he'd received as a private investigator. I hadn't googled Duncan Hobbes before driving over, but I should have. Maybe Kenneth Croy's stories had sold the old guy short. It looked like he may have been a big deal back in the day.

We walked by the kitchen and there wasn't a stray bowl, plate, or piece of silverware to be seen. Even the table tops looked freshly buffed.

We passed two hallways and came upon a big, glass sliding door which looked out on a huge pool. There were probably eight recliners sitting around it, all perfectly equidistant from each other.

"I thought we could talk outside by the pool," Duncan said.

"Sounds great."

He led me to one of the two tables. I took a chair and an umbrella protected us from the Vegas sun. On the table was a pitcher of water with a few sliced lemons in it. I poured myself a glass.

"So, I got a call from Abel yesterday. He said you might be contacting me."

"I was wondering why you were so eager to meet."

"I'm here to help."

"Thanks."

"And when Abel calls, I answer. I've known him since he was in diapers."

"Really?" I asked.

"You don't know my connection to their family?"

"He said you were a relative. That's all I know."

"My wife Ellen, who passed on a few years ago, was a Peters by birth. She was the aunt of Chance and Abel Peters."

I think that meant Duncan was Abel's uncle, but not by birth. I'd always been lousy with familial relationships.

"Is that why you investigated Emmy's disappearance for Chance?"

"For about a week," he said. "And then they brought in someone a little younger."

"Oh. I don't think Abel told me about him."

"They didn't get along with him very well."

I realized there was still much I needed to learn about the case.

"Let's start at the beginning of your investigation, I guess. When did you hear about Emmy?" I asked.

"Poor, Emmy. I still worry about that young woman every day. And just pray, somehow, someway, she's still alive."

It was obvious he thought she was dead.

"I'm so sorry," I said.

"I got a call from Chance the day she went missing," Duncan said. "Although, at that point, he was just asking if maybe she'd come over to my place. She did that on occasion. I said no. He called me back an hour or two later and asked me to go check out her show at The Remington. When she wasn't there either, a knot in my stomach started to form. I started asking some of her fellow showgirls if they'd heard anything, if Emmy had been hurt, etc. Nothing. So I called back Chance. It was already getting late at this point, so he and his wife Liz flew to Vegas early the following morning."

"That must have been a brutal few days."

"Brutal isn't even strong enough. Despite our age difference, Emmy and I had a bond from early on in her life. I really loved that young woman. And she loved learning from me. I think she was fascinated by my career as a private investigator."

"I saw some of your awards hanging up. You must have been pretty good at your job."

Duncan managed a smile, but I knew he was still thinking about Emmy.

"I was the best," he said. "Of course, I was a much younger man back then. I could tell you some stories about Vegas back in the day."

"I'd love to hear them," I said, meaning every word of it.

"We might have time for those later. But let's focus on Emmy for now. And by the way, Abel says you've got a brilliant mind and are going to make a great PI. I hear this is only your second case, however."

"I have a lot to learn," I admitted.

"Well, maybe I can give you a pointer or two along the way."

Duncan took a sip of his water and looked out on his pool.

"I'd appreciate that," I said.

"Okay, back to my poor little Emmy. My God how I hope she's still alive. And I know I already said that. Don't worry, I'm not going senile, I just worry about Emmy all the time. Anyhow, Chance flew in that next morning and I picked him up. Some might think that's impulsive, but he knew his daughter. If she didn't respond for several hours, and then missed her showgirl engagement, something was wrong. She was never without that phone of hers. And she was responsible. She would have called her father back."

It checked out with what Kenneth Croy had said.

"And that's when Chance hired you?"

"I guess you could say that, but there was never a doubt I was going to help out. Chance didn't have to hire me."

"I understand. So you started following Kenneth Croy? I met with him last night, by the way."

"A little smug," Duncan said. "But not a terrible all-around guy. And I don't think he killed Emmy."

That made two of us. And yet, during my first case, I'd made so many wrong assumptions about who was and wasn't a suspect. I wasn't going to eliminate anybody this time.

"He told me that you followed him around in a white Cadillac."

Duncan laughed so hard I thought he was going to fall out of his chair.

"What's so funny?" I asked.

"That was completely intentional," he said.

"I'm lost."

"You've got a lot to learn, Quint. Didn't they teach you anything?"

He wasn't talking down to me, despite how it sounded. He was saying it like he'd love to teach me.

"My PI license was expedited a bit. I'm kind of learning on the fly."

"Nothing wrong with that. Anyway, intentionally letting myself be seen was part of the old bait and switch," he said. "I made it obvious I was following him, so when he didn't see a white caddie, he'd let his guard down."

Brilliant. Utterly brilliant. And he was right. I did have a lot to learn.

"So how did it work?"

"I made it obvious within the first twenty-four hours I was following him. It was all part of the plan. We were hoping when he didn't see my car he might go somewhere that would lead us to Emmy. Or, possibly a co-conspirator. I have an old friend who works as a PI on occasion, and he used his nondescript car to follow Mr. Croy around when the caddie was nowhere to be seen."

I wanted to punch myself for thinking Duncan Hobbes had been some inept old man. He knew all the tricks. It was me who was the amateur.

"It's very creative," I said. "But did it lead anywhere?"

Duncan became serious again.

"No, it didn't. Like I said earlier, I don't think Mr. Croy is the killer. Or, the abductor. And if he is, he's an iceman, because we got nothing from him."

"Did the cops suspect him?"

"Originally, he was probably their number-one suspect. Part of that was Chance. He's very convincing when he wants to be. And obviously, because Mr. Croy was a lot older than Emmy, Chance immediately hated him."

He confirmed my suspicions.

"Understandable," I said.

"Of course. Any father would. Yet, as a PI, I can't think like that. I can't let emotions get in my way."

"How long did Chance stay in Vegas?" I asked.

"Probably three days and then he flew back to LA. He's got a big-time job and had to work, even though I'm sure he couldn't concentrate with his daughter missing. And he does fly back every time he can. Probably twice a week, even to this day."

"So where does the investigation stand?"

"She's a missing person. And the police don't have a suspect. It's like she vanished into thin air."

It's the second time I'd heard that phrase.

"This is horrible," I said.

"It is. I hope I live to see the day where Emmy is found alive."

"Do you think she is alive?" I asked, knowing he didn't.

"What choice do I have?"

He sighed and I understood perfectly. He thought she was dead, but would go on hoping she was alive.

"Any advice for me on what to do next?" I asked.

"Stop breaking the law," he said.

I took a sip of my water, almost instinctively.

"What do you mean?"

"Your PI license is from California. While you can ask questions as a private citizen, if you get deeply involved in this case, the authorities might take notice."

I was about to open my mouth, when Duncan continued.

"Don't worry, I've taken care of it. I did some paperwork and said you were working under my authority."

"I really appreciate it," I said, feeling like a nitwit. "How can I thank you?"

"Thank Abel. He asked me to do it and I quickly agreed."

"Well, thank you."

"You seem like a smart guy, Quint. You are a little wet behind the ears when it comes to being a PI, however. Hopefully, we can change that in the days to come."

I was floored. This was not what I expected.

"I'd be grateful," I said.

"Why don't we meet again tomorrow. Meanwhile, I've got you a copy of the police reports regarding Emmy. Maybe you'll find something I haven't."

'I'll see what I can do."

"Wait here a second."

Duncan slowly made his way back in the house and reemerged a minute later with a three-inch stack of papers in a manila envelope.

"Usually, a missing girl like Emmy would have a seven or eight inch file. That's how little there is to go on in this case."

"I'm ready to dive right in," I said.

"I appreciate the bravado. Now let's see if it's more than just bluster. We'll talk tomorrow and you can tell me what you've found."

"Thanks for everything, Duncan."

"Abel says you've got great instincts. Now go prove it!"

CHAPTER 5

The police reports were sprawled out on my bed at The Cosmo. I'd spent the last two hours going over them with a fine toothed comb.

And yet, nothing.

In my defense, there was very little to go on.

It's just like Duncan and Abel had said. *"She'd vanished into thin air."*

There were statements by Kenneth Croy and a few of Emmy's friends, including her roommate, of whom I planned on meeting soon.

There was a timeframe laid out by the cops that coincided with what both Croy and Duncan had said.

Obviously, there were no crime scene photos. For that, you need an actual crime scene and we didn't have one in this case.

There are plenty of cameras in Las Vegas, but none of the ones they'd looked at showed any evidence of Emmy Peters being abducted. Nor had any even picked up Emmy walking around. Which made it less likely it happened on the Strip, where cameras were everywhere.

Finally, something clicked.

And it was less from the police reports and more from information I'd accumulated. Chance Peters had texted Emmy at four p.m. but never heard back. And yet, the authorities had put her estimated time of disappearance at six p.m., because that's when her phone had powered down.

Everyone who I'd spoken to said Emmy always had her phone on her and was very considerate in texting back. So my guess, and that's all it was at this point, was that whatever happened to Emmy occurred a lot closer to four p.m. than six p.m.

She'd likely have texted her father between four and six if she really had her phone the entire time.

Maybe her captor, or killer, turned her phone off at six, but I think she was in trouble way before then.

What did it mean? I didn't know, but it was a start.

I'd talked to the two men on the list Abel had given me, but it was time to talk to some of the women. I decided to start with her roommate, Nia Solomon.

I called her.

"Hello?"

"Nia, my name is Quint Adler. I'm a private investigator and I'd like to ask you a few questions about Emmy Peters."

"Okay, I guess. I hate doing these interviews. But alright, if it might help you find Emmy."

Skittish was the only way to describe her.

"Thanks," I said. "Where is easiest for you?"

I didn't want to make this harder than it already was for her.

"Probably talking on the phone," she said.

I thought about it. Obviously, you can learn more from a face-to-face interview, but that could wait. Nia lived in Vegas still, and I'm sure I'd be talking to her more than once.

"That's fine," I said.

"What do you want to know?" Nia asked.

"Everything," I said, hoping in telling it again, she'd include something she'd forgotten to tell the authorities.

Nia said that she and Emmy hit it off right away as freshmen in the dorms. She was surprised, having grown up poor and black, while Emmy was white and obviously had some family money. None of that mattered, however, and they had become close from day one.

They remained good friends even after moving out of the dorms and remained so through all four years of college. When they graduated last year and found out they both were staying in Vegas, they decided to become roommates.

On the day she went missing, Nia had last seen Emmy around three p.m. when Nia had headed to her boyfriend's house for a few hours. She texted Emmy a little after four telling her she'd be back in an hour or so, but Emmy didn't respond.

She came back around 5:30 and Emmy was gone. Never to be seen again.

I'd let her talk, mostly uninterrupted, but it was time I interjected myself. My first question was predicated on my thinking that Emmy went missing closer to four p.m.

"What was Emmy's daily schedule like around four p.m.?" I asked.

"Hmm," Nia pondered my question. "It was a Friday. She had her show at The Remington, but that wasn't until later in the night."

The next woman on my list to call was a fellow showgirl, so I'd get more into life as a showgirl with her.

"Did she usually take it easy on the day of a show?" I asked.

"I'd say that's probably true. She didn't hit the gym. Those shows were exhausting and they had two a night. So yeah, she was generally pretty mellow on Fridays."

"Maybe some writing?"

"Probably, although she wrote most days."

"Did she write at cafes or at home?"

"Both."

"Could she have been headed to a cafe to do some writing on the day she went missing?"

"Makes as good a sense as anything I've heard," Nia said.

"Did she have a favorite spot?"

"There's a few coffee shops that are within walking distance from us. I know she wrote at them occasionally."

Who knew if it would amount to anything, but I already felt us getting somewhere.

"Can you text me those names when we get off the phone?"

"Sure."

"I'm going to assume Emmy would not have been hitting a Happy Hour with a show that night?"

"No chance. She was very responsible. There's no way she's even having one drink on the night of a show."

"What about to meet some guy?" I asked.

"It's possible, I guess," Nia said. "But I think she genuinely liked Kenneth Croy. And I know she didn't meet him because the police said he was working that day. Plus, I never heard her mention another guy. Like I said, we were pretty close."

"Did Emmy have a car?"

It was a question I knew the answer to, but helped move the conversation along.

"Yeah, but she didn't use it that day."

"Nor was there a record of her catching an Uber that day," I said.

"No. She just..."

I thought Nia was going to say 'vanished into thin air', but she didn't.

"...was never seen again."

Close enough.

"Were the coffee shops you were referring to within walking distance?"

"They were probably about a half of a mile."

"Do you know if she usually walked to them or drove?"

"I'd seen her do both, depending on the day," Nia said.

"With a show that night, I'd be willing to guess she's not going to walk a mile round trip. I don't think she'd want to tire her legs out."

"I think that's probably a good guess."

"And since her car didn't move on the day in question, my guess is Emmy wasn't going to a coffee shop."

"You're pretty good at this stuff," Nia said.

It was nice to hear, even if Nia Solomon knew nothing about being a private investigator.

"Nia, I'd like to meet in person at some point. But I'll let you go for now. Just one last question. Since she didn't drive, probably wouldn't be walking, and there was no record of her calling an Uber, maybe someone came and picked her up. Any idea who that could have been?"

"I would have said Kenneth Croy, but he was working. And if it was any of her girl friends, they would have told the police. I'm sorry, but I really don't have a good answer."

"That's alright. Thanks, Nia. I hope you're okay with me hitting you up again soon?"

"Yeah, that's fine."

"Thank you," I said and ended the call.

I tried to go through what I had learned, and determine if any of it meant anything.

CHAPTER 6

I made my first mistake later that night. Although, it had nothing to do with the case.

And truth be told, I'm not sure it should be categorized as a mistake. I'm still going back and forth on that.

I'd set up a meeting with one of Emmy's friends, Carrie Granger, for the following morning. She was the lone showgirl on the list of women Abel wanted me to contact, so I was hoping the meeting would prove fruitful.

The other two women on the list, besides Carrie and Nia, didn't even live in Vegas when Emmy went missing, so I was less concerned with them at the moment. Abel had said they'd be more helpful for background information on Emmy. Things she liked, her personality qualities, things like that. I told myself I'd call them tomorrow.

Instead, I spent my time re-reading the police report probably five times. And finally, when my head was basically mush and I couldn't process any more information, I decided to go have a few drinks.

I assumed it was going to be one of the few down times left in the case, so I was going to make the most of it.

So, I guess what I'm saying is that my guard was down.

I took the elevator to the casino floor and took in the sights and sounds of the gambling around me. Slot machines were making noises, people were yelling on the craps table, and Roulette players were imploring their number get hit. I could see why people might think it's all too much, but I enjoyed it. You couldn't help but feel alive in Vegas.

I headed to the Chandelier Bar, far and away The Cosmo's most well-known spot. It was a three story bar in which a gigantic chandelier spiraled from the roof of the third story down to the casino floor. You had your choice of taking the staircase or the elevator. I'd seen many a group take the stairs up and then, after several drinks, decide to take the elevator back down.

On previous visits, I'd always preferred the top level, knowing the further you got up from the casino floor, the less busy it would be. That's where I found myself.

I ordered a drink at the bar, choosing my standard drink of late, a Jack and Coke. And then I meandered to one of their little velvet love seats and took my first sip.

Eighteen minutes later, one drink turned into a second drink. And fourteen minutes after that, drink number two had become drink number three.

I told myself I'd return to my room after finishing the drink in front of me.

It didn't turn out that way.

A minute before I was going to close my tab, a table of women in their 30s invited me to join their table. Well, that's not exactly true. One specific woman asked me to join their table.

Looking back, I wonder if I would have accepted if I was still on my first drink.

As the woman approached my table, I was immediately reminded of Heather Graham. Their features were similar and they shared blond, curly hair, a pretty face, and a knockout body.

"All by yourself in Vegas?" she asked.

My heart rate accelerated ever so slightly.

"Taking a break from the reason I'm here," I said.

"And what would that be?" she asked.

"You don't want to know," I said.

"Actually, I do."

She was wearing a beige dress that was on the longer side of the ones you'd see in Vegas. I took that as a good sign. If a woman's skirt is too short, I am probably too quick to hold it against them. I guess I'm old fashioned and prefer when they leave some things to the imagination.

"I'm here investigating the disappearance of a young woman," I said.

I thought she'd be taken aback. She wasn't.

"That sounds interesting."

"That's one way to describe it."

"How would you describe it?"

"Sad. Scary. Suffocating."

"All the S words," she said and managed to smile.

I responded in kind.

She extended her hand.

"I'm Heather."

"No joke, when you were walking over here I was reminded of Heather Graham."

"I get that a lot," Heather said.

"I'm Quint."

"Like the shark hunter in Jaws?" she asked.

My heart rate accelerated further.

"You know your stuff. Yup, that's who I was named after."

"My parents love that movie," Heather said.

I took a quick peak at the table she'd come from. They seemed lost in their own fun, except for one woman who was trying to nonchalantly peer over at us.

"My parents saw it on their first date."

"Ah, that explains it."

"I'm impressed, though. Very few people get the reference immediately."

"I've been known to surprise people," Heather said seductively.

If I was still in a relationship with Cara, I might have jumped on the chandelier, ridden it to the first floor, proceeded to sprint to the elevator, locking the dead bolt in my room once I'd arrived.

But we'd broken up. And a very attractive woman in her mid-30s was flirting with me, the same me who was finishing up on his third drink and might have a little less inhibitions than usual.

"Oh, yeah. What surprises do you have in store for tonight?" I asked.

"That will have to wait. For now, I'll invite you to come join our table. If we just left together this quickly, my girls would call me all sorts of names."

I smiled.

I joined her table and was happy to see it wasn't a bachelorette party. That would have been too cliché. Each woman individually introduced themselves.

It was a very nice group. They weren't sloppy drunk and they weren't on the prowl, like so many groups of women you see in Vegas. And the men were worse, slobbering over groups of women, giving catcalls, etc. That was a part of Vegas I didn't like.

I was wrong about one thing. There was one of them on the prowl. And I was her intended victim.

"So what do you do, Quint?" One of them asked.

There were six of them and I'd already forgotten a few of their names. When they come rapid fire like that, it's hard to remember them all.

"I'm a private investigator," I said.

That would take some getting used to. Part of me still felt like the reporter for the *Walnut Creek Times*. After all, I'd held that position for ten years. I'd been a PI for a few months.

"You're not investigating any of us, are you, Quint?" she asked.

I laughed.

"No, you are all above reproach," I answered.

They smiled.

"Don't be so sure," one of them said.

"What are you gals all doing here?" I asked.

While I'd ruled out a bachelorette party, they hadn't told me what they were gathered for.

Heather spoke.

"It's Marilyn's 35th birthday."

Marilyn raised her hand. She had pitch black, straight hair.

"Happy Birthday," I said.

"Thank you, Quint!"

They seemed to remember my name.

"Finally hit your sexual prime!" one of the women said, and the table erupted with laughter and some chants of '*Cheers!*'

A server made his way to our table and the women all ordered a drink. No shots. Another thing that set them apart from many groups in Vegas, both male and female. Getting drunk quickly is a cornerstone of most Vegas groupings.

I ordered my fourth Jack and Coke.

Heather brushed her shoulder up against mine. It wasn't an accident.

It was hard to describe how I felt. She was a beautiful woman and I was excited. I'd be a liar if I denied that. However, it was impossible not to think of Cara. I kept reminding myself she'd broken up with me.

"So what do you guys have planned for tonight?" I asked.

Marilyn, the birthday girl, spoke.

"It's going to be a mellow night. We've got a cabana at the Circa pool tomorrow, and it's going to be a long day."

Although, Marilyn said it as "*It's going to be a loooooooooooooooooong day.*"

"You can swing by Circa tomorrow if you'd like," said one of the women, who's name I couldn't remember.

Circa was a new hotel downtown that supposedly had a hip pool area. It also had one of the biggest T.V.s in the world. I'd heard good things. I hoped it helped further regenerate downtown Las Vegas, which had become a dump over the last decade, but was showing signs of coming back to life.

"I've got a busy morning," I said. "But, maybe I could stop by in the afternoon."

"We'll be there most of the day."

"How long are you guys in town for?" I asked, thinking about Heather's legs the whole time.

She spoke.

"They're all leaving on Monday. I'm considering staying till Tuesday."

"I see," was all I could muster.

We talked for another ten minutes and I found myself enjoying their company.

"Alright, I'm calling it after this drink," Marilyn said.

The others nodded in agreement. This was truly the most responsible group of females I'd ever met in Vegas. Maybe their wild side would come out the next day at the pool.

Several minutes later, after paying their tab, everyone stood up.

I said my goodbyes to each and every one. They all hoped I'd join them at Circa.

No one seemed surprised or mentioned that Heather was going to stay with me. They were a well oiled machine.

Once everyone had departed, I turned to Heather.

"No guilt trips. No sarcastic comments about staying with me. You've got a pretty solid group of friends," I said.

"They're all married. And I'm the lone single girl."

"That explains it. So they're all happy for you?"

"Look down," she said.

We looked off the third floor and towards the casino floor. Her friends were laughing and smiling as they walked.

"That's them talking about me," she said.

I smiled.

"I hope they liked me," I said.

"Do you really care?"

"A little bit," I admitted.

"They did. If you were a turkey, they wouldn't have invited you to the pool."

She grabbed my hand.

"Show me around Vegas," Heather said. "I don't want to just go straight to your room."

I agreed wholeheartedly. It would have felt cheap. Heather seemed like a smart, fun woman. I'd be happy to chaperone her around.

~

A few minutes later, we left the Chandelier Bar, taking the stairs.

"What's next?" Heather asked.

"Do you have anything against rooftop bars?" I asked.

"Who doesn't love rooftop bars?"

"Acrophobes, I guess."

She paused.

"People who fear heights?" she asked.

"You got it."

She laughed and leaned her head into my chest.

"Let's go get a cab," I said.

~

We arrived at the cab stand and I, as was my custom, gave the guy a dollar for flagging down our cab. Not sure they deserved it, but it was just something I always did.

"Where to?" he asked.

"The Rio."

"To the Rio," he told the cab driver, earning his money by merely repeating what I'd said.

And we were off.

I knew I could have kissed Heather in the cab on the way there, but I was enjoying the back and forth flirting. We were going to end up together that night, so there was no need to rush it.

I wanted this to be on the more romantic side of Vegas one night stands, if that was possible.

~

The Voodoo Lounge was on the rooftop of the Rio and had the best views in Vegas in my humble opinion. The elevator ride up, which is a straight shot to the 50th floor, has scared a friend or two over the years.

Heather was unfazed and seemed to enjoy it.

Once we arrived on the 50th floor, we walked up one story and arrived at our destination. There's an inside area that has 360 degree views of the strip, and it's fantastic in its own right, but outside is where you want to be.

I took Heather's hand and led her outside. As soon as I opened the door, we got that warm Vegas air, and a phenomenal view of the Strip.

There were probably around fifty other people up there, the majority wrapped around the perimeter taking in the gorgeous sights.

"This is breathtaking," Heather said.

"I thought you'd enjoy it," I said.

We didn't order a drink for several minutes, instead we walked to each section of the rooftop. Each view was more amazing than the previous one.

Finally, after taking in the views, I asked what she wanted to drink.

"I'll take a Seven and Seven."

An old-school drink. I liked it.

I'd known Heather for all of an hour, but she'd already pleasantly surprised me several times.

I ordered her drink and my fifth Jack and Coke of the night. I was done drinking after this. As much fun as I was having with Heather, and I hoped it continued, I had an important morning tomorrow. I couldn't be in a haze. I had to remind myself, more than once, that I was in Vegas to investigate Emmy Peters's disappearance, not to try and bed women just because I was newly single. In my defense, Heather had approached me and had definitely been the one pushing this.

We found a spot where we could sip our drinks up against the railing and peer off at the views below.

"It's romantic up here, isn't it?" I said.

"It sure is," Heather replied.

"I have to ask. Why'd you approach my table tonight? Was it because I looked like an easy mark?"

"Not at all," she said. "I think I found you attractive because you were sitting alone."

"Is there a difference?" I asked.

She laughed.

"That's not what I meant. I think sitting and drinking alone shows confidence. Especially in Vegas where people act like they are part of a herd."

"I agree with that part," I said.

"Plus, you were cute."

"Anything else?"

"You may not love this part."

"Hit me with it," I said.

"I was lonely. I kept hearing my friends talk about their husbands and their kids. It was tough being the only single one."

"I could see how that would be tough."

"It can be. It seems to hit me more in Vegas than other places."

"I have no idea why," I joked.

"Are you single? Please say yes."

"Newly single," I said, and left it at that.

"If I'd seen a wedding ring, I wouldn't have approached. I'm not that type of girl."

I put my arm around Heather. She was good people.

She leaned back from the railing and turned towards me. She grabbed my drink and set it down.

"Kiss me," she said.

While Cara was surely in the back of my mind somewhere, I did exactly as Heather asked. It lasted a solid ten seconds and was exhilarating, like most first kisses.

After we finished, there was a bit of silence, although it wasn't awkward.

"So where do you live and what do you do for work?" I asked.

"Do you really want to know?"

"Yes. I'm not a one-night stand type of guy. If I get to know you a little bit, this will seem more appropriate."

A gust of wind came out of nowhere and blew Heather's curly hair every which way.

"I respect that," Heather said. "I live in Minneapolis and am a lawyer."

"Are all your girlfriends from Minneapolis as well?"

"Yeah, why?"

I smiled.

"That explains the pale complexion of each and every one of you."

Heather laughed. "How dare you?"

"You and the girls better watch it at the pool tomorrow. You might look like a bunch of lobsters when the day is over. I'd recommend SPF 7000."

"Are all PI's this funny?"

It was my turn to laugh.

We were having a nice back and forth. I knew there was no future, but this was more substantive than it had any right to be.

Or, maybe that's just what I was telling myself.

"And where are you based?" she asked.

"The Bay Area. Although my first two PI cases were in LA and now Vegas."

"You're a newbie."

"I am. And I'm feeling it. Although I've met this old retired PI who I think I'm going to learn a ton from."

"Very cool."

"So you're staying until Tuesday?"

"That's the plan. I have court on Wednesday so that's the latest I can stay."

"What type of law do you practice?"

"I'm a divorce attorney."

"No wonder you're single. You probably see all the shit that can come with a marriage."

She playfully punched my arm.

"I think you're on to something, Quint the shark hunter," she said. "But that doesn't mean I wouldn't trade in my single status if the right guy came along."

Heather had a sad look in her eyes. She wasn't saying I was her knight in shining armor, merely suggesting she was lonely in Minneapolis.

"You seem like a good woman, Heather. You'll find the right guy."

"I can worry about that when I get home. For now, I'm looking at a pretty darn handsome guy right in front of me."

I turned around.

"Who? Where?"

"You're soooooooo funny," she said.

I laughed, happy to be distancing ourselves from talk of marriage and me thinking about Cara.

"Do you want another drink?" I asked.

"I think I'm alright. Thanks. Do you?"

"No, I've got an important meeting tomorrow. I want to have all of my faculties working."

She leaned in and whispered.

"You'll need those tonight as well."

I kissed her again. We looked out on the strip, instinctively knowing we wouldn't be on the roof much longer.

"I think I've seen enough of Vegas," Heather said. "Show me where you're staying."

If this were a movie, it's the spot where I'd yell "Check, please!"

Instead, we finished our drinks, walked back inside the Voodoo Lounge, and caught the shuttle elevator back towards the ground floor.

The cab ride to the Cosmo did involve a few kisses this time.

Tacky for a forty-year-old? Maybe, but it wasn't anything egregious.

We arrived back and went straight towards my room.

By the time I opened the door to the hotel room, we were ready to rip each other's clothes off, which commenced a few seconds later.

I unzipped the top of her dress as she worked on my jeans.

Heather shimmied out of her dress and stood there in her bra and panties looking at me.

She had a lovely body.

I walked towards her and unlocked the back of her bra and she pushed down the front of my jeans.

I took my shirt off and she started kissing my chest. I was doing the same to her moments later.

We made our way to the bed and she pushed herself back up against the baseboard of the bed. I moved towards her and our hands started exploring each other's bodies. She was very into this, which in turn, only made me more excited.

After a few minutes of rapturous kissing, she reached for my boxers and took them off. I slid her panties off.

We kissed for another minute, knowing sex was imminent.

She took me in her hand and guided me inside of her.

Her moans and my groans filled the hotel room.

CHAPTER 7

SUNDAY

When I finally woke up the next morning, I looked over at the old school digital clock on the dresser. 9:38. I was late.

Fuck!

We'd had sex twice that night and it must have exhausted my forty-one-year old body. I never ever sleep in this late.

I looked over and Heather was still asleep. Which I guess meant I'd tired her out too.

But what the hell was I doing? Late for my interview with one of Emmy's friends? This was very unprofessional and I felt like a jackass. And I was only referring to my oversleeping. I'm sure I'd be tough on myself for having slept with Heather as well.

I went to the bathroom and dialed the number of Carrie Granger.

"Hello?" she answered.

"Carrie, this is Quint."

"You're late."

"I'm terribly sorry."

There was no excuse worth telling. And I certainly wasn't going to tell her the truth.

"Are you still coming?"

"Yeah, I'll be there in a half hour."

"Okay. See you then."

I walked out of the bathroom and Heather was just waking up.

"Are you sure you're not married?" she asked.

"Yes. That was a woman I have to see for the case I'm working on."

"And you're late?"

"Yes."

"I'm sorry."

"It's not your fault. You were fantastic."

She smiled and leaned up and kissed me.

"Should I go?" she asked.

"Maybe we'll hang out later," I said. "But I really do need to go now."

She sexily slid the comforter off to expose her breasts.

"Not one more session before you go?"

It would be next to impossible to say no, but I had to.

"It's not a no, but a to-be-continued. I have to meet this woman," I said.

"I understand," Heather said and got out of bed to change.

She didn't give me a guilt trip and realized this was important to me. I appreciated that.

I grabbed some clothes from my bag.

"One piece of advice," she said.

"What's that?" I asked.

She smiled.

"Take a quick shower. You smell like sex."

After a three minute shower, I got dressed and noticed that Heather had left. There was a note with her number and telling me to call her later. She said I was great and this didn't feel like a one-night stand. While I agreed with her sentiment, it's not like this was going anywhere. And I still loved Cara.

Whether I called Heather back or not was up in the air.

Carrie Granger lived in Veer Towers, a high rise in the middle of the Strip and walking distance from The Cosmo. It must have been a desirable place if you wanted to live smack dab in the center of Las Vegas Boulevard.

She was waiting for me when I approached the front door.

"You must be Quint," she said.

I didn't know how she recognized me immediately. Maybe she'd googled my name. I was still easy to find on the internet because of the Bay Area Butcher case. Or maybe she'd talked to Nia Solomon who had described me. I guess it didn't really matter.

Carrie herself was very attractive, with extremely long, tanned legs. I guess I shouldn't have been surprised. She worked as a showgirl with Emmy and long legs were a necessity.

Her hair had been dyed red and she must have stood out in a crowd, even in a city where standing out is an art. She had on denim shorts and a short sleeve top, dressed for the hot day that was coming. It was already approaching 90 degrees when I finally arrived at 10 a.m.

"You must be Carrie," I responded.

She smiled, but it felt more perfunctory. I guess I couldn't blame her. I was the guy here to talk about her missing friend. No one would look forward to that.

We headed to the elevator and she pressed the button to the 14th floor.

"Thanks for meeting with me," I said.

"You're welcome."

The 14th floor was our destination and she led me to her apartment.

I'd suggested a coffee shop, but she'd been adamant she'd rather do it in private and suggested her place. Whatever made her more comfortable was fine with me. I just wanted her to be as talkative as possible.

She opened the door and let me in. The place was magnificent with views looking up and down Las Vegas Boulevard.

"Great spot," I said. "Can't be cheap."

"No, it ain't cheap. But being a showgirl pays pretty well."

I reminded myself that Carrie Granger was the lone showgirl on Abel's list of people to contact. It's why I hadn't asked too many questions of Kenneth Croy, Duncan Hobbes, or Nia Solomon regarding Emmy's job. I knew I'd get that information from the woman standing in front of me.

She pushed two chairs together near the window. It was quite the view for an interview. It was the second great view I'd had in the last twelve hours. And I was referring to the Voodoo Lounge, not Heather's naked body.

"So what would you like to know?" Carrie asked.

She seemed a little bit nervous. Maybe it was just because she had to speak to a PI.

"As you know, I'm here investigating Emmy Peters's disappearance. I've talked to a few of her friends, but I know nothing of her life as a showgirl. That's what I'd like to learn from you."

"I'll tell you everything I know. But just a heads up, I've also told this to the police, to Emmy's father, and to a different private investigator they hired."

"That's fine. It will be the first time for me."

She didn't love my answer, but started talking anyway.

"I met Emmy about nine months ago, when she was first starting as a showgirl. She'd just graduated from UNLV. She was different from most of the other girls. Her goal was to be a novelist and dancing was just a way to pay the bills in the meantime. I've met many showgirls in my three years of doing this, and heard all sorts of reasons why they'd become one, but to become a novelist was a first. Emmy was a natural showgirl. She was a fantastic dancer and had legs to die for. And yes, I know most of us do, but Emmy's legs really stood out. As we became friendlier, Emmy told me she'd been dancing since a young age and it definitely showed. She had better instincts than girls who'd been doing it for years. She was never out of rhythm. And that's a big deal. Most people just think we get out there and kick our legs in the air, but I can assure you, it's a much tougher job than that. It's very physical and can be emotionally taxing as well. You sure don't want to be the one who fucks up when you're out there on stage. That part is tough. And yet, Emmy never once screwed it up. She was a natural from the beginning."

Carrie paused and took a deep breath. This was all very interesting, but it wasn't the information I was looking for. I decided to let her continue, however. Even the smallest detail might be important.

"So she started working in the actual shows quicker than anyone else. Again, her history of dancing was a big factor. And we started working together. We had two shows each on Friday and Saturday night."

Now we were getting somewhere and I had to interrupt.

"What time were your Friday shows at?" I asked.

"I figured you'd ask that since she went missing on a Friday. The shows were at seven p.m. and ten p.m."

"Did you notice Emmy was missing that night?"

She took a slight pause that I didn't like. Surely, she must have remembered one way or another.

"I didn't notice until our first show was about an hour in."

"Even though you were good friends with Emmy?"

"I was, but you're kind of in your own little world when you're preparing for a show. You say hi to the girls warming up next to you and that's about it."

I was surprised she wouldn't look for Emmy before the show started, but her reason seemed pretty legitimate. Plus, there was no reason to lie about it.

"So you said halfway through the show you noticed she was gone?"

"Something like that. And then, when the show ended, and I didn't see her, I knew for certain. I didn't think much of it. Maybe she was sick or had become injured. Like I said, it happened fairly frequently. We finished the first show a little after nine. And then I knew something was wrong, because there was some old private investigator backstage asking me if I knew where Emmy was. No one got backstage. And I mean no one. So I knew this guy must have known a VIP or something."

Duncan Hobbes continued to surprise. Getting backstage to talk to some showgirls couldn't have been easy. He must have used up one of his favors around town.

"And what did you tell him?"

"That I had no idea, obviously."

"Had you talked to Emmy at all on that Friday?"

"No. I'd seen her at the walkthrough on Thursday night, but not since then."

"What is the average showgirl's schedule like?"

"We have practice on Tuesday and Wednesday, a walkthrough on Thursday, two shows each on Friday and Saturday, and then we have Sunday and Monday off to rest our bodies."

"Sounds like a lot of work. Did Emmy have the same schedule."

"Yeah. All the showgirls did."

There was something about Carrie Granger that I didn't fully trust. I couldn't exactly place it, but I just felt she was holding something back. It could have been something completely unrelated to Emmy's disappearance. But if I became a PI in part because of my ability to read people, I had to trust my instincts. And they told me Carrie wasn't being completely truthful.

I'd felt that Kenneth Croy, Nia Solomon, and obviously, Duncan, had been forthright with me. I didn't feel the same with Carrie.

I didn't suspect her in Emmy's disappearance, at least not yet, but my radar was up for the first time.

"Were there any creepy guys who would hang out around the showgirls? Any stalkers you heard about?"

I stole a peek out the window that overlooked the Strip. It didn't look like much was going on, but it was barely after ten. Once day turned into night, you'd probably see some wild stuff from this window.

"Not really," Carrie answered. "The Remington, that's the hotel where we performed, was very protective of us. Sometimes as many as fifty beautiful women are training together at once. It would be a creepball's dream."

"How about once shows are over?"

"We go backstage, change, and then usually leave. It's just us girls, the director of the show, maybe a few bigwigs from the casino, and security. That's why I was so surprised when that private investigator showed up that night."

I'm glad Carrie had brought it back to the night in question.

"Did you talk to the police?"

"Not that night. The next afternoon I got a phone call, though. And I went to the Las Vegas PD and answered some questions. And then I had to do a show that night, knowing Emmy was missing. It was terrible."

"I have no doubt. Do you know why they picked you?"

"Emmy's father had come to town. And apparently Emmy had told him that I was her best friend amongst the showgirls."

"Did you meet with Emmy's father, Chance?"

"Yeah. He was literally waiting for me outside of the police station when I finished answering their questions."

"And what did he ask you?"

"Pretty much the same things the cops asked. And, if we're being honest, the things you're asking now. When did I see her last? Were there any guys I was suspicious of? Did I have any suspects myself? Had she seemed different lately? All that stuff. And I answered every question her father had. I can't imagine how he felt, knowing his daughter had just gone missing in the last twenty-four hours. Obviously, we all hoped she'd been found. Sadly, that's not what happened."

Carrie seemed very earnest in that moment. It made me think maybe I'd read her wrong. It was possible she just didn't like being interviewed by a PI. That would be natural and might explain my suspicion.

And yet, I know what I'd felt earlier and couldn't dismiss it yet.

"How did your fellow showgirls take it?" I asked.

"Not well, obviously. First and foremost, we were scared for Emmy. And it also enters your mind that it could be some lunatic who has it in for showgirls. Even to this day, four months later, there's still some anxiety. The hotel added security for the girls. And they now escort you to your car or your Uber once the show ends."

I felt myself slowly running out of questions.

"Did you know Kenneth Croy?" I asked.

"I met him once. A bunch of girls were out on the strip. It was mostly Emmy's older friends, so it was nice to meet them. Her mind was on Kenneth, though. I could tell. Emmy called it kind of early and I think the other girls and I knew why."

I was somewhat surprised she used his first name.

"And that's the only time you'd met, Kenneth?" I asked, responding in kind.

She noticed.

"Would you rather I called him, Mr. Croy?"

I laughed.

"Yes, that's the only time I met him," Carrie said. "I feel like you don't like me, Quint. See, there's a first name."

I laughed again, mainly to appease her.

"Sorry to jump on you. I'm just trying to get some facts on Emmy. I like you just fine, Carrie."

It was her turn to smile.

"Is there anything else you can think of?" I asked. "Maybe something I neglected to ask?"

"I can't think of anything. But I've got your card now. And I'll call you if I think of anything."

"Thanks," I said. "You know what, I do have one last question."

"Sure."

"Do you think Emmy is still alive?"

She seemed to weigh her decision.

"My heart and my brain have two different answers."

I knew exactly what she meant.

CHAPTER 8

"Quint, how are you?" Duncan Hobbes said, greeting me at his front door. "Shall we go to the pool again?"

"That would be great," I said.

It was obviously his go to spot for visitors. And who could blame him? With the beautiful Vegas weather, sitting under a canopy next to a giant pool was hard to beat.

We walked through his house and made our way to the same seats as we had the last time. Once again, there was a huge pitcher of lemon-filled water with ice cubes filling up three-quarters of it, surely to prevent them all melting in the Vegas sun.

It was ninety-six degrees and a few minutes after noon. Summer didn't officially start until June 20th, but Vegas didn't get the memo. They never did.

"So, have you learned anything since the last time?" he asked as we took our seats.

I figured why beat around the bush, so I started with a hot take.

"I don't totally trust Carrie Granger. I feel like she's holding something back."

Duncan took a sip of his water and leaned back in his chair.

"Really? I met with her a few times when Emmy first went missing. I found her to be truthful."

"I respect your opinion, Duncan, but I have to stick to my guns."

"I understand," he said. "What gave you that impression?"

"It's hard to pinpoint it. It's just in my gut. Her answers were fine. She didn't tell any obvious lies. I just felt she was holding something back."

"I only met her once or twice and it's been several months. So I might be willing to trust a more recent opinion of her."

"It's odd. If you asked me if she had something to do with Emmy going missing, I'd say no. But if you asked me if she knew more than she told me, I'd say yes."

"We can circle back to her. Did the police report lead anywhere?"

"Yeah, I think so."

Duncan looked at me intently.

"What is it?"

"The police are listing six p.m. as the likely time that Emmy went missing. I think it's closer to four p.m. It's true that her phone was turned off at six, which led police to think that's when she was abducted. However, Chance called his daughter a little before four p.m. And from what everyone has told me, Emmy was very good at getting back to people."

"I see where you're headed," Duncan said.

"Yup. If Emmy really had her phone until 6:00 p.m., she almost assuredly would have gotten back to her father by then. Probably much earlier. She didn't have a show until seven that night, so there was no reason to not get back to him. And it wasn't just her father. Her roommate Nia texted her also, around 4:15 p.m., and never heard back either. It's possible she could have been mad at her father and decided not to return a text, but why not respond to her roommate from 4:15 p.m. to 6:00 p.m.? It seems unlikely. If I had to guess, Emmy was abducted, or whatever happened, some time much closer to four, which would explain why she never texted either Nia or her father back. I can't answer why the phone wasn't powered down until six, however."

"This is good work, Quint."

"Thanks. For an amateur, you mean."

"No, that's not what I meant. It's good work for any PI."

I paused, wondering if it was the right time for my next question. Why not?

"When I met you yesterday morning, you said you'd give me some pointers. Well, I'm all ears."

"What would you like to know?"

"Everything," I said. "I know what they taught me in the lead up to getting my PI license. But I want to know what the real PIs do. Do you tap phones? Do you put honing devices on cars? Do you break into houses to get information?"

I was throwing out some wild things, but I just wanted to get his juices flowing, maybe have him tell me some of the more nefarious things he'd done or could get away with.

"C'mon, Quint. I don't break into houses. As for the first two, you're kind of straddling the line between legal and illegal."

The Polaris rose out of the pool and shot water high in the air, hitting about ten feet from us.

"I positioned all of the recliners and canopies just out of range of the Polaris."

"I'm not sure I agree with that decision, Duncan."

"Huh?"

He had no idea what I meant.

"I think it might feel good to get sprayed on a hot Vegas day."

Duncan laughed.

"You may have a point."

"It would feel good today, that's for sure."

"Why don't we take a walk? If I get some blood going to my brain, you might hear some of my more devious ideas. Wasn't that your intention?"

"You read me like a book," I said. "You sure it's not too hot out?"

I hated asking, but the guy was an old man.

"You'll learn that I'm a pretty tough guy. A sunny day isn't going to do me in."

I smiled.

I liked Duncan Hobbes and was looking forward to learning from him.

We walked around his neighborhood for twenty minutes. One time Duncan stopped mid-story when a couple walked near us, but for most of it, I just let him talk. And I listened. And I learned.

Being a PI in the 70s, 80s, 90s, and even early 2000s sounded like the Old West. There were way fewer restrictions, everyone carried a gun, and you really had free rein to do whatever you wanted.

They were tapping phones. using tracking devices on cars, and recording conversations.

Unfortunately, in my case, these things were now either illegal, or had to be confirmed by a law enforcement official and oftentimes a judge.

There were slight loopholes.

For example, if you were in a public place, i.e. a bar or a restaurant, you could record someone on your phone because they didn't have an expectation of privacy. However, if they were at a corner table, they could argue they had that expectation. Duncan said it got a little dicey in those situations.

This was the type of information that, while you studied it in a book to earn your PI's license, you didn't know how it worked in real life. That's why this type of conversation was so helpful.

I asked him if there was any way around getting a tracking device on a car. It turned out there was, but it wasn't easy.

For example, if you were investigating a husband, you could only install a tracking device if the car was under his wife's name and got her consent. If the car was under his name, you were shit out of luck.

"Have you ever slashed a tire to ensure the husband would have to drive his wife's car?" I asked Duncan.

He looked on like a proud father.

"I plead the fifth," he said, confirming my suspicions.

I laughed.

"Do most PIs still carry a gun? Things seem different these days."

"Different PIs will give you different answers. In Nevada, I would say most of us carry them. It's certainly much easier to get them here than it is in California."

"CCWs are done by counties though, correct?" I asked.

CCWs were the ability to carry a firearm. It stood for Carrying a Concealed Weapon.

"Yes," Duncan said. "But it's easy to get a gun in any county in this state. San Francisco County may be a little more difficult."

"I don't think they want everyone carrying a gun."

"After some of the things I've seen, I can't say I blame them."

"One last question on guns. If I haven't yet received one in my home state. Can I get one here in Nevada?"

"I'm not sure, to be honest. And since I helped get you licensed here, I'd advise against it. We don't need the authorities bringing added attention and realizing you are the one actually doing all the work and not yours truly."

"Understood," I said.

"If things change and you actually feel threatened, let me know. I'll see what I can do."

"Thanks, Duncan."

"Any other questions?"

"I'm sure I'll have more as this case progresses, but that's it for now."

"Don't be afraid to ask."

~

We headed back to his house and talked more about the case and Emmy Peters. Before I knew it, it was late afternoon and it was time I headed back to the Strip.

"Some hot date?" Duncan asked.

I didn't mention Heather. It wouldn't be a good look if Cara came up at some point.

"No, I think I'll just do some more research on the case. Maybe I'll read the police report for a twelfth time."

"You'd be surprised. Sometimes it is that fifth, ninth, or twelfth time reading it when something finally clicks."

"That's what I'm hoping for," I said.

"Keep me posted, as I know you will. And you know Chance is coming to Vegas tomorrow night, right?"

"I know. Anything I should be nervous about?"

"He's a bit intimidating, but just be yourself. He knows you're doing a great job."

"How would he know that?"

"Let's just say I've put in a good word."

"Thanks."

"Hit me up after you talk to Chance. We'll go over a few more things, including some more tools of our chosen trade."

"Looking forward to it," I said.

We shook hands and I headed back to the Strip.

Around 7:00 p.m., Heather called.

She was out with her friends and invited me to join them. I'd had fun with her, without question, but I was a bit tired after our late night. More importantly, I had been feeling guilty throughout the day. No, Cara and I weren't currently a couple, but I still loved her very much.

It was almost like I could rationalize a one night stand that happened after a few drinks. A second night where we planned things out? That might be tougher to explain away.

I told Heather how much fun I'd had and then politely declined her invitation.

She understood.

I'm sure at some point I'd regret it, but I was making the right decision.

CHAPTER 9

MONDAY

I received a three-word text message at noon on Monday.

"*Investigate Sidney Remington.*"

"*Who is this?*" I texted back.

But as I looked down at the phone, I saw that the message was not delivered. I tried calling the number, and not surprisingly, the call would not go through. The message came from some sort of burner phone where you couldn't call or text back.

I stared down at my phone, a sinister feeling coming over me.

Who knew I was in Vegas? I'd interviewed Kenneth Croy, Duncan Hobbes, Nia Solomon, and Carrie Granger. Anyone who was following the case of Emmy Peters closely might know who I was by now.

And I didn't like getting investigative advice from unknown numbers.

On the other hand, maybe this was a blessing and the break I'd been waiting for.

I wavered back and forth and decided I couldn't just ignore the text. I'd proceed with caution, but proceed I would.

There was no need to Google Sidney Remington. I knew exactly who he was, being one of the most famous men in Las Vegas. He'd built three or four mega-hotels along the Strip. He was somewhere around sixty years old and always looked like he was dressed for the Oscars or a heavyweight title bout, of which I'm sure he'd attended many.

He always had a beautiful girl on his arm, usually decades younger. I knew he'd been married and had several kids, but he'd either been separated or divorced for a long time.

The man was undoubtedly charismatic, and the cameras followed him everywhere. Any red carpet, any awards show, any grand opening and you'd likely see Sidney Remington there.

Some famous people shun the limelight. Sidney Remington was not one of them.

And while Remington had built several hotels, Emmy's gig as a showgirl was taking place at the first hotel he ever built. And it was called...the Remington.

So that's where I'd start.

The fact that Sidney Remington was one of the most influential people in Las Vegas and could squash me like a bug wasn't lost on me.

Not that it was going to stop me from investigating him.

Giddy-up!

I had a busy day planned, which included my first meeting with Chance Peters. There was time to swing by The Remington, though.

It was a ways down the strip from the Cosmo, so I decided to cab it. My rental car would be for trips outside of the Strip, like to Duncan Hobbes's house. There was no need to drive down Las Vegas Boulevard when you could get a cab quicker than you'd ever get your car. Plus, in Vegas, you never knew when a random meeting might turn into a boozy lunch.

Just another reason to keep the rental car at the Cosmo.

The Remington was definitely not a classic old Vegas hotel. Nor was it one of the new hotels that offered every amenity in the world. It was in its own little limbo, not old-school cool and not new-school hip.

Or was old-school now hip? So hard to tell these days.

My cab pulled up in front of the mahogany red facade of The Remington. It was just one building and looked almost like a semi-circle, definitely concave in the middle. It wasn't a rinky-dink hotel, but it wasn't all that elegant either. It was only about ten stories and was the least prestigious of any Remington properties, despite it being his eponymous hotel.

Most importantly, it's where Emmy had worked as a showgirl, which was the reason I'd started here.

Sadly, showgirls were a dying breed in Las Vegas. At their peak, they were every bit as recognizable in Vegas as the Rat Pack. The Strip had gone in a different direction however, and now shows were more lights and lasers and less long-legged girls dancing.

There were only a few spots in town that still employed showgirls and the Remington happened to be one of them.

I tipped my cab driver and walked to the front entrance of the casino. There was a man there to open the door for me. It was classy. There was also only one main door at the Remington. This type of service would be impossible at the bigger casinos where fifty people walk in every minute or two.

The rug that covered the casino was also a deep red. The casino itself was really quiet, but it was a Monday and the majority of the tourists in town had either flown back on Sunday or early Monday. Vegas was an entirely different town come Monday afternoon than it was from Thursday through Sunday.

And I knew this because on many of my previous Vegas trips I'd intentionally stayed until Monday night, looking to avoid the madhouse that was McCarron Airport on a Sunday or Monday morning.

I found an employee wandering the casino floor, asked him where the show featuring the showgirls was performed, and headed in that direction.

A few minutes later, I found myself standing in front of the Remington Theater. I'm not saying Sidney Remington was a narcissist, but the hotel and the theater had the exact same name. God forbid the show was called The Remington.

It was not.

It's name was *Old School Vegas*.

I read a few of the posters and it looked to be an ode to Sinatra and the Rat Pack days, which also could be considered the showgirl days.

They had pictures of the people who played the parts of Sinatra, Sammy Davis Jr., and Dean Martin. I had to give them credit. The performers looked pretty damn close to the legends they were playing.

Each poster had a positive quote or two about *Old School Vegas*.

"The best reviewed show on the Strip!"

"You'd think you were actually watching Frank, Dean, and Sammy!"

"Nice to see that showgirls haven't died off just yet! They steal the show!"

The last quote couldn't help but make me think of Emmy Peters, who despite what everyone around her hoped, was most likely dead. Young women rarely go missing for over four months and then turn up unharmed. Does it happen? Yes. Just not very often.

I saw a security guard standing twenty feet away and approached him. He was extremely heavyset and approaching sixty. I'm sure breathing the cigarette filled air wasn't ideal for the man. And he certainly wasn't going to be running and catching anyone. He was there purely for show.

"Have you seen *Old School Vegas*?" I asked.

"Sure have. It's excellent."

"I was considering giving it a shot."

"You won't regret it."

"So the Rat Pack performers and the showgirls are the stars of the show?"

"They are certainly the headliners. But there's a fake Don Rickles, a fake Wayne Newton, even a fake Elvis. It's a lot of fun."

Being on the older side of Vegas employees, he might have enjoyed the real life people he mentioned.

I looked back at the sign with all the showgirls.

"Do you know how tall the showgirls have to be?" I asked.

"I believe 5′8″ is the minimum. But some of those girls are six feet tall. They sky over me, even without heels."

The man laughed and I smiled back. He was a nice guy who'd probably never had a shot with a showgirl type.

"Wow. Maybe I should see the show just for them," I said.

I was moving towards asking about Emmy, but had to keep the conversation going.

"They are a nice distraction from Sinatra and the boys."

"Indeed. Did you happen to know the showgirl named Emmy Peters?"

The security guard in front of me would have been a terrible poker player. His expression changed within a second of me asking the question.

"I don't think I've heard of her," he lied.

I guess I wasn't all that surprised. I'm sure employees were told not to discuss the case of a missing girl who performed in one of their shows. I can't say I blamed The Remington.

"She used to perform in this show, but she went missing."

"I'm so sorry to hear that. But I didn't know her. I think I have to go," he said.

I really wanted to ask him if Sidney Remington ever came around, possibly saw a show. But that might well put me on the radar of the hotel, if my questions about Emmy hadn't already done so.

"Thanks for talking to me. Think I'll check out the show soon."

He waved goodbye, but was done interacting with me.

Was I more suspicious than when I arrived?

Maybe slightly, but I shouldn't have been surprised about The Remington having a gag order when it came to Emmy Peters. Nothing good could come of it from their point of view.

I decided that I would be seeing *Old School Vegas* in the days to come.

I looked at the poster one more time. Showing Thursday through Sunday.

Looks like I'd have to wait a few days.

CHAPTER 10

I don't know why I'd been bemoaning meeting the guy who had ostensibly hired me. Not knowing what to expect had something to do with it. Was he going to be grateful? Pissed? Devastated?

After returning from The Remington, I'd gone over all of the information I'd discovered and read the police report one more time.

It was seven p.m. by the time Chance arrived at the Cosmo. Monday was flying by.

He wanted to meet in my room, the one he was paying for. He didn't want to risk people overhearing us at a cafe or a bar.

It made sense. I heard a knock at the door and went to open it.

"You must be Quint!" he exclaimed.

We shook hands. He did so ferociously.

Chance was a few inches taller, several pounds heavier, and seemingly fifty times more intense than his brother, Abel. His hair was darker than it should have been for a guy on the wrong side of fifty. Not a stray gray hair was to be seen. I suspected a dye job.

I understood how he'd become a successful businessman. He looked like he'd cut your balls off if you didn't do what he asked. There was a fervor about him and it wasn't just his vitriolic handshake.

"I am. Thanks for this opportunity, Chance," I finally said.

I didn't like my response. Opportunity? It sounded like I'd just been given a chance to play for the Lakers.

"Duncan told me that you've found a few things."

I escorted him into the room and shut the door behind him. We each took a seat that I'd set up by the window. The set up was very reminiscent of my meeting the previous day with Carrie Granger.

I then answered his question.

"While that's true, they're nothing major yet, so I don't want you to get your hopes up," I said.

"That's inevitable, Quint. This is the first progress I've heard of in two months. The police are walking in mud. But just because my hopes are up, that doesn't put any added pressure on you."

I'm not sure I agreed.

"I'm continuing to push forward," I said.

"That sounds generic. You're better than that. I want to know specifically what you've discovered. Or, at least, what your instincts tell you."

I told Chance about how I thought Emmy likely went missing closer to four than six. He liked my logic and agreed that Emmy would surely have texted him back earlier if she'd had her phone. I was afraid of Chance hamstringing my investigation, so when I told him that I was a bit suspicious of Carrie Granger, I asked him not to confront her.

"I respect your position, Quint, but I'm going to do what I want," Chance said.

I had to stand my ground.

"Listen, it's your daughter, and I don't blame you for anything you decide to do. But if you go talk to Carrie Granger now or send another PI to question her, you'll lose her. Despite my suspicions of her, we had a good meeting. I think she'll talk to me again and I'm better equipped to deal with her going forward."

Chance shook his head, but it was more a capitulatory shake.

"Okay," he said. "I won't bother her."

"Thanks."

"What else?"

I debated whether to tell him about the text I received. On the one hand, he was the father and deserved to know. On the other hand, if he heard that name, there's no way he wouldn't interfere. Carrie Granger was different. He could stand down on her. I doubted he could do the same with Sidney Remington.

Plus, it was from a random burner phone and who knew whether it was someone to be trusted.

I was going to wait until I had more time to investigate.

"There's nothing worth reporting just yet," I said. "I should know more in a day or two."

If this had been a week or so into Emmy's disappearance, a day or two would have felt like an eternity. But so many months had passed that a day or two didn't seem to give Chance Peters any pause.

"That's fine. It sounds like you're doing good work, Quint. And Duncan has praised you, which holds a lot of water for me."

"He's a very astute man. I'm going to be learning from him as well."

I kicked myself once again. It made me sound like some newbie who didn't know shit, which wasn't that far from the truth.

"Keep bouncing your ideas off of him. You could do a lot worse."

"I will," I said.

"I'll be back Wednesday with my wife. I'd like you to meet her."

That was going to be a tough one. A mother who had lost her daughter.

"Looking forward to meeting her," I said, a white lie if there ever was one.

"Keep up the good work, Quint. And if you don't have to involve the LVPD, I wouldn't. Talk to Duncan instead. The police department here has been terrible from the minute my daughter went missing."

"I'll try not to deal with them unless absolutely necessary."

"Thanks. You seem very competent. If my baby is still out there, I have faith you will bring her home."

"I will try my best," I said, having been burdened with unreasonable expectations.

"I'll see you Wednesday."

"Nice to meet you, Chance."

"You as well, Quint."

And he quickly rose and left the room.

The meeting had taken less than five minutes.

CHAPTER 11

TUESDAY

I didn't have much to go on, but I had more than when I arrived in Vegas on Friday. That's what they call progress, I guess.

I hadn't decided how to broach the impenetrable wall that was Sidney Remington, so I figured I'd take another shot at Carrie Granger. The reason was twofold: I was suspicious of her, and she was the only showgirl I'd met. If Sidney Remington was involved, maybe Carrie would know something, considering *Old School Vegas* took place at The Remington.

Hopefully, I'd get more information than from the geriatric security guard.

I texted her and she reluctantly agreed to meet me. However, she was busy until Wednesday afternoon so we couldn't meet until then.

I'd now met face-to-face with Kenneth Croy, Nia Solomon, Duncan Hobbes, and was about to have a second meeting with Carrie Granger. I'd not yet talked to the other two people that Abel Peters had mentioned. I'd been in Vegas for several days now. Even though neither still lived in Vegas, and I was skeptical about how much they could possibly know, there was no excuse.

I took out my phone.

The girls' names were Rose Bruskin and Jenny Appleton. Abel had left me a few notes on each.

Rose had lived with Emmy for two years in college and was likely her best friend at the time. When they both graduated last summer, Rose decided to move on from Vegas and now lived in LA.

Similarly, Jenny had lived with Emmy during their time at UNLV and had left Vegas after graduation. She lived in Santa Barbara.

These girls left Vegas last summer. They aren't going to know anything about a disappearance in January.

That's what I told myself. Or, more likely, I was just rationalizing why I'd taken so long to reach out to them.

And it's not like they wouldn't have kept in touch with their good friend. Maybe Emmy dropped some important information during a phone call.

I reprimanded myself. You shouldn't head into an interview expecting nothing to come of it. It's a sure way to overlook something.

So I put my game face on and called Rose Bruskin.

"Hello?" she answered.

I considered that a win. I didn't usually answer phone calls when I didn't know who was calling.

"Hello, Rose. My name is Quint Adler and I'm a private investigator looking into the disappearance of Emmy Peters."

"I thought you might be calling."

"How did you know?" I asked.

"Nia Solomon told me you talked to her."

"I did, indeed. Do you mind answering a few of my questions?"

"Of course not. I'd do anything to help find Emmy. Or her killer."

"So you think she's dead?"

"I hate to say it, but yes, I do."

"Any specific reason?"

"Because girls who just vanish don't often get found alive. And if they do, it's usually in some sex dungeon or something that might be worse than death."

I'd heard the "Girls don't show up alive" reasoning too many times now. The word "vanish" as well. Neither was necessarily wrong, I just didn't like hearing them.

"I hope you're wrong. Let's assume for the moment that she's still alive."

"Alright," Rose said, but she certainly wasn't convinced.

"When was the last time you talked to her before she went missing?"

"The day before."

"Did anything seem amiss?"

"No."

"And did you guys talk often?"

"Probably twice a week. She missed me and I missed her. Emmy was so much fun and everyone was attracted to her. Guys, for obvious reasons, but girls loved hanging out with her too."

"What did you guys talk about during your last conversation?"

"Guys. Vegas. A potential vacation together this summer."

"Was there anything specific that you discussed about Vegas?"

"Not really. Just how the city was, how we were always surprised how cold it got in January. Tourists who only come every summer don't realize it, but Vegas can have some pretty harsh winters, weird rainfall, and the occasional lightning storm."

"Did she seem happy?"

Rose didn't answer for a bit.

"Emmy always seemed happy. I guess, looking back, maybe there was an underlying feeling that not everything was perfect. It wasn't anything blatant though. She seemed fine as we were talking. And maybe it's just your questions that have me doubting what I'd heard."

I could have called Rose out. She'd just said that nothing was amiss. There was no reason to get on her bad side, however.

"Was it something she said or just a feeling you got?"

"I hadn't thought of it much till now. But, I guess just a feeling. I mean she told me about this guy Kenneth, who she seemed to like. She enjoyed her job in that old Vegas show or whatever it was called. She still had Nia in Vegas. And some new showgirl friend named Carrie. She really seemed to like her. I just thought she was a bit down maybe."

I'd never considered the possibility that Emmy had gone missing intentionally. Or, worse yet, harmed herself. I hoped beyond anything that wasn't what happened. Of course, the alternative wasn't much better.

I hated any and all possibilities with regards to this case.

"How was her writing going?"

"We didn't talk about her writing all that much. That's what she and Jenny would talk about."

"Jenny Appleton?"

"Yup."

"I'll be calling her next."

"She was a creative writing major so she and Emmy would always be talking about books. I'll tell you what, I think Jenny might have been a little jealous of Emmy."

"Why is that?"

"Well, Jenny was the creative writing major, but had to go take a real nine-to-five job. Meanwhile, Emmy got to lay around Vegas and work on a novel."

"I think a lot of showgirls would tell you they aren't just lying around. That's not an easy job," I said.

"Yeah, that was crass of me. I'm sorry."

"Have you ever heard of Sidney Remington?"

"Of course. I lived in Vegas for four years."

"Do you know if Emmy ever met him?"

"That's a weird question. Please don't tell me he's a suspect."

"He's not, and please don't spread that rumor around."

"Alright, Mr. Private Investigator," she said, intentionally pushing my buttons.

"Well...," I said, leading her to answer my latest question.

"I never heard of her meeting him. Although I know her Old Vegas show was at The Remington, so I guess it's possible."

My questions about Sidney Remington were going nowhere.

"Do you have any theory as to how she went missing?" I asked.

Rose paused again.

"I always just assumed it was some random whacko. You're probably out there investigating people she knew, when all along it was just some crazy guy who was all meth'd up or something."

There's certainly a chance Rose Bruskin was right. I was talking with all these friends of Emmy's, while meanwhile it was some scumbag who picked her up from off the street, killed her, and buried her in the desert.

A man I'd never find.

I couldn't focus on that possibility. At least, not yet.

"So there's no one in Vegas that Emmy was scared of?"

"Nope. The only person Emmy ever butted heads with was her Dad."

Great, just what I needed. To worry that somehow Chance was involved.

"Don't every father and daughter argue?" I asked.

"Yeah, I guess. But she and Chance really did butt heads a lot. Listen, I'm not saying he was involved. He loved his daughter. I'm just saying they didn't always see eye-to-eye."

"Did she rebel against him?"

"Not in the way most people would define it. She didn't rush out and do drugs or start dating a guy on a motorcycle. But I'd had many talks with her over the years, and I think she came to Las Vegas to get away from LA and her parents."

"Is that why she stayed in Vegas after she graduated?"

"That I'm not sure of. I was so concentrated on what I was going to do that those last few months before graduation kind of just flew by. I wasn't great about asking other people what they were doing. I was concentrating on my own future."

"That's understandable, Rose. Do you know if Emmy ever had a one night stand with a creep?"

"I think we all have at some point."

"Any that kept calling or texting her, or maybe started showing up unannounced?"

"No, she never told me about anyone like that."

I was continuing to grasp at straws.

"Did the police ask you all these questions?"

"I never talked to them. Remember, I wasn't even living in Vegas anymore."

I was a bit surprised, but I guess it made sense. The police aren't going to reach out to people who weren't even in Vegas at the time.

"Do you know why Chance and his brother Abel would put me in touch with you?"

"I was one of her best friends, but it is a bit odd considering I was no longer in Vegas when she went missing."

I'm not sure if 'went missing' sounded any better than kidnapped or disappeared or vanished, but maybe it sounded more innocuous to Rose.

I didn't feel like I was getting anywhere. She had told me one piece of potentially important information so I doubled back there.

"Just a few more questions, Rose. You said that Emmy may have been a little down on your last phone call together. Can you remember at what point in your talk you started getting that feeling?"

"That's a tough question. It was so long ago and you're asking me to remember a specific part of a conversation."

"I know. Just throwing it out there."

"Like I said, we talked about guys. We talked about Vegas. And then we talked about taking a vacation together."

"Okay, good," I said, trying to keep her mind focused.

"There was something, I guess. When I brought up taking a vacation together, she was initially excited, but then said it was going to be hard to find time."

"Because of her job as a showgirl?"

"No. She said it had more to do with writing her novel."

This wasn't the answer I expected and definitely got my attention.

"You can write a novel anywhere," I said.

"That's what I told her. I asked her how fun it would be to write a novel on the beaches of Hawaii."

"And what did she say?"

"She said there was too much research about Vegas to be done."

"No offense Rose, but this is some pretty important information for a guy like me. Why didn't you tell me right away?"

"We were talking about taking a vacation and some book she was writing. It hardly seemed relevant."

"You're right," I said, merely trying to placate her. "What was the novel about?"

"I think it was some thriller based in Vegas. As I told you, she talked with Jenny a lot more about writing than she did with me."

My upcoming talk with Jenny was now holding more weight.

"Is there anything else you can add?"

"I don't think so. I hope this last part helped."

It could be nothing, but I had a suspicion it was the best piece of evidence, if you could call it that, I'd received yet.

"It can only help. I may be calling you again at some point if that's okay."

"Sure. That's fine."

"Thanks for your time. Take care."

And I hung up on my end.

It was time to call Jenny Appleton.

CHAPTER 12

"Hello, this is Jenny."

I'd been sitting on the bed during my phone call with Rose, but now I found myself pacing around the hotel room, the extra adrenaline being the impetus.

"Jenny, this is Quint Adler. I'm investigating Emmy Peters' disappearance."

"I know who you are."

Word spread fast amongst Emmy's friends.

"Is it cool if I ask you some questions?"

I always asked permission. They'd appreciate me asking and I'd be starting off on the right foot.

"Of course."

"I just got off the phone with Rose Bruskin. She told me that of all Emmy's friends, you discussed writing with her more than any other."

"No question. The other girls seemed bored by it."

"But not you, right?"

"No way. I loved it. I was a creative writing major and I have dreams of writing a novel myself. Unfortunately, I don't have really long legs like Emmy and couldn't get a job as a showgirl. I had to go get a real job and put off writing."

It was an unnecessarily harsh response, especially considering the friend she was referring to had gone missing.

Rose was right. Jenny Appleton was undeniably bitter that Emmy was writing a novel.

Before I had a chance to respond, Jenny jumped back in.

"I'm sorry. That sounded horrible. I just get really defensive when everyone talks about Emmy being the writer, when I was the one who went to school for it."

I'm not sure her apology was any better.

I was afraid of this conversation derailing so I tried to keep her in the right frame of mind.

"You're young, Jenny. You'll have plenty of time to write a novel or ten."

"Thanks. Again, I'm sorry. I loved Emmy and hate thinking of what happened to her. The writing just cuts deep with me."

"Do you know what her new novel was about?"

"She kept the exact plot pretty close to the vest. It was definitely a mystery that took place in Vegas."

I looked out of my room and onto the Strip below.

"And there was definitely a murder or two," she added.

"A Vegas murder mystery. Interesting," I said. "So, obviously this was fiction?"

"Yeah. Emmy was always very fastidious, though, so I know she'd want to make sure every detail was correct. It was almost like you'd research a non-fiction book."

"She sounds meticulous," I said, trying to find a word that rivaled fastidious.

"Exactly. If she was going to write about organized crime, she'd make sure she knew everything."

"Was she writing about organized crime?" I asked.

"I have no idea. I was just throwing that out there because the book was some sort of murder mystery. Seemed apropos."

"I know you said she kept it close to the vest, but do you know any more of the plot? Even the smallest detail might help."

"Not much. I know a young woman was the protagonist. And I'm assuming she gets thrown in the middle of a few murders. But I don't know if she's a cop, a victim, or even a PI like yourself."

"Do you think Emmy didn't disclose much of the plot to you because of your creative writing degree? Maybe she was afraid it wasn't good enough?"

"I thought about that, but no. I talked to some of our friends and she hadn't disclosed the plot to anyone. I just think that's how Emmy is. Her Dad was a bit intimidating, and I wonder if that didn't create a little mistrust of others. No, that's not the right word. A little reticent of putting herself out there."

I understood Jenny's overall point.

"Emmy's father doesn't seem too popular with her friends," I said.

"He was extremely generous. I can't tell you how many dinners he took us out to. So I can't badmouth him for that. But he was kind of a blowhard and was always talking about how great his business was or the private jet he flew in on or a helicopter ride over the Grand Canyon. Things like that, and it drove Emmy nuts."

This was the second of Emmy's friends who'd been critical of Chance

Peters, but mostly for just being braggadocious. Not because he wasn't a good father.

"I guess I can't blame her," I said.

"He's not all bad, and I know how much he loved his daughter."

Again, someone using Emmy in the past tense.

"After his daughter went missing, he may well have changed."

"Of course. I hate to be coming off as the girl who badmouths Emmy and her Dad. I promise I'm not that girl."

"Don't worry about it. We're just talking. Back to the novel if you don't mind. Do you have any idea how far she was into it?"

"I don't. She didn't start until after we graduated in June. So let's say she started in July or August. And she went missing in January. Keep in mind, it's a first novel, which most every author says takes longer than any subsequent book. So, if I had to guess, I doubt she was even halfway through it, if that helps."

"I would guess you're right. Any chance she told you the title?"

"A snowball's chance in hell."

I was sure she was referring to the odds Emmy would tell her that, but I still had to ask.

"Just to clarify, that's not the title is it?"

Jenny laughed.

"No, that was me telling you she'd never tell me the title. But now that you mention it, that's a great title for a book. Maybe I'll steal that," she said.

"It's all yours."

"Thanks."

"You said she was fastidious by nature. Did she tell you about anyone she interviewed for the book?"

"No, she didn't, but I'm sure she was out there learning about the world she was writing about. Like I said, she'd want to make sure she got every detail correct. She'd walk somewhere just to know she got the distance exactly right."

I couldn't tell if Jenny regarded this as an attribute or a shortcoming.

"Did the cops ever talk to you?" I asked.

"No," she said and answered just as Rose had. "Probably because I wasn't living in Las Vegas any longer. She had enough friends who still lived there that they could interview."

"Do you know if Emmy kept a journal about her writings?"

"Don't all writers? Well, maybe not a journal per se, but surely she kept something and made notes on her writing, or how the novel was going to progress, or a synopsis."

Or a list of people she'd interviewed.

"You've been very helpful, Jenny."

"Thanks. Is there anything else?"

"I'm sure I'll have a question or two in the future, but that's it for now. Thanks for your time."

"You're welcome."

～

Within ten seconds of ending the call with Jenny, I called Abel Peters.

"Hey, Quint, how's the investigation going?"

I hated getting Abel or Chance's hopes up, so I decided to play it cool.

"It's moving forward," I said. "Listen, I was wondering what happened to Emmy's writing stuff? Her laptop. Possibly a journal. Maybe some old spiral notebooks. Whatever she wrote with."

"About a month after her disappearance, they took all of Emmy's belongings back to their place in Bell Canyon. I'm sure it's all there."

"Can I call Chance or is it better to go through you?" I asked.

"I heard you guys met, so you can probably just call him yourself now."

"Ok, thanks."

"Let's hope she didn't leave a bunch of notes on her iPhone," Abel said.

It was a great point. Her iPhone had never been recovered and it was as good a place as any to leave notes. They had an app named Notes, after all.

"Do you think the book she was writing had something to do with what happened?" Abel asked.

"I'm just following up on every potential lead," I said.

"C'mon, Quint! You have to be a little more up front with me. I'm your friend. And I helped hire you."

He was right.

"I talked to Rose and Jenny, and I found out Emmy was writing a murder mystery of some type that took place in Vegas. Maybe she interviewed the wrong guy or asked the wrong question. I don't know, but it's certainly something I need to investigate."

"That's all I wanted, Quint. The truth."

It was similar to the conversation I'd had with Chance Peters. They wanted to know everything. Me, I was a little reticent about divulging too much.

"I'm sorry, I just don't want to get anyone's hopes up. Especially when everyone seems to already assume that I won't be finding her alive."

"I'm not ready to concede she's dead, but if she is, and you found the killer, that's still doing your job."

"I know," I said. "But I'm going with the assumption she's still alive."

"Of course. So you're going to call my brother?"

"Yeah, I'll call Chance. Take care, Abel."

"Keep up the good work. I feel like you're getting somewhere."

"That might be overstating it, but thanks."

～

NINE DAYS IN VEGAS 69

It had been a morning of phone calls and Chance Peters was next.

"Quint, give me some good news."

"You guys picked up all of Emmy's stuff from Vegas, correct?"

"We did. It's all sitting back in her old room at our house."

"Did the police keep anything?"

"They kept her laptop. And obviously they would have kept her phone, but that was never found."

"Were there any journals or notebooks or anything that you brought back?"

"I'd have to go through her room and check. I'm still planning on flying back to Vegas tomorrow, so would it be okay if I brought them then? If you need them now, I could scan and fax them."

"I've got some other things I can do today, so why don't you just bring them with you tomorrow."

"I will. We fly in really early, so are you up for meeting around nine a.m.?"

"That's fine. Where?"

"We're staying at the Wynn. You can come meet us there."

"See you then."

"Bye, Quint."

CHAPTER 13

1^{3.}

I took the elevator to the lobby of The Cosmopolitan, picked up a coffee and a copy of *The Las Vegas Daily*. I sat outside the little coffee shop and enjoyed people watching. An early morning in Vegas is just about the best version of that, with some maniacs still up from the night before, while many others are nursing hangovers and making their way down for their morning coffee.

It was enjoyable to watch, although I've been on the other side, and that's not nearly as fun.

I scrolled through the paper and something on page two caught my eye.

Fourteen-year-old-girl has gone missing.

"A teenage girl has gone missing from Vegas. Her name is Dakota Jones. The family was from Tennessee and had brought a large group of relatives. At some point, while walking along Las Vegas Boulevard, her parents turned around and realized that their daughter was no longer with them. This occurred somewhere around the outside of the Linq. Dakota was five feet tall and approximately one hundred pounds. If you have any information regarding this girl's disappearance, please call the LVPD at 702-555-1825."

Emmy Peters wasn't fourteen-years-old, but is there any way these two were related? Kidnapping a young teen would certainly be easier than abducting Emmy, who was tall and in good shape.

But a missing girl certainly gets your attention.

I decided I'd ask Duncan Hobbes if he could arrange a meeting with a member of the LVPD.

With Duncan's history, maybe, just maybe, they'd let me know if there had been a string of girls who'd gone missing recently.

I shuddered at the possibility.

I grabbed the paper and took it with me as I walked back towards the elevators. People watching didn't hold much charm after reading about a missing teenage girl.

~

As I walked down the hall to my room, a new text came in.

I looked down .

"Sidney Remington was just a test. He had nothing to do with Emmy's disappearance. I just had to make sure you wouldn't go rushing to the police."

I was pissed!

I didn't like being jerked around and that's exactly what this felt like.

All those questions at the Remington were for nothing?

I arrived back at my room and chucked my phone onto the bed. It bounced off the comforter and hit the bed frame. I walked over and luckily there were no scratches on the screen of the phone.

I felt like a puppet, being dangled around by a puppeteer.

Say this! Do that!

And me, obliging every word.

I once again tried to respond to the text, but it wouldn't process. Same thing when I tried to call the number.

I was tempted to throw my cell again, but resisted the urge.

And as I white knuckled the phone, another text came in.

"If you continue to behave and tell no one, and that includes Emmy's family and that old PI, I will keep you in the game. If you spill the beans, and trust me, I'll know, you'll never hear from me again and this case will remain unsolved forever."

"FUCK!!"

I yelled it so loud, people from four doors down surely heard it.

~

The rest of Tuesday was largely spent in my own head.

I would be meeting Chance Peters and his wife the following morning.

Do I tell him about these mysterious texts? Do I go to the cops?

There were pros and cons on each side, but I came to the decision not to tell anyone. At least, not yet. The advantages of telling Chance or the police were outweighed by any potential bombshell I might receive from the mysterious texter, even if there was a chance I was just being played.

Something told me that this person was legitimate and not just some crackpot. They were also very honed in on my investigation. Maybe it was Emmy's killer. Maybe it was a cop. Maybe it was a friend of Emmy's who knew something. I had no idea. Above all, I believed this person knew what they were talking about. So I was going to sit on the information.

I decided to make a concession. If I didn't receive another text by Thursday, I'd tell both Chance and the LVPD.

I hated the entire situation, but I felt I came to the right decision.

I avoided the lights and action of Vegas on Tuesday night, opting for an early bedtime.

My intuition told me the next two days would be pivotal.

CHAPTER 14

WEDNESDAY

While The Cosmopolitan was a solid Las Vegas hotel, it had nothing on the Wynn.

Even at nine a.m., when Vegas is waking up from a collective hangover, the Wynn still exudes class.

The carpeting is clean. The air is filtered. And there's not a ragamuffin to be seen. The architecture, marbling, chandeliers, etc are all top notch. And that's coming from a guy who usually doesn't take stock of those types of things.

Chance Peters met me at the entrance to the elevators. You couldn't get on them without a key, so he came down to vouch for me.

We made some small talk on the elevator ride up, knowing it wouldn't last once we got to his room, which just so happened to be on the top floor. I knew I was in for something special.

He opened the door and I was greeted by the smiling face of Liz Peters.

She had light brown hair, was tall like her daughter, and had aged very well. She was a very attractive woman and probably somewhere in her mid-fifties.

While the smile was big, the eyes held a certain sadness in them. The reason was obvious.

"You must be Quint," she said.

"I am. Nice to meet you, Mrs. Peters."

"Call me Liz."

I extended my hand for a shake, but she hugged me instead.

It made me feel insecure, like she'd anointed me the savior, as if she expected me to find Emmy alive. I didn't tell her this, obviously, but I wished we could keep it more business-like.

"Chance tells me you are making great progress in finding our Emmy."

"I think great progress would be a stretch, but I'm doing all I can."

Chance jumped in.

"Let me show you the suite, Quint."

We were still standing by the doorway and they led me towards the heart of the room.

My opinion of the Wynn could well describe this suite as well. Stunning.

There were two spiral staircases leading to a second story. There was a ten-foot-long bar and five accompanying barstools. There was a massive chandelier smack dab in the middle of the suite. There was a view that rivaled the Voodoo Lounge.

They led me to the bathroom which had a huge jacuzzi, a shower that was probably half the size of my apartment, and four sets of mirrors for people to get dressed and prepared to go out.

Seemed excessive, but that's how opulent the suite was.

They walked me up one of the spiral staircases, where the master bedroom happened to be. It had a massive gold frame surrounding the entire bed. And you could look out on the floor below and below that, the strip of Vegas. A true bird's-eye-view.

"Spectacular," I said.

Chance approved of my adjective. So far, I'd liked the guy, but the showboating that Emmy's friends spoke of was always close at hand.

They led me back down to the main level and into a separate little room that had its own huge bay window overlooking the strip.

On a table, pushed up against the window, was a feast.

I saw Eggs Benedict, French Toast, Hash Browns, toast, and sides of bacon and sausage.

There was also a bottle of champagne and a carafe of orange juice if someone wanted a Mimosa.

It was enough food for eight people.

"Hope you're hungry, Quint. We might have ordered just a bit too much."

"It looks great. I can do some damage," I said.

Liz smiled, those sad eyes still very front and center.

We all took a seat and stared down on the Strip below.

I grabbed one Eggs Benedict (is that an Eggs Benedict?), a piece of French Toast, a segment of Hash Browns, and a side of bacon. I was sampling just about everything.

"Would you like a Mimosa?" Chance asked.

I didn't know how to respond. I didn't want to offend them by saying no, but would it look unprofessional if I said yes? I was on a job for them, after all.

"Don't feel guilty," Chance said. "Some of my best business deals have been done with a drink or two in my system."

"Well, then, I guess I'll have one. Thanks, Chance."

He took out a flute glass and poured champagne towards the brim, topping it off with just a little OJ.

"Are you enjoying Vegas, Quint?" Liz asked.

They were making an obvious decision not to bring up Emmy right away, to enjoy our meal first.

"I've had some nice moments, but the main reason I'm here is obviously to find out what happened to your daughter."

"There will be time for that," Chance said, nipping it in the bud. "Let's just enjoy our breakfast first. This is quite the view isn't it, Quint?"

I took a bite of the Eggs Benedict. Delicious.

"It's great. I'm afraid to ask how much this room costs for a night."

"It's free. As long as you give them tens of thousands on the tables over the years," Chance said and then laughed.

He was more carefree than when I'd met him two days previous. I'm sure with a missing daughter you have good days and bad days. Or, more likely, bad days and worse days. Whatever the case, he seemed a little more upbeat today.

I hope it wasn't because he was expecting miracles from me.

"They'll pretty much give us a suite every time we're in town, Quint." Liz said.

If you didn't know about Emmy, you'd say these two upper class citizens had the perfect life. But they'd surely give it all back for the safe return of their daughter. Some people think money can buy some form of happiness, but not when catastrophe hits. Their money did nothing for their broken hearts.

"Those Eggs Benedict hit the spot," I said. "A good Hollandaise is always key."

I next attacked the French Toast, trying to avoid thinking about Emmy and broken hearts.

"How's the Mimosa?" Chance asked.

I took my first sip and finally noticed it had come from a bottle of Dom Perignon.

"Slight step above the Brut Mimosa's we used to have in college," I said.

Liz laughed.

"You're a very nice young man," Liz said.

It had been a while since I'd been called a young man, so I gladly took it.

"Thanks. But don't think that means I won't do the dirty work for this case."

Everyone was quiet for several seconds.

"Alright," Chance said. "We've waited long enough. Is it time to dive in?"

"Sure," I said.

"Have you found out anything more since I saw you on Monday?"

I saw Liz set her fork down and stare at me.

"I talked to Rose Bruskin which led me to a conversation with Jenny Appleton. I hadn't heard much about the novel that Emmy was writing, but after talking with her two friends, I think it could be very important."

"How so?"

"Jenny said that it was a murder mystery based in Vegas. It was fiction, so it's not like she's describing real people who might get pissed. However, Jenny used the word fastidious to describe Emmy, saying she'd vehemently research every aspect of her novel. I think it's possible that Emmy ran into some problems while doing her research."

"Do you have any evidence of this?" Liz asked.

"No," I admitted. "But in a case with so little evidence, this sounds promising. Plus, I have to follow-up on any potential lead I get. There haven't been many."

"Of course."

"And that's why I asked Chance to bring all of Emmy's journals. Did you?"

"Yeah. They are in one of the closets and I'll give them to you before you go."

"Thanks," I said.

"What do you hope to find in them?" Liz asked. Once our conversation had moved to Emmy, she'd become very attentive, as would be expected.

"I don't know exactly, but I'm hoping she may have listed people she was interviewing for the novel. Maybe one of them was up to no good."

"It sounds like a stretch," Liz said.

She was skeptical.

"Possibly, but it's the best thing I have to go on right now."

I said it a little too forcefully. As if I was calling out Liz Peters. She didn't seem to take offense, though.

"Can I be frank?" I asked.

"Of course," Chance said.

"There's only so much I can control on my side," I said. "If some stranger grabbed your daughter off the street, I don't have much of a prayer. But I can investigate things that come to my attention. And if Emmy interviewed some people for her book, I certainly have to follow up on that. Especially since she was writing a murder mystery. Maybe, just maybe, she picked the wrong guy to interview. Or she saw something she shouldn't have. Whatever the case, this is the best direction for me to head at the moment."

Along with the texts I received, but I'd already decided against disclosing them.

"My husband and I are behind you 100 percent. I shouldn't have said it sounded like a stretch. It's absolutely the right thing to do."

"Thank you, Liz."

I took another sip of my drink. The Peters were on my side, but this was still a very stressful meeting. The mimosa was welcomed.

"How is Duncan?" Chance asked.

I knew to tread lightly here and not make it sound like I was some rank amateur. I'd already made that mistake on our previous visit.

"He's been very helpful and seems to like the direction my inquiries have headed."

They both nodded, obviously holding Duncan in high esteem.

"If it gets to the point where you need help, he knows a plethora of PI's. You just let me know and I'll add another one to the payroll."

If another PI joined the case, he'd quickly find out everything I knew. It wouldn't be ideal with the texts I hadn't mentioned.

"Thanks, Chance. And that may eventually be the case, but for now, I'm able to handle everything that's come in."

Chance turned to his wife.

"I feel like we are in good hands, Liz."

"I agree," she said. "Your brother Abel always had a good read on people."

"Abel is a good man," I said. "He was a lot of help to me in Hollywood."

"He speaks highly of you."

While I appreciated it, I didn't like all the fanfare. It just added pressure to an already difficult case. One in which an unhappy ending was still the most likely outcome.

I couldn't let this meeting pass without throwing one of my suspicions out there. I didn't want to alert them to me having Carrie on my radar, so I threw out all of Emmy's friends together.

"How well do you guys know Nia, Carrie, Jenny and Rose?" I asked.

Liz answered.

"Chance knows them better than I, since he flew out here more often and took the girls out to dinner sometimes. But I've had a lot of nice conversations with Carrie since Emmy went missing."

That got my full attention.

"Oh yeah, why is that?"

"She's just been very nice, always asking what the latest news was. She probably calls me twice a week or so. We've lost touch with many of Emmy's friends, so I really cherish the phone calls with Carrie. In fact, I don't think I've talked to any of Emmy's other friends in weeks."

"Sounds like Carrie is keeping on top of it," I said.

"She is. She keeps telling me that Emmy will turn up alive. And she always wants to know if we've heard any new info."

I had to tread lightly and not give away my suspicions about Carrie, so I just said, "Nice of her to stay involved."

I was now more than a little dubious. Was Carrie just being a good friend? That was possible. Likely, even. However, the fact that the girl I didn't entirely trust happened to be the only one who kept calling for updates? That gave me pause.

Maybe I could find a way to record one of Liz's conversations with Carrie and see if something caught my ear. The problem was, it wouldn't work if Liz was suspicious of Carrie.

So I was going to say nothing for now. In fact, I thought it was better to steer the conversation in another direction.

"I'm sure you two have answered this question a million times, but did Emmy seem scared leading up to her disappearance?"

"I don't think so," Chance said. "She seemed the same happy, yet determined, young woman."

"I'd agree," Liz said. "I didn't notice anything."

"I'm going to speak frankly again. I don't think Kenneth Croy had anything to do with her disappearance."

"I feel the same," Chance said, surprising me.

"I thought you suspected him."

"Only for the first week or so. And part of it was, I can admit this now, me being pissed he was so much older than Emmy. A guy almost forty dating a girl barely over twenty-one? I thought if his morals were questionable in that regard, maybe they were in other ways as well."

"I don't blame you. But he was working at the time she went missing. And I interviewed him and actually believe the guy. Duncan agrees with me."

"Anyone else you've been able to rule out?"

I could tell Chance didn't want to talk much about Kenneth Croy. He may have regretted coming down so hard on him.

"No, but it's not like there's been a multitude of suspects."

"That's the scary part, like you mentioned earlier. What if it was just some random junkie who grabbed Emmy off the street?"

I saw his wife cringe.

"Let's not talk specifics like that, please," Liz said. "I've got enough bad visuals going through my head."

She looked like she was about to cry and my heart broke for her. I couldn't imagine the games your mind would play on you, recreating your daughter being kidnapped, taken advantage of, killed.

"I'm sorry, babe," Chance said and hugged his wife.

Emmy's friends portrayed Chance as a blowhard and someone who thought he was Joe Cool. And while those were partly true, he also seemed to be quite loving towards his wife. It was a great attribute. My opinion of Chance had improved.

"How long are you staying for this time?" I asked.

"We're leaving tomorrow morning. We'll be back on Friday afternoon."

"That's a lot of back and forth for you."

"That will be the case until we find out what happened to our precious daughter. You're right, though, this week has been especially busy."

I nodded.

"And we'll make an assessment on Friday about whether you should continue. Money is no object for me, so I'm assuming we will keep you on. I appreciate all the work you are doing, Quint."

"Thank you."

"That goes for both of us," Liz said.

I nodded in her direction.

"What do you have planned for today?" Chance asked.

"I'm going to interview Nia Solomon again. I know it's been several months since Emmy went missing, but maybe she'll remember something."

"Anything else?"

"I might stop by Duncan's and bounce a few ideas off of him."

"Always a good idea. And Quint, if you ever need any money to help push this case forward, you just let me know. Like I said, money is no object. I don't care if it's a tracking device or paying off someone who has information on Emmy. We'll do or pay anything."

He was basically telling me I had free rein to do whatever I wanted. And who was I to blame him? If I had a missing daughter, I'd do anything within the law, and probably a few things just outside of it, to help find her.

"I'm not at that point yet, but let's talk Friday."

"I'll be in touch," Chance said.

The breakfast was over a few minutes later. I hugged Liz who looked to have a few tears in her eyes. Chance was stoic, but I knew just how much this was affecting him as well.

I'd really gotten the feeling of despair from the Peters. More than ever, I hoped that by some miracle Emmy was still alive.

With it being her only child, I wondered how Liz Peters would move forward if Emmy was found dead.

In reality, Chance would probably be losing his wife along with his daughter.

Before I left, Chance Peters gave me a box that was about two feet wide, two feet long, and two feet deep.

"It's probably more than just her writing, but I'll let you decide what's important. I hope something comes of it."

That made two of us.

CHAPTER 15

"Do you ever feel it necessary to withhold information from your clients?"
I was back at Duncan Hobbes' home for a meeting we'd already arranged. Part of me wanted to just sit at The Cosmo and read Emmy's journals, but I figured that could wait until later in the day. Plus, I didn't want to cancel on Duncan. I learned a few things about my new profession every time I talked to him.

Duncan was wearing yellow shorts and a yellow shirt that had the two top buttons undone. His white chest hair was showing and it was definitely a casual Wednesday for him.

It was a scorcher in Vegas, already topping one hundred degrees and it wasn't even noon yet. A heat wave was forecast for the next several days, like that was something new. We were sitting on a couch inside the house for the first time. There's only so much a canopy, some ice water, and sitting near the pool can do. And it was just too hot out.

The only conclusion Duncan could reach was that my question was about the Peters. And obviously, it was.

"Is there something you can't tell Chance?"

I decided to come clean. For the most part.

The texts I'd been receiving would stay my little secret, however. I wasn't ready to divulge that info, even to Duncan himself.

"I don't know if I can't tell him. I've just decided not to."

"What is it? Since you brought it up, I'm guessing you're willing to tell me."

"You already know some of it. I'm suspicious of Carrie Granger. I've felt it from the first time I talked to her and now I know something that only furthers that belief."

"What's that?"

"Liz Peters told me that Carrie is calling her frequently and always asking for updates about the case. I didn't like the sound of it. I may be reading too much into it, but it sounded like Carrie was more interested in updates on the case than Emmy herself."

"That's a fine line. And the two surely overlap."

"Sure, but since I've considered Carrie a potential person of interest from the beginning, I can't just ignore it."

"A little confirmation bias for your theory."

Duncan was a smart man.

"That's exactly right," I said.

"As to your original question, yes, there's times I've held off from giving my clients all the information I've accumulated. Many times, actually. My question to you would be, why is this something you want to withhold?"

"Because Liz seems like she's barely holding on. I can't blame her, God knows what I'd be like if I ever had a daughter who went missing. If I'm correct, though, and Carrie may somehow be involved, I can't risk telling Liz and having her give something away over the phone. Especially if they are talking a few times a week. Carrie may call today or tomorrow. And I don't trust Liz to play it cool."

"So is your plan to eventually set a trap for Carrie?"

"While a trap may be overstating it, yes, that's the general idea. I'd record a call between Liz and Carrie and maybe give Liz a question or two to ask and see if Carrie takes the bait or asks something that seems just a bit out of line."

Duncan took a second to think about it.

"I think you've thought this out long and hard, Quint. And I'm not going to disagree with you for sitting on your suspicions for now."

"Thanks, Duncan. I'm glad we agree."

"Start working fast. The worst thing would be to have Carrie clam up and decide not to call Liz anymore. You'd have missed an opportunity. So go out and investigate Carrie, and if you still consider her a suspect, you have to talk to Chance and Liz and set up a planned phone call soon. And this goes without saying, but I'll say it anyway. Don't let Carrie know you're looking at her. That's one sure way of those phone calls ending abruptly. If you talk to her, be subtle. Don't be accusatory."

"I appreciate all the advice."

"I should probably add that I myself was not suspicious of Carrie. I met with her twice and she didn't strike me as anything but a worried, grieving friend."

He'd already told me that, but felt it important to reiterate. It was one of the few things we'd disagreed on.

"I respect you greatly, Duncan. I have to go with my gut, though."

"You really think that seemingly sweet showgirl had something to do with Emmy's disappearance?"

"Sounds crazy, doesn't it?   And I'm not ready to jump into potential motives. Hopefully, it's not something outrageous like a rivalry in the *Old School Vegas* show. Like I said earlier, she's not a suspect. I'm just suspicious of her. There is a difference. Maybe she thinks she knows what happened and just won't tell me. Or she suspects someone herself, but is afraid to voice it. I actually think that is more likely than her being involved in the disappearance itself."

"I'm glad you said disappearance and not killing or murder. Keep thinking that Emmy is alive. It will make you work harder going forward."

"I'll assume she's alive until I see the body."

"Even then, double check," Duncan said.

He was trying to say that things aren't always as they seem, but the statement hit with a thud.

"You know what I mean," he said.

"I do."

"If you see or hear Carrie do something unexpected, come by tomorrow. We could do a few things that might skirt the whole legal/illegal line."

"Like putting a honing device on her car?"

"That's illegal without a warrant. We'll find something, though. I'm not yet sold on your suspicions of her, so you'll have to bring me something more before I condone taking a next step."

"That's fair," I said. "We'll talk soon."

"Be safe, Quint."

CHAPTER 16

I arrived back at The Cosmo and picked up two coffees on my way to the room.

I pushed a desk over towards the window so I could have a nice view while I did some research. No, it wasn't the view that Chance and Liz had, or even Carrie at Veer Towers, but it wasn't too shabby either.

I emptied all the contents of the box on the desk and set my coffees on a small little table next to it.

There were a few items that I was quickly able to discern were not Emmy's writings. One was a little photo album that I quickly thumbed through. There were pictures with Rose, Jenny, Nia, and several other young women. They all looked so happy. There were zero pictures of Kenneth Croy, who I hadn't thought much about lately. A second interview with him couldn't hurt, I told myself. Nor were there any pictures of Carrie Granger, but that's likely because they'd only met each other when Emmy started working as a showgirl. These pictures looked to be all from her time at UNLV.

A few candles had made their way into the box. A small Barbie had me sadly thinking of Emmy Peters as a little kid. And finally, there were a few curling irons. I tossed those aside.

Chance Peters said he'd just thrown a bunch of stuff in a box and it truly was a hodge-podge of things.

After narrowing it down, I was left with a spiral notebook, a journal, and some stray papers that had been written on.

All in all, I was just happy that some of her work had been saved. I'd have preferred to have her laptop, but that was in the hands of the LVPD.

I started with the journal, feeling a little bit icky thumbing through a young woman's private thoughts. This was my chosen profession and things would get grimy from time to time, so it's just something I had to do.

I'd have to ask Chance if the police had confiscated this at one point and then given it back. It seemed like it would be a huge piece of evidence.

There were entries from around the time of her graduation, but they quite obviously had nothing to do with her future abduction.

I continued leafing through, but didn't find anything interesting until I got to January of this year.

The first few posts were about Kenneth Croy and how much Emmy liked hanging out with him. She never used the word love, and this wasn't an overly gushy journal like you might find from a fifteen-year-old. Emmy was measured and didn't profess her love, just said they had fun together.

Emmy was a very mature, thoughtful woman. She didn't seem the least bit impulsive. I'd already gathered this from others, but the journal entries confirmed it.

This was not a girl who just ran off, never to be seen again. Not a chance.

The entries on Croy weren't the treasure trove I was hoping for.

Emmy next started talking about her novel and my interest level heightened.

I found this entry interesting.

"Unlike most women my age, I'm probably more excited about a book I'm writing than the man I'm dating or some upcoming party. Probably because it's my book. It's something that's coming from my brain. It's something that will be out there in the world, even when I'm gone someday. I read a quote one time about authors being immortal and I agree wholeheartedly. Books never die.

I'll admit, my progress has been slow. My problem is that I was trying to make every paragraph perfect. It's an arduous process and I've recently decided to make a change. I'm just going to start writing. I'm not trying to achieve perfection with each chapter, or even each sentence. I can, and will, edit it at a later point.

It has made a big difference. I've only written six chapters since I started in July. And then, once I made this change, I've written another six chapters in only three weeks.

I'm happy with my recent progress.

Plus, I've got a few exciting interviews coming up. Once I know more about the subject I'm writing about, it will be easier to pick up the pace."

And then Emmy signed it, as she did with each journal entry.

There was a large E for Emmy and a large P for Peters. The rest of the letters were basically undecipherable.

The next several entries were about Vegas itself. She seemed to truly love the city.

One section stuck out.

"A lot of my friends thought I stayed in Vegas because my Dad can be a bit over-bearing. That's not the reason. I like it here. Even though I'm not much of a gambler, I like the endless action. I like the fact that tens of thousands of people from all over the

world are converging on this city every weekend. I feel like my city is constantly holding the world's biggest party. And even if I don't attend all those parties, I'm proud that people enjoy our city so much.

Plus, my Dad isn't as bad as everyone thinks. Sure, he's a bit loud and cocky, but I know he loves me. And so does my Mom, obviously. One of these days I'll write a novel that revolves around UCLA. That will make my Dad proud. Maybe not as proud as if I'd attended UCLA, but I think he's over that."

Despite a few of Emmy's friends voicing concern about Chance, I'd never considered him a suspect. He seemed like a very loving father. And that had been confirmed with my recent breakfast with him and Liz. Not that one breakfast and a journal entry could absolve him of any involvement, but it just furthered my opinion that he was a grieving father and nothing more.

I continued reading.

She talked about her friends in mostly glowing terms. There were never any suspicions directed at Carrie or any of the other girls. Emmy did mention that she thought Jenny Appleton was a little jealous of her writing, but I'd already come to that conclusion myself. I did not consider her a suspect. Killing over a writing grudge? I didn't think so.

Finally, something did catch my eye.

"Despite the lousy recent weather in Vegas, things are looking up. I nailed down that interview. I've been afraid to mention his name up to this point, afraid I might jinx it. And I'm sticking to that, at least for now. But once I've talked to him, I'LL BLAST HIS NAME IN ALL CAPS, JUST LIKE THIS!!!!"

As emphatic as Emmy was about her upcoming interview, that's not what got my attention. It was the missing entries that followed. That post had been made on January 12th and when I turned the page, I realized that was the last post in the journal.

Emmy went missing on January 17th. There were five full days that she went without writing a journal entry. I went back over the course of the last several months and she'd never gone five days without posting. She'd never even gone three days.

And then, I noticed something that horrified me.

I looked at the binding. It was subtle, and I easily could have missed it, but there was still a small segment where you could see the perforated paper in the pages that followed. Someone had ripped off a few pages, but had not severed them perfectly. There were still a few very small, probably only a fraction of an inch, pieces of perforated paper that hadn't been completely ripped off.

I pushed the journal as wide open as it could go and moved my finger down along the binding.

Fucking A!

Someone had removed the last two pages from Emmy's journal.

I felt there were three possibilities.

One, that Emmy herself had ripped them out. It didn't seem likely considering it was her journal, but maybe she hadn't liked what she'd written. I considered it a long shot, but it had to be considered.

Two, the police had collected the journal and ripped the pages out to keep as evidence. Wouldn't they just keep it all together as one? I doubted they'd tear a few pages out and keep them separately. I also considered this scenario unlikely, but not impossible.

Three, that whoever abducted Emmy knew about the journal and made sure to get rid of the part mentioning them. And then, a worse notion came to mind. Once they abducted her, they started asking questions, potentially even torturing Emmy. And then she admitted to the journal.

Again, why would they not just steal the whole journal?

I had no answer for that.

CHAPTER 17

I started taking inventory of the evidence I'd collected.

Not literally, but in the space between my ears.

The missing journal pages were undoubtedly the best evidence I had. The problem was that it didn't mean anything until I found out who Emmy had planned on interviewing. I was going on the assumption that's who the entries had mentioned.

I regretted having gone to Duncan Hobbes' place first. If I'd known the information about the journal, I'd have asked him to put me in touch with a member of the Las Vegas Police Department.

I'd like to know if the journal was ever brought in as evidence. Chance believes they only took Emmy's laptop, but I'm sure his mind was pretty occupied during those first few days she went missing. Maybe the LVPD had collected the journal and then returned it to him at a later date.

It was unlikely, but maybe the journal still had those two missing pages when it was tagged as evidence and the LVPD would let me see them.

I had more questions than answers.

There was still the Carrie Granger angle as well.

I texted her and asked if we were still meeting up tonight. She said yes.

It was only 3:30 p.m. and I was already exhausted.

I laid down in hopes of getting a nap in.

I was asleep within seconds.

~

I agreed to meet Carrie for a drink at the lobby bar of The Cosmo.

By the time I'd woken up from my nap, showered, and changed, it was approaching seven p.m. Vegas days moved fast.

It had been Carrie's idea to meet for a drink. I'd suggested coffee.

I was still of the opinion that if you meet someone for a drink, you're more likely to get a Chatty Cathy. Which is precisely what you wanted in my line of work. So, while having a drink with one of Emmy's friends had never been my intention, it might pay dividends for the case itself.

I found a corner table. Ironically, the same one I'd talked to Kenneth Croy at on my first night in Vegas. It had only been five days, but it felt much longer.

I saw Carrie approach with a short, light green dress. I really hoped she was going out later and wasn't wearing this to impress me. Her long legs were accentuated even more with the short dress and her high heels.

I saw a few heads turn from the guys playing automated five card draw at the bar.

They were probably wondering what a beautiful girl in her early twenties was doing with a forty-one-year-old man. Actually, scratch that. This was Vegas, I know what they were thinking.

She took the seat next to me.

"You look very nice," I said. "If not a bit overdressed."

"Sorry. I'm meeting friends after this."

Good!

"Emmy's friends?" I asked.

"No. Like I told you, I've only known Emmy since we started dancing together. I don't know her UNLV girls very well."

I'd debated whether to be the nice guy with Carrie or to just put her on the spot right away. I wanted to put her under duress and see how she reacted. But I'd also been considering recording a phone call with Liz.

And that would never happen if Carrie knew I suspected her of something.

I impulsively decided that one in the hand was worth two in the bush. I was going to confront Carrie while I had her in front of me.

Was it a mistake? Possibly, but the case was starting to move quickly and I didn't want to wait for a phone call that might not happen for days.

So I went for it.

"I find it odd that you've known Emmy for such a short period of time and yet you're always calling Liz Peters to ask for updates on the case."

I watched Carrie very closely. My words had obviously connected. Her face scrunched up like she was trying to hide her emotions. She brushed her hair aside, shuffled her feet.

I could see her trying to recover, knowing I'd seen it all.

"We were friends. I don't think what I'm doing is weird at all," she said.

"You don't think calling twice a week is odd?"

Carrie didn't answer for a few seconds. She was reeling. My suspicions were being proven true in real time. At least, that's the way I was choosing to look at it.

"They have a missing child. What's the proper amount of times to call a week? There must be some playbook that you know about that I don't."

She came back firing, and made a good point as well. Who was I to tell her how often to call a grieving family?

"It's less the amount of times you called, Carrie. Liz told me that you'd want to know details on the case. Are you trying to take my job?"

I was being an asshole. Intentionally.

I saw a waitress walking in our direction, but I raised my hand as if to stop. I didn't want to let Carrie have a break and get her thoughts together.

"I'm not trying to take your job. I'm trying to be a thoughtful friend."

"A thoughtful friend would be a shoulder to cry on, not asking about the forensics of the case."

Yes, I'd made that up.

"Forensics? What are you talking about? I never asked about no forensics."

It seemed like the wrong time to mention she'd used a double negative. Carrie's eyes already conveyed she was furious at me.

"Maybe not forensics per se, but Liz said you asked for particulars on the case. Particulars that no one else has been asking for."

"Because I want to know what happened to their daughter!" she yelled.

A few people looked in our direction.

We were discussing the case of a missing Las Vegas showgirl. It probably wasn't wise to have people hearing our conversation.

"Alright, let's keep it down, Carrie."

"You're the one who is riling me up! Don't blame this on me."

She was right. Not that I was going to admit it. I liked having her on her heels, and I don't mean the literal ones she was wearing, but on the defensive.

"I talked to Nia and Rose and Jenny. They haven't called the Peters in months. And you call them twice a week."

Another white lie, although Liz Peters did say Emmy's friends hadn't called in weeks. This was on the small side and certainly wasn't a whopper of a lie.

"Maybe I just care more about Emmy."

I smiled. It was a good answer. Even if I didn't entirely buy it.

"Why do you care so much? Like you said, you'd only known her for a few months. Her other friends had known Emmy for years."

I saw her face go from being angry to being a little bit sad. I wasn't sure why the change.

"Why are you attacking me? Do you really think I had something to do with Emmy's disappearance? You're crazy."

"Just following up on my suspicions," I said.

"So you do suspect me?"

"I suspect you of not telling the entire truth. I'm undecided on whether I think you had a part in it."

With that, I saw a tear appear in Carrie's eye.

Was I being a jerk? Yes. A little too forceful? Maybe.

But I was potentially getting somewhere and this was absolutely the right way to question Carrie Granger. I was doing my job. Well.

"I had nothing to do with her going missing," she said.

"Then why all the interest?"

"Because she was my friend, you asshole!"

A few more looks from the surrounding patrons.

We really should have continued this conversation elsewhere, but there was zero chance Carrie was going anywhere else with me.

In fact, she probably wouldn't be staying at the lobby bar very much longer.

"I'm sorry, Carrie," I said, hoping to keep our voices down more than anything else. "I'm just doing my job. And since I first met you, I feel like you've been holding something back. Have you?"

She wiped the lone tear away and looked back at me.

"I had nothing to do with her going missing," she said, for a second time.

It struck me as odd.

"That's not what I asked, Carrie. I asked if you've been holding anything back."

She looked at me and I could tell she had no comeback.

"Is there something you want to tell me?" I asked.

Just as I was getting my hopes up, Carrie Granger rose from the table.

"Don't contact me again!" she yelled.

And briskly walked away.

CHAPTER 18

I f I'd already been halfway convinced that Carrie Granger was hiding something, I was now all the way there.

As she walked away from The Cosmo Lobby Bar and into the abyss that was a Las Vegas casino floor, I had one thought. I really wished I had her phone tapped. The next few phone calls that Carrie made would have told me everything.

Things weren't going to be that easy.

∼

I decided to walk along the Strip for a while.

The sun was close to setting and it was a gorgeous time of night in Vegas. The temperature was now "only" in the upper 80's. Which may sound hot, but it was a dry heat, and much more comfortable than the upper 80's of, say, Florida.

I passed families on vacation and groups of guys who'd already had too much to drink. My body was present as I nudged through the masses of people outside of the Bellagio and then Caesar's Palace, making my way north along the strip.

My mind was somewhere else entirely, however. I was focused on three things: the anonymous texter, the pages missing from Emmy's journal, and Carrie Granger.

I continued heading north, passing The Mirage and Treasure Island. There was a slight breeze and it was perfect Vegas weather to get lost in thought.

I'd already been walking for almost a half hour. Aimlessly, you might say.

When my mind wandered away from the case at hand, it gravitated towards Cara, my mother (who I needed to call), and even to Heather, whom I'd really enjoyed my time with. Even if it was meaningless in the end.

The irony of thinking about these three women within seconds of each other was not lost on me. My mother loved Cara and would have hated that I'd hooked up with some random woman in Vegas. I'd have to explain that Heather was not some Vegas slut, but actually a really good person. She'd tell me that Cara was better than good and we'd always been great together.

She would have been right, if we just excluded the last few months of our relationship.

And then I remembered Cara's warning to me before I left for Vegas.

"Private investigators always become assholes. Don't become a stereotype, Quint."

I hadn't called Cara since I'd left for Vegas. I hadn't told my mother that I was no longer with my girlfriend of ten years. I hadn't even had the balls to say goodbye to Heather.

It looked like Cara's prognosis was coming true.

My mind tried to revert back to thinking about Emmy's case.

It almost seemed easier.

I'd walked half the strip by the time I turned around to double back.

I saw a man in his sixties holding a yard long frozen strawberry daiquiri that I knew came from a bar called Fat Tuesday. Making matters worse, he was wearing a sleeveless jersey of his favorite player. That was never a good look for a man of a certain age. And he was undoubtedly past that age. Yet, the guy had the biggest smile I'd ever seen. He and his friends were having a blast. Who was I to judge?

And I'll be honest, it made me a bit lonely.

Vegas was a weird city when you were by yourself.

In real life, I would drink occasionally. Nothing too crazy, but I certainly wasn't a prude when it came to alcohol.

And yet, in Vegas, I'd see these yard long frozen cocktails, and want to have one or two myself.

I don't know if it was being lonely without Cara, or whether the case was driving me nuts. Whichever the case, I wanted a night to go out and get drunk.

A night of debauchery, of forgetting about everything for a few hours, sounded heavenly to me.

And as I got closer to The Cosmo, I'd convinced myself this was going to be that night.

But then I got a text that changed everything.

PART 2: BONES IN THE DESERT

CHAPTER 19

I read the text.

"If you don't go to the police, or call Emmy's family, I will tell you where her bones are buried. If you contact anybody, I will know and you'll never discover what happened. Nor hear from me again. Be ready tomorrow morning."

As I read the text a second time, I almost ran directly into someone on the Strip. I found a nearby bench that paralleled the walkway and sat down.

I think I was a bit in shock. Mainly, because I believed the person texting me. They'd misguided me about Sidney Remington, but for some reason, I thought they were telling the truth this time.

Besides shock, I also felt sadness, my fear that Emmy was already dead was confirmed. I hated to admit it, but there was even a slight level of satisfaction, knowing my asking questions all around town had likely brought this person out from the woodwork.

But mostly, there was sorrow.

I tried to imagine the conversation I'd have with Chance and Liz. It hurt my heart. I don't know how the police told family members that their loved ones had passed away. It had to be the most thankless job in the world.

I tried to concentrate on my situation at hand.

I knew I wasn't going to call the cops. I couldn't risk this person disappearing forever, like Emmy herself.

I would call the cops once I found the body, but I couldn't risk not getting to that point.

Also, and maybe I was wrong to keep trusting these texts, I believed they'd know if I contacted anyone, including the police.

So I wasn't going to tell Chance or Liz or Duncan or anybody else.

I would have a lot of things to answer for when this was over. And maybe Chance and Liz would completely disagree with my decision.

But I'd been hired to find Emmy Peters. And by keeping my mouth shut, that's what I was going to do.

It wasn't going to be the happy ending the family and myself had hoped for. There would be closure, however. And that might be the only thing that was left for Chance and Liz.

After I'd gone through a range of emotions on the bench, I stood up to make the trek back to the Cosmo. My knees hurt and my whole body ached. It's like I'd aged ten years in the five minutes since receiving the text.

And I knew tomorrow was going to be much worse.

I arrived back at The Cosmo and saw people drinking and enjoying their time throughout the casino.

Fifteen minutes earlier, I had been ready to join them. No longer.

I took the elevator up to my room and started re-reading some of Emmy's journal. Was the person texting me someone that Emmy was going to meet?

Even though I assumed it was a male, I found my brain using the word *person*. My suspicions of Carrie Granger kept open that possibility. And yet, despite my inklings when it came to Carrie, I highly doubted she killed Emmy.

So I still went on the assumption that a man was texting me.

I grabbed the police reports and started leafing over them as well.

I read and read and read until my brain became mush. It was probably for the best as I had become very tired and was able to fall asleep at a decent hour.

At least I slept for a while, until a nightmare took over my unconscious mind.

I was standing above a plot of land, getting ready to dig my shovel in. That's when the soil began moving and a hand started poking its way out of the ground and into the air towards me.

As if that wasn't bad enough, there was a faint voice that, even though I'd never heard her talk, I knew was Emmy.

"You're too late," the voice said. "I'm already dead."

CHAPTER 20

THURSDAY

I woke up the next morning in a sweat, remembering the terrible nightmare I'd had.

I didn't feel much like dealing with people on the casino floor, so I ordered some room service and waited for the text I was dreading.

It came in at 9:30.

"Last warning. Come alone or you'll never hear from me again. You'll be off the beaten path and it will be obvious if anyone is with you. Take I-15 South until you're about twenty minutes outside of Vegas. Use Exit #25, take a left, go back under the freeway, and follow that for ten miles. You'll come to a slight break in the road, where I've put a red ribbon on a cactus. Turn right there. Follow that two more miles. There will be a yellow ribbon this time. Take a left there. You will learn the rest if you arrive alone. Leave The Cosmo ASAP. Oh, and bring a shovel."

The tidbit that I was at The Cosmo was their way of showing how much they knew.

Not that it was necessary. I believed them. Or him. Or her.

I might be headed off towards my execution, but there was no turning back now. I was going deep into the heart of the desert.

∾

With a growing pit in my stomach, which I knew was only going to get worse, I retrieved my rental car and started driving. I had one stop to make along the way, at a hardware store to get a shovel. A fucking shovel!

What the hell had my life become?

I dreaded what lay ahead.

The idea of what I might see disgusted me to no end.

I was going to where the dead bodies were buried in Vegas. It had long been a joke in the public lexicon, but for me, it was all too real. I was going to dig up a dead body. Literally.

I hoped, beyond reason, that the text messages were wrong. But deep in my gut, I believed them to be true.

I hated being at the whim of this person texting me, but I didn't feel like I had much choice. If my goal was truly to find Emmy (dead or alive), then I had to make this trip. If it was all a ruse and I was going to be shot dead, then so be it. I wasn't going to stop investigating just because there was a chance of danger. If that were the case, I'd entered the wrong line of work.

Nor was I going to call the cops. I'd given it a brief consideration, but I believed the person texting me. If they saw anyone else but myself, they would immediately stop texting me. And the chance to bring Emmy home, even if it was just her dead body, would be lost forever.

As much as I tried, I couldn't escape thinking about the worst possible scenario. What if I was shot in the middle of the desert without anyone knowing? The killer would never be found.

After stopping off to get the shovel, and grabbing a gallon of water, I decided to make one more stop. The Post Office.

I wrote a brief letter to Duncan Hobbes. I explained the texts I'd received about finding Emmy's body. I included the phone number that the texts were coming from. And the directions to the place I was going.

I ended the letter with this message.

"If you haven't heard from me in the last few days, I was likely killed. Please give this information to the police in hopes that they will catch my killer. Thank you."

I sealed the letter and sent it to Duncan's address in Las Vegas.

I'd intercept the letter in a few days.

If I was alive to do it.

If not, then Duncan would know what to do with the info I'd given him.

I made my way from the Post Office on Las Vegas Boulevard to Interstate 15 South which headed towards Barstow. If you were going that far, which I wasn't.

I'd checked my GPS and Exit #25 was eighteen minutes away. As I drove down the freeway and passed the Mandalay Bay, it hit home just how different the Strip was from the geography it was built on.

This truly was a desert and the lights and action of Vegas were incongruous with the nature of the setting.

I passed the South Point Casino, which I knew was the last casino until you hit the Primm resorts at the California/Nevada border. I wouldn't be going that far, either.

As I got closer to my destination, I began to fear my reaction to digging out

Emmy Peters' body. What would it look like? What would it smell like, being buried in the desert for months?

I figured I could deal with the smell. I just hoped I wouldn't be burdened with the visual of Emmy's rotted body for the rest of my life.

During my drive out there, I came to the conclusion that this wasn't a trap. I didn't think I was going to be killed assassination style once I arrived.

What if I told the police and they were scoping out the area from afar? What if the police had put up a roadblock at every possible exit?

The risk was just too great on their end. If they/he/she really wanted to kill me, they'd do it when I was leaving Duncan Hobbes' house or some other random spot in Vegas. They would never do it at a place where the cops could potentially be waiting.

I started to breathe a little easier.

I looked down at my GPS and was five miles away.

With a mile or so to go, I started moving from the far left lane over to the slow lane. A minute later, I exited the freeway. A few hundred feet up, I took a left, going back underneath the freeway, and then started heading away from I-15.

I kept following the road and felt myself drifting further from civilization. That may sound odd, being only a few miles from a much used Interstate, but it's how it felt. There were no other cars on the road I was on. What there were, were a bunch of cacti, tumbleweeds, and rough soil that looked like it hadn't seen rain in years. I'm sure a poisonous snake or two were nearby.

I continued driving for what seemed like an eternity, even though it was only a little more than ten minutes. No wonder people buried the bodies out in the desert. There was literally no reason to be out where I was. Unless you were up to no good.

I followed the road for another few miles and came upon the cactus with a red ribbon wrapped around it. I took the right turn that I'd been instructed to take and started following a new road. To be honest, calling it a road was overly generous. I was driving over dried dirt. This was a path.

I continued for two miles longer where I saw a huge cactus, this time with a yellow ribbon wrapped around it. I took a left and followed it for another mile or so. I knew I was getting close.

Another mile down the road, there was a third cactus. There wasn't a ribbon on this one, but a piece of paper instead. I had to get out of the car to read it. It said, *"You're here. You'll see the X several feet ahead."*

My heart was in my chest as I parked the car. I saw no one else around, which I took as a good sign. But I was still scared shitless.

Was I going to be shot by a sniper? I didn't think so, but was it still in my head? You're damn right it was.

I decided there was no point belaboring my decision to come here alone. For better or worse, I'd arrived at my destination. It was time to get down to business.

I stepped out of my car and grabbed the shovel from the trunk. I walked fifty feet forward and saw a huge X drawn in chalk over the desert dirt. It was probably fifteen feet long and just a tiny bit less wide.

No explanation for the X was given. It was unnecessary. It's where Emmy Peters' body was buried.

I raised the shovel to my waist and was ready to lunge it into the unforgiving, dried out dirt.

"Here goes nothing!" I yelled.

The shovel hit and almost bounced off the ground. There was zero acceptance from the soil. I realized this was going to be a longer process than I'd ever imagined. I wondered if the gallon of water I'd brought would be enough. What if my rental car wouldn't start up? I looked down at my phone. No reception.

"Great," I said, talking to myself for the second time in a minute.

I raised the shovel again and was met with resistance once again as I struck the dirt. I didn't have a rototiller, a hoe, or even a rake. A rookie mistake by yours truly. A shovel in the desert isn't like a shovel on watered soil.

I started stabbing the ground with the shovel, not as much to remove dirt, but more to loosen up the topsoil. It seemed to work. Several stabs and then I was able to dig into the dirt a bit.

I went to my car and grabbed a few sips of water. I was only ten minutes in and already drenched in sweat. I knew it was approaching 100 degrees already. I guess I could have waited until later in the evening, or even the next morning, but this really wasn't information you could sit on. If Emmy Peters' body was out here, I needed to excavate it.

The ground became easier to navigate once I'd learned to stab it a few times first. It was by no means easy, merely not as difficult.

I worked for the next hour and still was probably only about a foot deep in an area covering about fifteen feet square. If the huge X was correct, I was covering a big enough area where I wouldn't miss the body.

I was halfway through my gallon of water. I could have pounded the rest in two huge gulps, but I needed to save some. It was now a few minutes past noon and it was north of 100 degrees. I was yearning for the air-conditioning of the Strip.

Another forty-five minutes passed and I was now at least two feet deep, possibly more. I was making quicker progress. The soil was proving to be easier to navigate once you got through the first several inches.

I was down to the bottom of my gallon of water, however. I was sweating like a hooker in church, or however that phrase goes.

It was so hot I was truly risking my own health every minute I continued shoveling.

I could see the proverbial finish line, but I worried I might pass out first. I agreed to give myself ten more minutes and then drive somewhere and get some water before coming back.

And then it happened.

I raised the shovel and brought it into the ground with a lot of force.

It hit something hard, which I immediately presumed was either rock or bone. I took the shovel and started scraping the soil above whatever I'd just hit. It seemed a safer way to proceed.

After a minute of vehemently scraping back and forth, my biggest fears were realized. This was no rock.

I saw the skin first, a rotting mess that had been annihilated by worms and whatever else lived in the soil of the Vegas desert. It was barely dangling from the bone, which is why the shovel's contact had been more with bone than skin.

It looked like it was a shin and an ankle, but I honestly couldn't be sure. It could have also been an arm and a wrist.

"I'm so sorry, Emmy. What a horrible death you must have experienced."

I knew the more I saw, the worse it would get. What would Emmy's face look like?

I was afraid to find out.

I entered the shovel a foot up from what I thought was the ankle/shin and struck bone again. I scraped the soil off the top and a few minutes later, the bone was visible. It was longer than the previous bones and I was now pretty sure I was staring at a femur, which meant I'd been right about the ankle and shin bones.

The femur was covered by even less skin.

I hoped the skin was missing from what had been Emmy Peters' face. I'm not sure I could handle seeing that.

If there were any positives, it's that Chance or Liz Peters were not present. As bad as this was for me, I couldn't imagine being a parent in this situation.

My mind continued to wander.

Was my time on this case coming to an end? Would finding her body be enough for Chance Peters? Or would he continue to employ me to try and find out who did this? That would usually be the job of the police, but Chance probably trusted me more at this point.

I needed to stop thinking and get back to the business at hand.

I scraped more soil off the bones. This was starting to look like an archaeological dig, with the bones visible and the soil all delicately manicured around them. It was time to make my way further up the body. Which was mostly just a skeleton at this point.

Seeing Emmy's face, or what was left of it, was mere seconds away.

I began to scrape the shovel over what I assumed to be the pelvic bone, when I was greeted with the biggest shock of my life.

CHAPTER 21

"His name was Victor."

I thought I was hallucinating at first, maybe hearing voices or having a Jim Morrison like drug trip in the middle of the desert.

I turned around.

No, this wasn't some peyote trip.

Standing in front of me was none other than Emmy Peters.

I couldn't have been more shocked if God him/herself had been there.

Her hair was entirely different, now in a pixie style and bleached blonde, but there was no mistaking it was her. She was wearing jean shorts and a light blue t-shirt that had seen better days.

I'd seen a hundred pictures of Emmy, and now, here she was in the flesh.

And not the rotting flesh in the ground below me.

She looked me over, as if this was a poker game and she was trying to get a read on me.

When I couldn't muster a word, she continued.

"He brought me out here to murder me. I'm sure he'd have either buried me or left my body for the vultures. Probably the former, but when I have nightmares, it's the vultures gnawing at my dead body."

She walked a few steps closer to me. I still hadn't said a word.

"You might be wondering how I escaped almost certain death out here. A bit of luck, to be sure, and some quick thinking, I'd like to believe."

She inched closer and was only a few feet from me now. The shovel dropped from my hands. My mouth might have been agape for all I knew.

I finally found the will to speak. Sort of.

"I don't know what to say," I said. "I'm in shock."

"I have no doubt. One second you think you're digging up my bones and the next I'm standing in front of you."

"Pretty much, " I said, slowly getting my bearings back. "Everyone who loves you will be shocked as well."

"Well that shock is going to have to wait."

"What do you mean?" I asked.

"Haven't you asked yourself why, if I'm alive, I haven't returned to society?"

"To be honest, I haven't had much time to think of anything."

"That's fair. I'll give you time now."

She was silent for several seconds, allowing me time to think.

"My guess is that someone must be after you."

"Correct."

"And you can't turn yourself in?"

"Correct."

"Can I ask a favor, Emmy?"

"Maybe."

"Can we continue this conversation in my car? I'm about to keel over from heatstroke."

"You have to promise me you won't forcefully take me to the police."

She reached into her jean shorts and held up a can of what I assumed to be mace.

"My word means that much to you?"

"I've been following you from afar. If you say it, I'll believe you."

"I have every intention of listening to all you have to say. I may try to convince you to turn yourself in, but I will not forcefully take you to the cops."

"That's all I needed to hear. Let's go to your car. I took an Uber out here."

I had so many questions, including what the Uber driver must have thought, dropping a woman off in the middle of nowhere. I also had many questions that were more pertinent to my actual investigation.

I was very close to passing out, however, and for the moment that took precedence over any questions. The sweat was dripping off of me like a fountain.

We headed towards my car.

I was walking alongside Emmy Peters, someone I'd assumed was dead only a few minutes earlier. Surreal wasn't a strong enough word.

We walked the hundred feet from the decaying body of Victor, whoever that was, to my car. Usually, I'd be worried that someone might happen upon the body, but we were so far off the beaten path, the odds were basically nil.

I opened the passenger door and Emmy jumped in. I took my seat behind the wheel and turned on the air-conditioning. My body was a sticky mess.

"How do you want to do this?" I asked.

"What do you mean?"

"Do you want me to ask questions or do you want to just start from the beginning?"

"I think the latter would be easier."

"Alright, the floor is yours."

And Emmy Peters began telling her story.

∼

She started in early January of this year.

Emmy was four chapters into her debut novel and had just finished her first week as a Las Vegas showgirl. It was a happy time for her.

The book's introductory chapters, which she'd lamented over for far too long, didn't need any research. They came from her imagination and laid out the groundwork for the characters' actions that followed.

As she began writing chapter five, she knew it was time to start doing some fact-finding. The novel revolved around a young heroine who was helping take down a criminal enterprise, and Emmy wanted the novel to sound authentic.

She started asking around to see if people would sit with her and talk about the underworld crime that takes place in Las Vegas. And if they said no, she'd ask again. Sometimes a third time. She admitted to being very persistent.

She asked a professor from UNLV, a Pit Boss at a casino, and even an old Italian guy who owned a restaurant, hoping he might have some stories. They all turned her down.

Vegas was a city where people knew how to keep their mouths shut. Emmy would tell them that the novel was fiction, and she wouldn't mention real names, but they wouldn't budge.

"Finally, after a few weeks, I'd procured my first interview," Emmy said. "It was from someone who was in your field."

"A PI?"

"No, your old field. A reporter for a local Las Vegas magazine."

I didn't bother asking Emmy how she knew I'd been a reporter in a former life. It was obvious that she'd done her homework.

"I hope he was helpful," I said.

"I think he was scared of me. He didn't want to elaborate on how much organized crime was entrenched in Vegas. He was afraid it might get back to him after I wrote my book. Like everyone else, I told him it was a work of fiction, and I wasn't going to reference any real person or event. That didn't help. He wasn't very forthcoming."

"Giving my old profession a bad name," I said.

Emmy smiled.

"You seem to be pretty good at your new one," she said.

"I'm not so sure. I only found you because you wanted me to."

"That's not exactly true."

"What do you mean?" I asked.

"We'll get to that, but it involves Carrie Granger."

I knew it!

Emmy tried to push her hair further up, but they were bangs and just fell back down. It didn't appear Emmy was fully used to her new hairstyle.

"New haircut?" I said.

"My third one since I went missing. All done by yours truly."

I nodded. There was no need to point out the bangs were crooked and anyone could tell it wasn't professionally done.

Emmy continued.

"So, after I met with the reporter, I secured a second interview. The date was Thursday, January 15th. This time with a local businessman, someone who hung around with us showgirls."

I noted the date was one day before she went missing.

"Really? Carrie made it out like the showgirls were pretty insulated from outsiders."

"If your father owns the casino, you're not exactly an outsider are you?"

"One of Sidney Remington's kids?"

"Sidney Remington Jr. You see, my text to investigate Sidney Remington wasn't completely a wild goose chase. Although, I'm sure you instinctively thought of the father."

"I didn't even know he had a junior."

"Which is exactly what they call him...Junior Remington. No one calls him Sidney or Remington. That's reserved for his father."

"Well, what exactly did Junior tell you that changed everything?"

"You just want to get down to it, don't you, Quint?"

I believed it was the first time she'd used my name, but I'd been in a state of shock for ten minutes, so who knows.

"I've been on this case for almost a week and I'm finally going to find out what happened."

"Well, I've been missing for four months, so you can wait a few extra minutes."

"You don't take shit from anyone, do you?" I asked.

"I was already pretty tough. This experience has made me tougher."

"You say *experience* like it's a roller coaster."

"It has been a roller coaster. Just a lot more downs than ups," Emmy said.

We were talking in circles.

"So what happened with Junior Remington?" I asked. "I'm completely in the dark."

She didn't look flustered. More like she was enjoying letting me squirm on the hook.

"It's more fun like this," she said.

"You're enjoying this more than I expected," I said.

"This is the longest conversation I've had in months. And if you'd been through all I have, you'd try to enjoy moments like these."

"Of course. I'm sorry."

She was hard-headed, just as Abel had described. I was leaning towards saying it was endearing, assuming she'd get to the point soon.

"So I met with Junior at his luxurious office at The Remington," she said. "He approached our meeting as a date, flirting with me from the moment I walked in. He kept saying how he'd seen me dancing with the other showgirls. I had the best legs of the entire group. It was creepy. I hadn't expected him to go there, but I could tell he was drunk from the moment I'd walked in. And I don't mean two or three drinks deep. I'm talking seven or eight drinks in. Not that it's any excuse, I'm just stating facts. So, after ten minutes of his unrequited flirting, he eventually asked me why I was there. I'd told him about my novel when I first asked for the interview, but since he was drunk, I reiterated it. *I'm here to learn how crime works in a city like Las Vegas. And I don't mean your common, everyday crime. I'm talking about the underworld; the crime that most people don't hear about.'"

Emmy paused and I knew something important was on its way.

"Junior slurred his response. It went something like this. *People always call it the underworld, but I'm not sure why. It's not like these guys are hiding below the surface. They are easy to find. In plain sight. Shit, how do you think we've brought The Remington back from the dead? Luck? Hardly. More like the fact that the casino next to us went under.'* That's when he looked at me and knew he'd said too much. Even in his drunken state, he was aware he'd crossed the line."

Emmy peered at me, making sure I was taking it all in.

"What was the casino that went under?" I asked.

"It was called The Gambler's Gambit."

"And it was right next to The Remington?"

"Yeah. There was a big space between those two casinos and the next few on the Strip. So they were in constant competition."

"Do you know why they went under?"

"Only from what I've read online. And it's nothing specific. Just that they were struggling financially. And I guess there were a lot of drug busts going on there, with some occasional fights thrown in. There was an article in *The Las Vegas Daily* every week or so outlining all the bad dudes hanging out at The Gambler's Gambit."

"When did they go under?"

"Late last year."

"So you were already training to be a showgirl at The Remington. Were there any rumors about why they were closing?"

"No. Honestly, that's not what we talked about."

I realized I'd gone off on my own little tangent.

"I'm sorry. I got distracted. What happened next with Junior?"

"He made some comment saying he was just joking, but he looked genuinely worried. He knew he shouldn't have said what he said. I tried to play dumb and told him he was slurring his words and I couldn't understand what he was saying. He gave me a knowing smile like he knew what I was doing. It was the only time he appeared sober the whole meeting."

"Were you scared?"

"Not so much of Junior. At least not at the moment. He's a bit of a buffoon, a drunken flirt who models himself a playboy. He seemed genuinely afraid, though, as if he'd be in serious trouble if anyone knew what he'd said."

"No one else was with you, correct?"

"Just us two. I guess it's possible someone was listening."

"Could someone have tapped his office? Or maybe he recorded his own conversations?"

"I wasn't thinking of either at the time, but when you're almost murdered a day later, you consider each and every possibility, including those two. The reporter and Junior were the only two people I talked to before I was almost killed. Unless this is the world's worst case of mistaken identity, it has something to do with one of those two interviews. And I'd place a sizable bet that it was the Junior interview that precipitated it."

Emmy paused.

"I guess I'm getting ahead of myself," she said. "You probably want to know what happened on Friday, January 16th."

"If you're up for it, yes."

"Let's get it over with. What do you say, Victor?"

Emmy motioned to the plot of dirt where the body and bones of Victor Smith sat. I shook my head, afraid to hear what she went through.

"Whenever you are ready," I said.

"I remember it being a lazy morning and early afternoon. I had two shows every Friday and Saturday, so that was pretty standard. There's no reason to waste my energy on those days. I remember Nia left to go somewhere, her boyfriend's apartment, if memory serves. I was just lying around the house when I saw someone approaching the front door. It was probably around 4:00 p.m, give or take fifteen minutes or so. He had a package underneath his arm and looked like a delivery driver. Keep in mind, even though my meeting with Junior had been weird, I never, ever, ever expected someone might be after me. I had no reason to be suspicious. I mean, this was less than twenty-four hours later. So the guy knocks on the door. I saw that his uniform said Amazon, blue and black shirt, I believe. I said thanks through the door, but he said I had to sign it. You're probably going to think I was an idiot for opening the door, but it was 4:00 p.m. in broad daylight and the guy had a package and an Amazon outfit on."

Emmy wiped her nose with her sleeve.

"I don't think you're an idiot," I said. "Anyone would have opened the door. How could you know?"

"Thanks. So I opened the door, and he immediately head butted me in the forehead. I later realized he'd probably intentionally avoided my nose. That would have been more likely to leave some blood, evidence he was trying to avoid. I fell back and before I knew it, he was on top of me. He grabbed some duct tape and a set of handcuffs from his pocket. He put a strip of tape over my mouth. He was about to put the handcuffs on my wrists, but thought better of it and locked them around my ankles. The reason was obvious. My feet were a bigger threat than my hands. I could run away with my feet. For good measure, he forced my wrists behind my back and wrapped them several times with the duct tape. I wasn't going anywhere. A second later, he was gone. I hoped and prayed it was over, knowing deep down that wasn't possible. What he did, and this was smart, was that he backed his van up so it was basically touching our garage. He then came back inside the apartment and carried me to the garage. This way, no neighbors would see what was about to happen. The van would be blocking what he was doing. He pressed the remote for the garage door, opened the back of the van, and threw me in, shutting the door behind me. The van was windowless, so I couldn't see out, and trust me, I was as scared as humanly possible. A lot of things run through your mind in a situation like that. A minute or two later, we were driving away from my apartment. I was sure he'd shut my front door and locked the garage door behind him. And it was then I realized that he'd been wearing gloves. Maybe that should have been a red flag as he approached the door, but being abducted was the last thing on my mind. As we headed out toward the desert, and I was being thrown around in the back of the van, I remember thinking it was the perfect crime. It would look like I just vanished."

It was a lot to take in and I couldn't imagine the fear that Emmy had been feeling in the moment, with her mouth and wrists duct taped and her ankles handcuffed. All in the back of a windowless van. It was almost inconceivable, only it was real.

"I don't think the police ever suspected you'd been taken from your home," I said. "Probably because there was zero evidence of a struggle."

"I didn't stand a chance. I was head butted and taped up within seconds."

"I'm so sorry, Emmy."

"Just wait. We haven't even gotten to the desert yet."

I nodded.

"Please continue," I said.

"That drive was by far the most petrifying time of my life. Looking back, I know it was probably about thirty-five or so minutes from my apartment, but it felt like three hours. I didn't know if I was going to be raped, killed, or tortured. They all were on the table. And I couldn't even talk or try to convince my captor to let me go. The duct tape on my mouth had made sure of that. Making things worse was that there was no seating in the back of the van and I was being tossed around like a rag doll. I tried to brace my legs against the walls, but it didn't seem to help much. I was at the behest of the angles of the van and the road ahead. Finally, after probably twenty minutes of feeling like I was in the middle of a dryer, I came up with an idea. I always had a small bottle of mace that I carried with me, like the one you saw earlier. Luckily, I had some in my jeans when I was kidnapped. It was my only chance. However, my hands were duct taped behind my back, so what was I to do? There was a divider between the front seat where my abductor was and the barren back of the van. The next time I was sent back into the divider, I vowed to grab on as hard as I could. My wrists were tied, so it would have to be with my fingers. Hopefully, that was going to be enough. A minute or so later, I was sent from the back of the van towards the divider. I leaned down with my fingers and grabbed hold for dear life. My grip loosened within seconds. It wasn't going to last. My fingers themselves weren't strong enough. I had to slide my wrists up against something that would hold them in place. I was sent careening towards the back of the van again, hitting it with a lot of force. I was woozy from the head butt and the violent collisions against the inside of the van. This time I had a better plan, though. A few seconds later, as I was sent sliding up towards the divider, I took my wrists, and wrapped them around the steel that the divider was made of. I realized that, besides keeping me in place, there was the potential to slide my wrists up and down the steel. I might be able to cause the duct tape to rip. I slid my wrists up and down. There was no way my abductor could see me. The divider was at least two feet above my head. I furiously moved my wrists back and forth and after a minute, the duct tape ripped a bit. At that point, it was just a matter of time. A few seconds later, the whole thing ripped and my wrists were free. I grabbed the mace from my pocket. It would be my one opportunity. And I knew, even with it, I'd be very lucky to escape. I had a chance now, but it wasn't a very good one. I put the mace back in my pocket, knowing I couldn't risk it falling out and finding some nook or cranny of the van. I started to prepare myself. Whenever we arrived at our destination, I'd only have a few seconds to try and save my life. I did think I had one advantage on my side, albeit a small one. The guy wasn't going to shoot me in the back of the van. He could have done that when he first threw me into it. No, I imagined he'd wait to kill - or rape or torture - until I was out of the van. So that would give me the fighting chance I needed."

I knew Emmy was alive, she was sitting right next to me after all, and yet the story felt like it was playing out in real time. It was terrifying.

She took a deep breath and continued.

"Several minutes later, I knew we were getting closer and I'd have my chance. The car must have exited the freeway because we started driving slower, going over more rocky roads. I made sure the mace remained in my jeans until it was go time. A few minutes later, the van took another turn and slowed down even more. I knew we were arriving at his destination, wherever that was. The van came to a stop shortly thereafter. I took the mace out of my jeans, knowing this was the moment of truth. My heart was beating out of my chest. I tried not to imagine what would happen to me if my plan didn't work. I just hoped he didn't have a gun pointed at me when he opened the door. He'd duct taped my mouth, my wrists, and handcuffed my ankles together. He couldn't have considered me much of a threat. It gave me a slight ray of hope. A very slight ray. I heard my abductor get out of the van. The next few seconds took forever. He opened the rear door and saw my back flush against the divider. I had my wrists behind my back as if they were still duct taped. He inched closer, but didn't say a word. I looked at his hands, but didn't see a gun. He moved closer and I readied the mace behind my back. He went to grab my legs and I realized he was going to drag me out of the van, feet first. He wasn't going to get close enough to mace. I had to do something! 'I can't move,' I yelled, hoping he'd hear me through the duct tape. He leaned forward quickly and ripped off the duct tape. I realized I may have lost my chance. He'd been close enough to mace, but he'd done it so quickly, I didn't react in time. I had one more chance. 'The tape wrapped around some of this steel,' I said. 'I can't move.' He started towards me again and this time I was ready. When he was a mere foot from my face, about to reach down behind me and release my wrists, I swiftly moved the mace towards his face, pressing the plunger as I did. He wasn't ready for it and I got him straight in the eyes, blinding him immediately. He started swinging in my direction and I shimmied to the other side. I kept spraying the mace right at him for a good four or five seconds. As well as it was working, I knew it was only temporary. I had to get the key for the handcuffs or I wouldn't have a chance. And that's when I saw it. The man had a gun holstered on his side and he was reaching for it. This was it. I shuffled towards the man. I had to get close enough to knock the gun loose, but I couldn't let him get ahold of me. He'd get me in a bear hug and I'd never escape. So, I had to move quickly. As he began to raise the gun from its holster, I brought both hands down on it as hard as I could. He didn't see it coming. Couldn't see it coming. And because of that, it worked. I knocked the gun out of his hand and it fell to the floor of the van. Gravity then took over and it quickly slid to the back of the van. I shuffled in that direction. My ankles were still obviously handcuffed, so it was the only way I could maneuver. However, my captor still couldn't see, so my knowing where the gun had slid made all the difference. The man said his first words since knocking on my door. 'I was only paid to kill you, but what the hell, now I'm going to torture you too.' As he said this, I grabbed the gun. He heard the sound of the metal being taken off the floor of the van and knew I had the gun. In a split second, he lunged in my direction, knowing where the sound had come from. I had no time to think. I raised the gun in his direction and fired. I knew immediately that I'd struck him. He fell back into the divider. Blood started to appear on the left side of his chest. His eyes told me was dead, but I couldn't take any chances. I shot him a second time. This time there was no doubt. He was dead."

Emmy took a moment to gather herself. I was still in awe of the story and of the young woman reciting it.

"Let me know if you'd like to take a break," I said.

"No, we're close. I might as well finish."

A few seconds later, she continued.

"Like I said, I knew he was dead. His eyes were bug-eyed and he was no longer a threat. I pushed the van door fully open and saw that we were in the middle of the desert. That was meant to be my final resting place. I grabbed my phone from my pocket and was ready to call 9-1-1, but I had no service. I hoped maybe his phone would work. I went through his pockets, trying not to look at his face. I dug out some keys, a wallet, and his phone. I tried 9-1-1 again, to no avail. That's when I decided to look at his wallet. I saw his Nevada driver's license, saying he was Victor Smith and fifty-two years old. That didn't interest me, but then I saw something that gave me pause. A members card saying that Victor Smith belonged to the Las Vegas Police Department alumni association. As if that wasn't enough, the real shocker came next, the reason I could never go to the police."

I waited with bated breath, utterly transfixed by Emmy's story.

"A phone call came through on Victor Smith's phone and the name lit up. Valentine."

"Jesus," I said.

"Yeah, exactly. Jesus."

Bo Valentine was the Chief of Police for the Las Vegas Police Department. Even if you didn't live in Las Vegas, you'd probably heard of him. He loved the limelight and always made a big show of speaking to the media when they caught a bad guy or two. He had a handlebar mustache that made him immediately recognizable. I think he was in his fifties, but couldn't be sure.

"And I don't want to hear it was some coincidence. Bo Valentine just happened to call Victor Smith at that exact time he was about to kill me?" Emmy said. "Or that Victor Smith had a girlfriend whom he'd nicknamed 'Valentine?' I'm not buying any bullshit explanation like that. It was Chief Bo Valentine calling to make sure I was dead. I had zero doubt then and I have zero doubt now."

I surely would have thought the same if I'd been in Emmy's situation.

There are coincidences in this world, but Bo Valentine calling at that exact time would be an all-timer. I think Emmy was probably right and it scared the hell out of me.

"Do you see what I'm dealing with? There was absolutely zero chance I was going to call the police after seeing the name Valentine on the phone."

"I don't blame you. So what did you do?"

"I buried Victor Smith right over there," she said, pointing to the bones I'd dug up. "Luckily, he wasn't a very big man. I grabbed his feet and carried him out of the van, the same way he planned on doing with me. I then dragged him about twenty more feet, taking a few breaks as I went, and then started digging. Remember, this was January, so there had been rain and the soil was much easier to navigate. There's no way I could have done what you did today."

I was going to ask her why she let me dig for so long, but the answer was obvious. She wanted me to find Victor Smith's body.

"And then you drove Smith's car somewhere else, didn't you?"

"I assumed he'd be reported missing. And if they found his car out here, the police would probably start digging themselves. So, yes, I had to move it."

"Where did you take it?"

"It's out in the desert, about two miles from The Bored Cactus, the motel I'm staying at. I'll probably have you drop me off, so you'll get to see the complete shit hole that motel is. Anyway, Victor Smith had a thousand dollars in his wallet. I really hope that wasn't all my life was worth. Maybe it was only a down payment. Regardless, I knew that was enough money to last a week or two, hopefully longer, at some rundown hotel. Or motel, as it turned out. After I buried Victor Smith, and put the dirt back over him, I drove the van far, far away from his body. I did write down the turns I had to take from the freeway to get back to Smith's body. Not on my phone, obviously. I knew I had to power that down or they could locate me. I used a pen and paper that was in the glove compartment."

"What time was this at?" I interjected.

"It was probably about six or so at that point."

This case was coming full circle. Emmy had powered her own phone down around six p.m.

"Thanks. Sorry for interrupting."

"I also knew my credit cards were now worthless. Just another way the police could track me. No thanks. If I found the right motel they'd take cash. And after an hour or so of driving around, I found The Bored Cactus. I parked the car at a gas station across the street, walked over, and asked how much it was for a week. They said they had a weekly rate of $350. I told them I'd take it. I knew there was no way that either Victor Smith or me had been reported missing yet, so I drove the van to the store and bought some feminine essentials, and also picked up some bleach, scissors, and other things to change my look. I got some cheap, crappy clothes as well. After I dropped the supplies off at my motel room, the sun had already set. It was unlikely people were looking for me yet, but I needed to ditch Victor Smith's van. I took another shitty, bumpy road, reminiscent of the one you took to get here. After driving on it for about two miles, I saw a couple of trees a few hundred yards from the road. Keep in mind, there's not too many trees in the desert. Mostly just cacti and low lying plants. So I drove the van and parked it between the two trees, which shielded it from the main road. And I do say 'main road' with a grain of salt. I then walked back along that road, in the dark mind you, for a few miles until I got back to The Bored Cactus."

I shook my head.

"This is all so crazy, Emmy."

"I know. I was thinking if I get out of this alive, I couldn't write this as non-fiction. No one would believe it."

"True. If you'll allow a compliment, you were exceptionally calm and made some great decisions."

"I can assure you, I wasn't calm."

"Maybe, but your actions say otherwise."

"Thanks."

Emmy pushed her hair up for what seemed like a third time. The bleached blonde bangs returned to their natural spot a split second later. Gravity is undefeated.

"Sorry, old habits die hard, even with this new haircut."

"No need to apologize. Speaking of your hair, did you change it up right away?"

"Yeah, that first night, once I got back from hiding the van. And like the van, I've been hiding ever since."

I decided to bring up something she'd alluded to earlier.

"And Carrie Granger has been giving you the money to survive?"

It was Emmy's turn to be surprised.

"Very good, Quint. How did you know?"

"I didn't think she was being completely forthright with me. And you've been missing for months, so obviously you'd need some money, which wasn't coming from your parents or Duncan. Carrie seemed the logical guess."

"That's some good PI work."

"Thanks," I said.

"That's what brought me out of hiding, by the way."

It made sense now.

"You were afraid I was going to turn Carrie in?"

"She called me on my burner phone last night, right after your meeting with her. She was scared you'd go to the police with your suspicions about her. I couldn't include Carrie any more than I already had, so I had to meet with you myself. Plus, I couldn't risk her accidentally alerting the cops to the fact that I was alive."

"Of course," I said. "I'll stop bothering her now."

"Thank you. She's been a godsend for me. I picked up a burner phone about a week after getting abducted and texted her, saying I was alive and to please, please, please, not tell anyone. It took some convincing her that it was me, asking questions only I knew the answer to. Once she was convinced it was me, she agreed to meet, and has been lending me money ever since. I told her once this all ends, I'd be paying her back double."

Something clicked for me. That's why Duncan and I had drawn different conclusions on Carrie Granger. When Duncan had met her, she was the grieving friend. Carrie had nothing to hide at that point. By the time I came around, however, she had this huge secret. And that's why I sensed something disingenuous about her.

"I'm sure the money isn't Carrie's number one concern," I said. "Did she try to convince you to turn yourself in?"

"The first few times, but I made it clear my life would be at risk if I did. So she finally just let it be. She'd mentioned turning myself into a neighboring county and I told her I'd just be transferred back to Vegas."

"I'm sure she wanted to tell your parents."

"Of course, but I couldn't risk it. At least, not yet."

"So what's your endgame, Emmy? Stay at this Scared Cactus motel your whole life?"

Emmy laughed.

"What?" I asked.

"It's The Bored Cactus."

I smiled.

"Whatever."

"Well, now that you've met me, I assumed we could solve this shit together. We could figure out why Victor Smith was trying to kill me. Was Junior Remington involved? Bo Valentine? Did The Gambler's Gambit going under have something to do with it? It sure sounds like it. And once we finish, you can tell my parents I'm alive and be the big hero, but not until then."

It felt like we'd been talking for five hours. There was so much to digest.

"I won't say anything to your parents. For now. That is subject to change, however."

"Thanks."

"I have a question," I said.

"Sure."

"Did you mention your meeting with Junior in your journal?"

"You've read my journal?"

She seemed hurt.

"Yes," I admitted. "It was merely to try and find some clues as to what happened to you. I've already forgotten the parts about Kenneth Croy."

Instead of getting mad, Emmy blushed.

"We had fun together. And he had nothing to do with this."

"I never thought he did. Your father was tough on him."

"I heard that from Carrie."

"You didn't answer my question."

"Yeah, I mentioned the meeting with Junior in my journal. Why?"

"Because there were two pages ripped out at the back of your journal. Was there anything else you wrote that someone wouldn't want others to see?"

Emmy thought for a moment.

"I'm trying to think what else I wrote before I went missing. It's been a while, obviously. I probably mentioned the meeting with the magazine reporter. I can't even remember his damn name. I might have talked about how my novel was moving along. I don't think I mentioned any other people besides Junior and the writer."

"Did you mention the awkward things that Junior said?"

Emmy nodded.

"I did. That's got to be it, right?"

"Seems likely," I admitted.

"Why would they only rip out the last two pages?" Emmy asked.

"I've been wondering that myself and don't have an answer."

There was about a ten second silence, the longest since we'd started talking.

Finally, I asked a question, even though she'd somewhat answered it earlier.

"Why didn't you try to contact your parents early on? At the very least, to just tell them that you were alive?"

"What if the police were tapping their phones? Or, if my parents stopped coming to Vegas, would the police get suspicious? Would they accidentally let on that I was alive? There's no way their behaviors wouldn't change. I just couldn't take the chance."

"I understand," I said.

"You know what also started to frighten me? There wasn't a single story on the local news about Victor. How can that be? Did Valentine tell the media not to report on it? Or, at least, talk to a few important people to make that happen?"

Once again, I had no answer. Emmy's disappearance itself had received way less publicity than I would have expected. She was young, attractive, and came from a well-to-do family. Usually, that would be a ratings bonanza. I wondered why the media hadn't rolled with it more than they had. I decided a visit to a local Vegas TV station couldn't hurt.

I didn't want to add that concern to Emmy's plate. She had enough on it.

"I don't know why the news didn't report on Victor," I said. "But I do know your parents are dying a little bit each day. If you're really scared of tapped phones, I can tell them. Or, I can set up a meeting in a place of your choice."

"I don't know, Quint."

I decided to go with a guilt trip. And it was an extreme one.

"If something happened to one of your parents, they'd go to the grave thinking their daughter died a brutal death."

"Don't say that!" Emmy yelled.

"Or, worse yet, something happens to them while they are investigating your disappearance, when they don't need to be flying to Vegas every few days."

"Stop with the guilt trips. Don't you think I've been through enough?"

She had a point.

"I'm sorry, but I'm just imagining what a reunion would do for Chance and Liz's psyches."

I used their first names intentionally.

"What if people are watching my parents?"

"Do you want your parents flying to Vegas twice a week for the unforesee-able future?"

"No."

"Well, what then?" I asked.

"I want to catch whoever ordered me killed."

"And so do I. And if I ever get out of this godforsaken car, that's what I plan on doing."

Emmy managed to laugh.

"Maybe we should end this sometime soon."

She said what we'd both been thinking. There was surely more we had to discuss, but this initial conversation had gone on long enough.

"Agreed. We can continue this soon. Let me drive you to that Cactus motel."

"I'll let you drop me off close," she said. "I can't risk someone seeing you at the motel itself."

"That's fine," I said.

"I'm sure there are things I've left out," Emmy said.

"We'll be talking a lot over the next few days. You can tell me then."

"And we'll discuss a potential meeting with my parents next time."

"Alright, I can live with that," I said.

"Somehow, my life is about to get more complicated."

"Mine too," I said and smiled, hoping to make her feel better.

"Sorry to burden you."

"Finding out you are alive is a burden I'll gladly carry. Although, I'll tell you what. You almost gave me a heart attack when you said, '*His name was Victor.*'"

"I had to go through all of that to make sure you hadn't gone to the cops. Plus, I wanted you to find the body. "

"What if I had gone to the police?"

"If I'd seen them, I'd have gone deeper into hiding. I'd have assumed if I talked to you, I was talking to the police."

I shook my head. This case was freaking bonkers.

"Are you ready to get out of here?" I asked.

"Aren't you forgetting something?"

"Shit! The body."

"We can't risk someone coming out this way, as unlikely as that is."

Emmy was right. Luckily, with the soil already loosened up, it was going to be much easier to re-bury his body.

Ten minutes later, we'd done just that.

And as we headed back towards Interstate-15, we picked up the ribbons that had adorned the cacti. We had removed the road map to Victor Smith's body.

∾

Twenty-five minutes later, we arrived at a gas station across from a motel. I don't know if there were actual fleas at her motel, but it was a shit hole, just as she'd relayed to me.

And this time I remembered the name. The Bored Cactus.

The building was ancient and the paint job was puke yellow and peeling all over the property. I'm guessing many of the inhabitants had a drug problem. Prostitution was likely as well. It was no place for a woman like Emmy.

Despite being at the gas station across the street, I was able to get a good look at it. I asked what she did for food and she said she'd order delivery and just have them leave it outside the door. She'd order a lot so she only had to order twice a week.

I gave her the $347 I had in my wallet. It was a lot more than I usually carried. You can thank Vegas for that. I didn't mention that I'd won some of the money on Kenneth Croy's blackjack table.

At first, Emmy didn't want to take it, but she could tell I was adamant and finally, she relented.

"Stay safe," I said, on the verge of getting emotional.

"I will. You too. Assume everyone is watching."

"One last thing" I said. "Can you input my number to allow your burner to receive my incoming texts or phone calls?"

"I can and I will."

"Thanks. We don't know what might come up."

"Agreed."

"Alright," I said. "Talk soon, Emmy, and stay safe."

I said it for a second time. Even that probably wasn't enough.

"Goodbye, Quint. Thank you."

She gave me a quick hug, exited the car, and started walking across the street toward The Bored Cactus.

It had been the most bizarre morning of my entire life. As I headed back towards a main highway, I ran through everything we'd talked about.

I tried to focus on the positive. Emmy was alive!

Personally, I couldn't wait to see the expression on Chance and Liz's faces upon being reacquainted with their daughter.

That's assuming Emmy would allow it, and someone didn't get to her first.

CHAPTER 22

I t was quite the drive back to The Cosmo with 5,927 things going through my head. Give or take.

I was ecstatic that Emmy was alive. That was the most important thing, without question. And yet, I shared her fear. If the Chief of Police was truly part of the plot to kill Emmy, my investigation going forward would be very dangerous indeed.

There was so much I had to do. I almost didn't know where to start.

I valeted my car, and when I arrived at my room, laid down on the bed to think and formulate a plan of attack.

I decided to text Duncan first.

I was interrupted mid-text by the phone ringing.

It was Cara. It wasn't ideal timing, but I hadn't talked to her since arriving in Vegas and had to take her call.

"Hi, Cara," I answered.

"How are you, Quint?"

"If I told you all I've been through, you'd almost feel a tiny bit of pity for me."

That could have been construed as being rude, but I'd said it in a playful way.

"Anything you want to tell me about?"

"I'd like to tell you every single thing, but I'd be breaking the trust of the people who hired me."

And Emmy herself.

"I won't push it. Are you any closer to finding the missing girl?"

I hated lying to Cara a minute into our first conversation since breaking up. I didn't really have a choice, though. It was time for white lie number one.

"I'm making progress," I said. "But nothing imminent."

"I can tell you don't really want to talk about this."

"I'm sorry, Cara. Thanks for understanding."

"Of course."

"How have you been? Enjoying the time off from teaching?"

"It's been alright. If I'm being honest, I miss you."

"I miss you too, Cara. I didn't want to break up."

"I'm not sure I did either. Everything just came on so quickly. I wanted to work on our relationship, and then you dropped the bomb that you have a job in Vegas."

"I needed the money."

"I'm not here to relitigate it, Quint. I just want you to know that I care for you. That's not fair. It's more than that. I still love you."

"I still love you too, Cara. I probably always will."

"Are we going to get through this?"

"I hope so."

"Technically, we are broken up. So it's probably more than just getting through something."

Another deep conversation wasn't what I needed. Not after my talk with Emmy. I decided I needed to lighten up the mood.

"What does broken up mean to us? We've been there, done that many times over the years."

I heard Cara laugh. Her great, operatic laugh. If you could make a song of it, I'd listen to it on a loop.

"That's true," she said. "We break up like other people have arguments."

"I'm in Vegas, the betting capital of the world. They'd probably make us a favorite to get back together."

"You'd probably bet against us and then try to sabotage the relationship."

"Ouch, " I said, knowing she was joking.

"So you haven't found some Vegas floozie to shack up with?"

It was time for white lie number two.

"I've got no time for anything besides this case. How about you?"

"A Vegas floozie? No."

It was my turn to laugh.

"No, but maybe a tennis club pro. He comes over to our apartment after a lesson and he's all sweaty in his white shorts."

"Looks like you've spent some time thinking about this?"

"Just imaging my worst case scenario," I said.

"This is the back and forth I miss, Quint. We could always push each other's buttons. People thought we were mocking each other, but it was really our way of flirting."

"Yeah, pretty much. Although, I usually don't mention you sleeping with tennis pros when I'm flirting."

"You know what I mean," Cara said.

"I do."

"So when are you coming back?"

"I'm supposed to meet with Emmy's parents tomorrow and find out if they are keeping me on a little longer. I'm assuming I'll be here at least a few more days, but I can't be certain."

"We'll have a nice long talk when you get back. You can tell me everything then."

"That sounds really nice, Cara. I mean it. I miss you."

"I miss you too. Has it been a busy morning?"

"One day soon I'll tell you about it."

"That crazy?"

"Whatever you find yourself imagining, multiply it by a hundred."

"Are you in danger?"

"Life's a risk."

"That's not an answer."

"It kind of is," I said.

"You're scaring me a little bit."

It was time to change the subject again.

"I'll be fine. I'm assuming you are still at our apartment?"

"Yeah, I wasn't going to just move out."

"You did threaten to."

"Did I? I probably made a lot of threats that day."

I was afraid we were veering back towards the break up.

"We both said some things we regret. Let's remember the good times. How about that trip to Vegas where we took the Ferris Wheel?"

"They call it The High Roller," Cara said. "And yeah, didn't we almost have sex on it?"

"We were making out and were certainly very touchy feely, but that second time around they picked up some people."

"That's right. We had the whole segment to ourselves on that first rotation."

"Yup."

"And then we lost our chance."

We both laughed at the memory.

"This has been nice, Cara."

"Thanks, Quint. Now tell me I have nothing to worry about."

It was time for my third and final white lie.

"You have nothing to worry about."

Truth was, she did.

~

I didn't want to also lie to my mother over the phone, so I started typing a text, telling her the case was moving along rapidly and I hoped to be back in the Bay Area in the next week, if not sooner. I promised to take her out to dinner.

Although I said I'd be back soon, I really had no idea how much longer I was going to be in Vegas. The only thing I did know was that I had no plans on leaving. Now that I'd found Emmy, or more precisely, she'd found me, I needed to see this thing to its conclusion. We were about to start a new portion of our investigation and I wasn't going to miss out. Even while conceding that it would be dangerous.

I pressed send on the text to my mother and went back to finishing the one to Duncan. I told him I'd like to see him as soon as he had time. I tried to keep it casual so as not to alarm him.

He responded that he'd be free that evening around six p.m. and I could come by then. I told him I'd be there.

CHAPTER 23

"You look like shit," Duncan Hobbes said as he opened his door to me.

"What do you really think?" I asked.

"I've never been good at sugarcoating things. Sorry."

"Don't change. It's part of your charm."

"In my old age?"

"I didn't say that. I'm sure you were charming at my age."

"More like a bulldog. Not exactly synonymous with charisma."

I laughed.

"No, I guess not."

"Any news?" Duncan asked, as he led me through his now familiar house.

I'd been both blessed and burdened with the earth shattering news that Emmy was alive. The blessing was obvious and the burden was not being able to tell anyone.

Duncan Hobbes was an obvious person I wished I could tell.

"Nothing of consequence," I said, my white lies growing in size by the minute.

As a smart, perceptive man, I worried that Duncan would notice a change in me. I told myself to just play it cool.

Duncan was wearing a red Tommy Bahama shirt with some white cargo shorts. He always dressed the part of a retired Las Vegas local.

We stayed inside the house for a second straight visit, the Vegas weather doing its thing. It was still hot as hell even after six p.m.

It was hard for me to accept this was the same day that I'd dug up Victor Smith and learned Emmy was alive. My space time continuum had been altered once I'd heard Emmy's voice.

"So, if there is nothing of consequence, what can I help you with?"

He was testing me out to see if I was hiding something.

"Besides the police reports, what are some other ways to know more about the police investigation into Emmy?"

"What exactly do you mean?"

"I mean, the inner workings of the case."

"That's what the police reports are for."

"I know I'm not explaining myself well, but I've got one of my feelings again. And I want to know who made the final decisions on Emmy's case."

"What type of decisions?"

I decided to just come out and say it.

"For a case that should be high profile, Emmy's disappearance has received very little attention from the media."

"That seems like a media problem."

"Maybe. And yet, from the beginning, the police don't seem to have put all their resources into this case. I've read the police reports inside and out. Why are they not all over town questioning people? If Emmy had been a runaway or a junkie, I could almost understand it. But that's obviously not what's going on here. I'm suspicious of the LVPD, if we're being honest."

Duncan sighed.

"I've butted heads with them before," he said. "Many times. Overall, though, I've found them to be a pretty good bunch of cops. I've become friendly with several of them as well."

It was time for the real reason I'd set this meeting up.

"Is there one officer you trust above anyone else?" I asked.

"You're not asking what I think you're asking, are you?"

"If it's wanting to meet with one of the officers of the Las Vegas Police Department, then yes, I am."

Duncan smiled.

"You've got a lot in common with Emmy. Tenacity. Persistence. Whatever you want to call it."

Now that I'd met her, I wholeheartedly agreed.

"I imagine you had it as well," I said, changing the subject from Emmy.

"Shit, I've never lost it!" Duncan said.

I laughed.

"Still that bulldog?"

"You know it. With a little of that charm thrown in."

"Channel that inner bulldog and you'll know why I'm asking this favor."

"Trust me, Quint, I get it. It just becomes complicated for me, having a long time relationship with some of the guys on the force."

"We don't need to offend anyone. Just give me the one guy that you completely trust. And hopefully, he's not too entrenched in the hierarchy of the police force. I want someone who would be willing to voice their opinion, not toe the company line."

"Then there's only one guy. Trent Ebbing. He definitely doesn't toe the company line. In fact, I know that he hates Bo Valentine, the Chief of Police. Trent joined when he was in his early twenties. Probably been there two decades by now. He's definitely a rebel within the force. He's more of an agitator, really. He speaks to power and does not suffer fools gladly."

Once Duncan said that Trent Ebbing hated Bo Valentine, the rest didn't matter. Not that I could tell Duncan that.

"I like him already. Could he keep a meeting quiet?"

"Yes. Without question. He owes me a favor or two."

"I won't ask," I said.

"I wasn't going to tell anyway."

I smiled.

"I'd like to meet him."

"You're a pain in the ass, Quint! Let me make a call," Duncan said and disappeared down one of the hallways.

∼

He returned a few minutes later.

"Trent Ebbing will meet with you."

"Thanks so much, Duncan."

I felt guilty. Here Duncan was, going out of his way to help me out, and I couldn't even tell him that Emmy was alive. I told myself that he'd do the same in my shoes, but it didn't make me feel much better.

"Just in case you're right and something stinks at the LVPD, I told Trent you guys could meet here. Better than at a coffee shop where people might see you. Word can get around quickly in this town."

"You've thought of everything," I said.

"Trent said he's busy today, but can meet tomorrow morning around eight a.m. Why don't you come back then?"

"Of course."

"Can I make one suggestion?"

"Sure."

"I know I said he's a rebel, but don't just come out and accuse specific people within the LVPD. Trent might not take that well. You don't know who he's friendly with, even though you can rule out Valentine. I'd approach it in a more general way and ask him if he's seen any malfeasance, etc."

"I won't mention names. Truth is, I don't even know any officers on the force. It's just an overall feeling I have. But I will be talking about the investigation into Emmy's disappearance and he probably knows which officers were assigned to it."

That wasn't entirely true. I did know one officer on the force. The Chief, Bo Valentine. And a former officer, Victor Smith.

"That's fine," Duncan said. "Just let him say the names."

"Like I said, I've got no names to name."

"No names to name. I like that."

"Thanks for all of this, Duncan," I said.

He smiled and nodded in my direction.

"What are you going to do when I'm not around for your next case?"

I laughed and patted him on the shoulder.

"Maybe you can follow me around from case to case," I said.

He smiled.

"This old guy is staying put in Vegas."

"Maybe I'll start up a PI firm here."

He laughed and gave me a push.

"Get out of here. I'll see you tomorrow morning."

CHAPTER 24

FRIDAY

Trent Ebbing was fifteen minutes late.

I was worried he wouldn't show, but was proven wrong by a knock at Duncan's door at exactly 8:15 in the morning.

Duncan let him in and introduced the two of us.

We exchanged pleasantries.

Trent Ebbing was an African American man who looked to be in his mid-forties. He had a thin goatee and was starting to go gray.

He was built like a statue, strong and immovable. His personality wasn't much different, at least on first impression. I had a feeling he was going to be a tough egg to crack. In fairness, all he knew about me was that I had a bad feeling about the police force he worked for. I guess I couldn't blame him for not being bubbly with me right off the bat.

Whatever the reason for his curtness, I wouldn't want to be on the bad side of Trent Ebbing. I'm not even sure I'd enjoy being on his good side. It wasn't that he was rude, just extremely intense.

Duncan escorted us to the pool where he set down his standard pitcher of lemon infused ice water.

"I'll leave you two to it," Duncan said and started to walk away.

Duncan knew what he was doing. He felt that either myself or Ebbing could be more direct if he wasn't around. My respect for Duncan increased every day.

I poured water for both of us.

"So, Quint, what can I help you with?"

"First off, Mr. Ebbing, or Officer Ebbing, thanks for meeting me."

"It's neither. Call me Trent."

And then he smiled and I wondered if I'd too quickly pigeonholed him as a joyless cop.

"I'm sorry. Trent it is."

"Thanks."

"I assume Duncan told you which case I was working on?"

Trent nodded.

"He did."

This is where I had to tread very lightly. I couldn't just come out and tell him about the call from Bo Valentine. I had to get to the Chief of Police in a roundabout way.

"Emmy's father thinks the police haven't paid enough attention to her case. He feels he's getting the runaround half of the time."

"Is there a question there?"

I wanted to say 'It's implicit', but didn't want to piss Trent off. Not due to his intensity, but because I needed him.

"Have you heard anything that makes you think the higher-ups in the department would prefer if Emmy's disappearance wasn't investigated fully?"

So much for subtlety. I'd thrown most of my cards out on the table.

I could feel Trent thinking it over.

"Nothing that obvious," he said. "Although it does strike me as odd this case hasn't garnered more attention. I've met Emmy a few times through Duncan. And she's a striking young woman."

His meaning was obvious and I'd thought the same thing myself. Beautiful girls who disappear tend to garner more attention. And if we are being even more precise, beautiful young girls. And even one step further; Beautiful, young, white girls. It's a sad, but undeniable fact.

The black guy in front of me surely knew that was the case.

"She certainly looks so from her pictures," I said, careful not to say anything suggesting I'd met Emmy.

"Prettier in person, I can assure you," Trent said matter-of-factly and not in a creepy way.

"So that leads back to my question. Doesn't it seem surprising this case hasn't garnered more attention?"

"Yes, but that's not all on the LVPD. Why haven't the local media covered it more? Do you think this is all some big conspiracy?"

"I don't know," I answered honestly. "But let's focus on the LVPD end."

He stared me down, but I think it was more out of respect than anything else. He realized I wasn't going to give his department a pass.

"The answer to your insinuation is yes. I thought we would have devoted more man hours to it. They never gave us some ultimatum not to investigate it, though. I kind of just assumed they thought Chance Peters was an asshole and didn't jump through hoops to help find his daughter."

"That's quite an indictment."

"Whether you like it or not, politics always plays a part. Even in police work."

"I guess. Not investigating a crime because you don't like the father of the victim seems a bit much."

"Remember, we're talking about levels. The case is still being investigated. Just not with the full force of the force behind it."

I couldn't tell if using force twice was intentional or not. I didn't care. Trent seemed to be confirming my suspicions about Emmy's case.

The question was if there was something more sinister going on, or if it really was just that they didn't like Chance. I tended to think it was the former.

I decided to play dumb.

"What's the name of the Chief of the LVPD?"

I was assuming Duncan hadn't told Trent that I knew he didn't like Bo Valentine.

"Wow, you really haven't done your homework, have you?"

"I guess not," I said. "Let's pretend tomorrow is the midterm and you can help get me prepared."

Trent laughed, a minor win for me.

"His name is Bo Valentine. He's an asshole!"

Duncan might have undersold his hatred.

"In what way?" I asked.

Trent poured himself another glass of water. I looked towards the home and didn't see Duncan peering out. He'd truly left us alone to our conversation.

"In every way. Smug, hard-headed, probably some latent racist tendencies. Although, to be fair, he's never said anything about the color of my skin. It's just the way he conducts himself around white suspects vs. black suspects. But enough of that. That's not why I hate him. The dude is just an arrogant asshole."

"How old is he?"

It's a question I knew the answer to, having Googled Bo Valentine after what Emmy had told me, but I had to make it sound like I knew nothing.

"He's around fifty-five, I believe."

"How long has he been Chief?"

"About fifteen years. He's lived in Vegas his whole life and became an officer in his early twenties, like myself. When I said everything is political earlier, I meant it. He became Chief at forty, which rarely happens. But he's politically savvy, so it happened for him."

"Any loftier goals for him?"

"Are you saying the Chief of a Police for a big American city isn't a good job?"

I looked over and Trent was smiling. He seemed to be loosening up by the minute.

"I'm sorry," I said. "Loftier political goals? Mayor? Governor?"

"Yes, there's been some rumors he might run for mayor next year."

Interesting.

"Is he more than just an asshole?"

"I assume you're asking if I could see him involved in criminal activity."

"Yes," I answered.

"If he is, I'd love nothing more than to take him down. He's not a big fan of mine. But in the interest of honesty, I've never heard him accused of any impropriety. At least, not on the level you're talking about. And someone better be damn sure if they accuse Bo Valentine of something. They wouldn't be around long if they were wrong."

"Do you mean kicked off the force or six feet under?" I asked.

Trent stared at me and I couldn't read his reaction.

"I meant kicked off the force. Why, is there something you'd like to tell me?"

"If something fishy was going on at the LVPD, would it have to come from Valentine?" I asked, not ready to answer his question.

"He's certainly the head of the snake, or in this example, the head of the fish. But it's not like there aren't officers who can't do appalling things without Valentine's urging."

I tried to understand his last sentence. He took notice.

"Too many double negatives?" Trent asked.

I laughed.

"I thought my head was going to explode," I said.

"Sorry."

"Don't be."

"And by the way, I'm going to assume this conversation will stay private."

"The only person I'll talk to about this conversation is sitting inside," I said, motioning to Duncan's home.

"Duncan is a good man. You can learn a lot from him."

"I already have."

"Well, maybe he should teach you to do your research first."

I laughed. Trent did have a softer side, that much had become obvious.

"I won't forget the name Bo Valentine from here on in."

"No, I don't think you will."

"You may not be able to answer this," I said. "But I'm going to ask anyway. What's the latest you've heard on the Emmy Peters case?"

"Nothing. Nothing for a few months now. We're not even getting any new calls on our tip line. We used to get people saying they'd seen her around town, or she moved to Europe, or she's buried in the desert."

I made sure not to flinch when he said his last sentence.

"It's like the public has lost interest," I said.

"It does feel that way," Ebbing said.

Which is exactly what the people who tried to kill her would want.

"Well, I'm not giving up. I'm just trying to see what sticks," I said.

"Duncan was the best at that. He'd talk to officers of the LVPD and throw five theories out there and see if we bit on any of them."

"Smart," I said.

"He most certainly is."

Trent was obviously a big fan of Duncan's.

"How did you two meet?" I asked, seeing if giving him the floor would elicit some information. Turns out it did.

"I'm going to tell you this once and then we won't talk about it again. Do you understand?"

Intimidating Trent was back.

"Yes," I said.

"He found me in a compromising position with a woman he was tailing. I was single, but the woman was married. I should have known better. Duncan told me that her husband was a hot head and if I didn't end it immediately, I might end up with a toe tag. I listened to Duncan, and a few months later, the woman and her new boy toy were killed by her husband. I've been loyal to Duncan ever since."

No wonder Duncan was able to get me a meeting with Trent. He'd basically saved his life.

"I won't bring it up again," I said. "One question, though. Is your loyalty more to Duncan or to the LVPD?"

"It's not one or the other. I do take my job seriously, and for that reason I have great allegiance to the LVPD. But if my department is rotten, then I'm all about taking it down. And if it ever came to push or shove in choosing Duncan or Bo Valentine, well, that's an easy one."

That's what I wanted to hear. I had an ally.

"Can we meet again soon?" I asked. "I think I'll have some more information that I'd like to run by you."

"Go through Duncan. You'll have a better shot at getting me over here. I don't need some newbie PI calling me at work."

He laughed and I responded in kind.

"Thanks for your time, Trent."

"You're welcome. Be sure to thank Duncan. He's the reason."

Trent Ebbing rose to his feet. I'd intentionally waited until this moment to ask my final question. I wanted to make it look like a throwaway question.

"There was one last thing, actually. Have you heard of a former police officer named Victor?"

"Sure. Victor Smith. He retired about five years ago. Disability, I believe. Haven't heard what he's been up to since."

There was a pause.

"Why?" Trent asked.

"Someone told me to check him out, is all," I said. It sounded weak.

"I never dealt with him very much, but I knew the guy. He didn't leave much of an impression one way or the other. I think he was a bit of a recluse outside of work."

"Do you know who he was close to on the force?" I asked.

"Hmmm, let me think. His partner was a guy named Rat. Rat Stallings, I believe. And yes, it's because his face looked like a Rat. He worked in Northwest Vegas a lot, whereas I was usually working the Strip. So I can't be of too much help."

I debated whether to ask the next question. As I often did, I said 'Fuck it', and decided to let it fly.

"Do you have any idea if Victor Smith was close with Valentine?"

Trent stared at me intently.

"This seems less like a fishing exhibition and more like you've got some real suspicions."

I didn't confirm or deny his statement.

"So, were they friendly?" I asked.

I watched as his face pondered the question.

"I seem to remember hearing about an incident."

My heart rate accelerated.

"I'm listening," I said.

"I don't know much about it. Rumors were that Victor might have been a little forceful during an arrest. And if the rumors were correct, little would be the wrong adjective. He was allegedly quite forceful. I was told Chief Valentine had to sit him down. Keep in mind, these rumors happen all the time in a police department. This one persisted, though. A couple people told me that Valentine had saved Victor Smith's job."

It was all I needed to hear. It was a reason that Smith might have been indebted to Valentine. The pieces of the puzzle were starting to come together.

"Do you remember the name of the case or the victim of Smith's alleged tormenting?"

"I don't," Trent said.

I'd received more information than I'd ever expected.

"Thanks for everything," I said.

"Anything else?"

"No, that's it."

Trent turned to go for a second time when I had one last request.

"It's probably better if you don't ask around about Victor Smith."

"What is going on here?"

"I have to do a little more investigating first. Just don't mention Victor Smith to anyone. Please."

"This is getting weirder and weirder."

"I promise I'll have more for you next time."

Trent shook his head.

"Duncan was right. You're going to be a pretty good PI. I feel like I gave away everything and didn't get any information in return."

It was a backhanded compliment.

"Next time, I promise," I said a second time.

"I'm going to go now," Trent said and walked towards Duncan's house.

We hadn't ended on a high note, but it's not like I could tell him that Victor Smith tried to kill Emmy Peters. And overall, we'd gotten along pretty well. I hoped Trent didn't hold the last few minutes against me.

I saw Duncan open the sliding glass door - maybe he had been watching - and Trent disappeared into the house.

~

I thought back over our conversation.

Trent had all but confirmed that Valentine and Smith had a connection. More than that, Valentine had likely saved his job. Would that be enough to forever keep Smith in Valentine's debt? Maybe.

And that wasn't even the most shocking information I'd received.

Unless he was some great actor, Trent Ebbing had no idea that Smith was missing.

How was that possible?

How could a cop not know that a former LVPD officer was missing?

Had they completely swept it under the rug?

And by they, I really just meant Valentine.

I had more questions I needed answered.

And I knew where to start.

CHAPTER 25

Before I reached out to Emmy, I wanted to inspect Victor Smith's van myself, just to make sure there wasn't any evidence left on site that might eventually lead back to her.

I drove from Duncan's house directly to The Bored Cactus and followed the road that Emmy had described on which she'd hidden Victor Smith's car.

It had been four months since Victor Smith had died. I had no idea whether the car was still there. And yet, my brain was telling me it was. If the media had learned that an ex-cop's car was abandoned in the middle of the desert, they'd have some questions, and when I'd googled Victor Smith the night before, I found nothing.

Then again, the media had been largely silent on Emmy's disappearance, so who the hell knew?

I followed the road for several minutes. Emmy had guessed it was about two miles, but I was starting to think it was even longer. I imagined Emmy walking this long stretch of road, long after the sun had set, on a day where she'd nearly lost her life. She was a tough SOB and I meant that in the most complimentary way imaginable.

After what seemed like ten minutes, I looked off to my left and saw two trees, probably half a football field away. I couldn't remember just how far Emmy had said they were from the road, but this seemed as good a possibility as any.

The terrain looked rough, so I parked my car on the side of the road, which probably wasn't even necessary. I hadn't seen a car since I'd started on the road.

I didn't have any gloves, but I grabbed a shirt I had sitting in the car. If I had to enter the van for any reason, better not to leave a fingerprint.

I walked towards the van, almost spraining my ankle a few seconds in, stepping on a tiny bush that bent my ankle to the side. I shook it off and kept walking.

When I got within about twenty yards, I finally saw the van.

Emmy had been correct. The trees definitely hid it, and there was no way that someone could have seen the van from the road.

I inched closer and walked around the two trees to get a better view. You could easily see the van from this vantage point, but all that occupied that side was a vast desert. There was literally no reason a human would ever come upon the van.

The first thing I did was take a picture of the license plate.

I looked around, making sure Emmy hadn't dropped any personal items or things that had belonged to Victor Smith. I saw nothing.

I reached for the door, holding the handle with my shirt, and pressed the button on the old school van, covering my finger with the shirt as well. It was locked.

Emmy would have locked the van after abandoning it. She's no dummy. I just hoped she'd taken his wallet, keys, phone, and any other valuables back to her hotel. I needed anything that might contribute to my investigation.

I walked around the van a few more times and found nothing, even getting on my hands and knees and searching underneath.

I wasn't quite sure what I'd hoped to accomplish with my visit out here. Mainly, I needed to verify Emmy's story, I guess. And now I knew, if push came to shove and I needed to prove she was telling the truth, I could show them Victor Smith's car.

Who would that be to, though? Like Emmy herself, I certainly didn't want to involve the police at this point. Not when the Chief was likely up to his neck in this.

With nothing more to do near the van, I texted Emmy's burner phone. I hoped she'd allowed the incoming texts from my phone.

"Can we meet in the next hour? I'm pretty close to The Bored Cactus."

I started thinking about Emmy and how well she'd done considering the circumstances. She was quite the young woman; determined, responsible, hard-charging. And yes, she was as beautiful as everyone stated. Not that it mattered. I was here to do a job and that was it.

As I thought about how capable she'd been, it prompted a question I hadn't yet asked myself. Did Emmy seem like the type of woman who would just sit in her motel day after day, watching the T.V. and letting time pass her by?

The answer was no.

In fact, she'd been nothing but proactive before this all went down. I didn't think she'd suddenly pull a 180. Would she be careful going forward? Yes, but I don't think she'd lose that fire in her belly. And that fire would lead her to finding more about why she was almost killed.

I came to a conclusion.

Emmy hadn't just been sitting in her motel room all day. She'd been investigating the people she felt had wronged her.

I was pretty confident.

Just then, a text came through.

"I'll meet you at the gas station in thirty minutes."

It was time to find out if I was right.

I drove from Victor Smith's van to the gas station, picked up Emmy, and started heading back in the direction I'd come from.

Emmy was wearing cutoff jeans again with a shabby T-shirt of some T.V. show I'd never heard of.

"Can I buy you some clothes?" I asked.

"To be honest, I'd rather look grubby and blend in with the people at the motel."

She had a point. Looking attractive was probably the last thing she wanted to do, being by herself at a shady motel.

"That makes sense."

"When you're shacked up in a motel all day, you don't really care what you look like."

"Actually, that's what I wanted to talk to you about, being shacked up in the motel."

Emmy gave me a curious look.

I slowed down as we were about to go over a particularly rocky part of the road.

"You can stop anywhere you want. I think we're far enough off the beaten path."

"I'm going to park where I just came from."

"You came from Victor Smith's car, didn't you?"

"I did," I said.

"The doors are all locked."

"That's another thing I wanted to talk about."

"I feel like I'm being cornered."

"Nothing like that, just some questions I had."

We approached the area I'd left only minutes before and I parked in roughly the same spot.

"Alright, fire away," Emmy said.

She seemed more defensive than yesterday, but it's not like I could blame her. She'd be suspicious of me texting her, picking her up, telling her I had some questions, and then driving to where she'd left Victor Smith's car. All of this took place in a very short amount of time.

"First things first. Did you hold on to Victor's wallet?"

"Yes. I considered burying it with him, but thought it might be important to have down the road."

"Smart decision. Can I see it?"

"It's at the motel, but sure."

"Alright, thanks."

"What else did you want to know?"

She wanted to get this over with.

"We're on the same side, Emmy. I'm sorry to be dropping this on you all at once."

"I know we are. It's just been a tough morning."

"I hope nothing happened," I said, quite concerned.

"Nothing like that. It's just that some days this can all be overwhelming, knowing my life might be at risk if I leave the motel. And shit, if we're being honest, my life might be at risk at The Bored Cactus as well, for different reasons. There are too many creep balls to name."

I saw an opening and pounced.

"Emmy, if you'd allow me to set up a meeting with your parents, I can guarantee you'd be out of The Bored Cactus within the hour. I could set up a room at a nice hotel and just give you the key. It wouldn't be under your name. I'm not saying you want to be on the Strip, but we could find something better than where you are right now. Shit, you could probably move back to Los Angeles."

"I'm staying in Vegas. If you think I'd leave after all that happened, you don't know me that well."

That's when I saw another opening.

"You've been doing your own research, haven't you? You can't leave because you're too immersed in it."

"Of course," Emmy said. "Did you think I was sitting around twiddling my thumbs?"

"No, not exactly."

"And it's not like I've found anything concrete on anybody. If so, I wouldn't still be on the run. The phone call from Bo Valentine is still the biggest piece of information I have."

"I've been doing a little research myself, about Bo Valentine specifically," I said.

"What did you find out?"

"I think he had dirt on Victor Smith," I said.

"Interesting. How'd you find that out?"

"I talked to an LVPD officer and he said there were rumors Victor had roughed up a suspect. And Valentine had helped him get out of it."

"That would explain why Victor was willing to do his dirty work for him."

"Which, in turn, would explain why no one seems to know that Victor Smith is dead. Bo Valentine would do anything he could to keep that on the down low."

"I searched the internet on my trusty burner phone and couldn't find a wife or kids for Smith. Not even an ex-wife."

"The officer told me that he was a bit of a loner."

"That would explain why no one has reported him missing. Still, you'd think a friend would be suspicious if they hadn't heard from him in months."

"Maybe Valentine was intentionally having any calls pertaining to Victor Smith sent to him. And I'm sure he wasn't rushing out to tell the press."

"Good point."

"That's assuming only Valentine and Victor Smith knew about their arrangement."

"Don't forget about Junior Remington. He's involved somehow."

Emmy was correct. From the moment I'd heard the Chief of Police mentioned, my mind had gravitated towards Bo Valentine.

"True," I said. "Although, there's a decent chance that Valentine wouldn't tell Junior who he hired to abduct you."

"Another fair point," Emmy said.

"Thanks."

Emmy surprised me with her next question.

"Can I guess the LVPD officer's name?"

"Sure."

"Trent Ebbing."

"I'd say impressive, but somehow I'm not all that surprised."

"You're too new in town to have those type of connections. You know who isn't? Duncan."

"You're good, Emmy."

"It doesn't hurt that I met him a few times. And he's been Duncan's go-to cop for a long time. Well, before I moved to Vegas."

"He despises Valentine."

"That could be very helpful."

"I'm supposed to meet him again."

"When?"

"Haven't set up a time, but I'd imagine in the next day or two."

"Tell him what I told you when we met yesterday."

"We talked about a lot of things, Emmy. Which part?"

"What Junior drunkenly said to me about The Gambler's Gambit getting shut down. Even though he didn't mention the casino by name, there's no doubt that's what he was referring to. It all comes back to that."

I could tell she wanted to say more.

"And..."

"And I think Bo Valentine was in cahoots with Junior Remington. They brought down The Gambler's Gambit to bring The Remington back to prominence. Or, at the very least, to make the extra money that would surely come with their rival casino's downfall."

"Would that make a huge difference?"

"Those two casinos dominated that section of the Strip. Now imagine if your next door neighbor is shut down. That section is yours and yours only. I'm not saying it would double your revenue, but it would certainly spike it in a big way."

"Any idea on how exactly they managed to get them shut down?"

"I told you there were some articles about drug deals, fights, things like that. But I never saw the official reason, so I did some further digging."

"I'd expect nothing less," I said, sounding like a proud father.

"I made up a fake email address and pretended to be from a newspaper. Then I emailed the Nevada Gaming Commission asking if they had any information on why The Gambler's Gambit was shut down."

"Any luck?" I asked.

"No response. I don't know if it's because they couldn't verify who the hell I was or if it's just against their protocol."

"You get an A for effort. Very industrious."

"Maybe you'd have better luck. You can actually go into these buildings and ask questions. That's still a bridge too far for me."

"Yeah, I'd keep laying low if I were you, especially if this involves some of the big wigs we've mentioned. The Chief of Police is no one to fuck with."

"Why do you think I've been shacked up at…"

I could tell she was tired of saying the name of The Bored Cactus.

"Have you been worried that someone might come knocking at your door?"

"Yes and no. Obviously, I think about it. And yet, I don't think Junior or Bo Valentine would risk it. Could you imagine them taking around a picture of me, a missing woman, and asking if anyone had seen me? They'd have a lot of questions to answer. Could they have hired their own PI to look for me? Sure, but then you're just adding more people to the conspiracy, something I'm sure they want to avoid. If I had to guess, their wet dream would be if Victor and I had somehow managed to kill each other, and then the vultures did the rest of the work. I'm sure they'd have loved that."

"I can't argue with any of that. But I'd say it's more likely they think Victor Smith killed you and then said 'Fuck it, I'm out of here.' They have to assume you are dead. Why else would you have never reappeared? Or gone to the police? Plus, your parents are out here twice a week trying to find information on you."

"I always knew that helped contribute to the notion that I was dead. I hate that I can't tell my parents, but it kind of works as confirmation that I'm dead."

"I'd agree."

"Are you starting to understand why I made the decisions I made?"

"Yes."

"I promise you, it wasn't easy. I hate when I start thinking about what my family and friends are going through."

"I'm sure that's very tough."

"It is, Quint. I've cried myself to sleep many nights thinking about my parents."

I didn't want to be unsympathetic, but I tried to steer the conversation in a different direction.

"Anything else you've discovered that might help me out?"

"Junior Remington has an ex-wife who isn't a big fan of his. I almost emailed her with my fake account, but I thought if that got back to Junior, he might start wondering if I was alive and I couldn't have that."

"Do you have her info? I could follow up on it."

"It's back at the motel."

"You ready to head back there?"

"Sure."

We both instinctually looked out in the direction of Victor Smith's car.

"It was him or me," Emmy said, unnecessarily.

"Emmy, I have zero sympathy for Victor Smith. None at all. He tried to kill an innocent woman. You saved your own life and have nothing to apologize for."

"Okay, thanks. Sometimes I still have a tough time with the fact that I killed a man."

"Well, don't. If not, it would have been you out in the desert. Now let's go back to your place so I can get Smith's wallet."

"I'd feel a little better about this if you let me go to my room first. I'll leave the door unlocked and you can walk in a few minutes later. I don't want to be seen walking in with a guy. No need to give the creeps at the motel any ideas."

I understood perfectly.

"Of course."

"Thanks."

I started driving back down the dirt road I'd now become accustomed to.

I parked at the gas station and Emmy said she was in Room #158 on the first floor. She asked me to wait a few minutes and make sure no one was watching when I entered the room.

Was it possible she was being overcautious? Maybe, but I didn't have to deal with the type of man who would stay at The Bored Cactus. Better to be overly cautious.

About five minutes after Emmy walked over, I did the same. I found Room #158, and after making sure no one was looking, I quickly entered the room.

Emmy was sitting on the bed.

"Can you lock the door behind you?" she quietly asked.

"Sure." I did so.

I looked around the room and it was as run down as I'd expected. It had ugly colors, stained carpets, and a television that was more reminiscent of an 80's model than the smart T.V.s of today. She extended me a chair to sit on.

"So, welcome to The Bored Cactus."

I'm not sure whether levity was appropriate, but I decided to roll with it.

"It reminds me of your parents' suite at the Wynn."

Emmy laughed.

"Good," I said. "I wasn't sure if your sense of humor was intact."

"You kidding me? I need it now more than ever."

"I hear that," I said.

"So you met my parents at the Wynn?"

"I did. I liked them both very much."

"I hope you never suspected my Dad was involved," she said.

"Never. A few of your friends think he's a bit of a showoff, but all I saw was a loving father."

"He's a bit of both," Emmy said.

The Bored Cactus had air-conditioning, a must in Vegas, but it was still very stuffy in the room. I don't know how Emmy did it day after day. Actually, it was month after month at this point.

I guess when you fear for your life you'll resort to almost anything.

"I'm going to ask one more time, Emmy. Can I set up a meeting? First and foremost, it will be the greatest day of your parents' life. And if you'd rather look at it selfishly, I'll get you out of this hell hole."

"That's a good way to describe this place," she said.

She walked to a section of the room where the wallpaper was curling up and ripped off a section, throwing it at me.

"A parting gift," she said.

I laughed.

"I'd rather have that retro T.V."

"It still says 'FREE HBO' on the marquee. I didn't know hotels still did that."

"Not many," I conceded. "You're staying at the last of a dying breed."

"When the potential of death is the other option, you kind of just roll with it. And it had become easy to just pay the front desk for a week or two and then disappear from sight. A new hotel would bring its own new set of headaches."

"I understand, but I'd almost have taken my chances with the cops."

I was trying to keep the light naturedness of the conversation going, but this one landed with a thud. Emmy looked back up at me and she had tears forming in her eyes.

"Do you think I wanted this?" she asked. "To stay at this horrible motel for months on end? To meet Carrie so she can give me cash to pay for my stay here? To order food delivery twice a week and store the rest in this fridge here? To have meth heads and probably sexual deviants walking around in this parking lot? To have..."

She couldn't continue, the tears getting the best of her. They increased and within seconds she was sobbing uncontrollably. I leaned in, hugged her, and she buried her face in my chest, barely able to control her crying. It almost sounded like she was hyperventilating.

It was uncomfortable for me, but I understood completely. Emmy had gone from a twenty-two-year-old with her whole life ahead of her to almost being murdered and then having to spend four months at this disgusting motel, fearing for her life daily.

After about thirty seconds, she removed her face from my chest.

"You can set up the meeting," she said.

It was barely audible, but I caught it.

I realized this event was likely necessary for Emmy to move forward and agree to meet with her parents. She'd probably needed this, but didn't have a shoulder to cry on. I'd become that proverbial, and now literal, shoulder.

"I'm sorry," she said as she continued to wipe the tears from her eyes.

"Don't be," I said. "You've gone through so much."

She went to the bathroom and grabbed a towel, using it to wipe her face clean.

"If we're being honest, that's been a long time coming," Emmy said. "Thanks for allowing it."

"You don't have to apologize, Emmy."

"I'm usually a lot tougher than this."

"You've been extremely tough, whether you realize it or not," I said.

She used the towel one more time.

"At least I'm not screwing up my makeup. No need to wear it when you are stuck at The Bored Cactus."

I looked at Emmy, not sure how to take her comment.

"C'mon, you can laugh," she said. "That was funny."

And I did laugh, because she was right, it was funny.

"No hot dates at The Bored Cactus?" I asked.

It was Emmy's turn to laugh.

"Not unless you like guys with one front tooth," she said.

"Touche."

The tears had given way to laughter and it was a welcomed relief.

"So, where were we?" Emmy finally asked.

"You agreed to meet with your parents."

"I did, didn't I?"

Her response was rhetorical.

A few seconds passed and I realized it was time to solidify the meeting.

"I won't tell your parents why I need to meet them."

"Good. I still worry that somehow their phones are tapped."

"Can I tell Duncan? I can easily do it at his house. That's the only other person I feel compelled to tell."

"Yes, but wait until I've met with my parents first."

"That's fair. They are coming into town early tomorrow morning. What do you say about setting up a time right now?"

"That's fine."

"How about nine a.m.?"

"Where?"

"I was thinking I could drive them out here, then pick you up at the gas station and drive around."

"No, that's not going to work."

"Why not?"

"I don't want my parents to see where I've been staying. That will only make things tougher on them."

"Then where?"

"At the Wynn."

"You're serious?"

"As a heart attack. They'll be shocked enough seeing me with short, bleached blonde hair. If they saw the vagrants who hung out at The Bored Cactus, I'm not sure they'd be able to erase that from their minds."

"This seems risky."

"Like you said, Valentine and Junior probably think I'm dead."

"I didn't say probably, I said it's a possibility. What if Valentine has some police officers on the lookout for you?"

"I won't look any cops in the eyes. Plus, they aren't looking for a blond pixie," Emmy said, flipping her bangs in the air.

She was trying to be cute, but I was deathly serious. Emmy on the Strip didn't sound like a great idea. I did understand where she was coming from, though. Her parents would be aghast if they knew where Emmy had been shacked up.

"Alright, let's do this," I reluctantly said. "I'm assuming you know the Wynn?"

"I sure do. My Dad would stay there every time he visited."

"Then meet me at the bottom of the elevators where they check your key. Nine a.m. tomorrow."

"I'm excited," she said.

"I'm nervous," I replied.

We'd shifted positions.

"And don't be late. You'll probably give me a coronary," I said.

Emmy got up from the bed and walked to the lone closet in the room. I saw her reach on to the top shelf and return with Victor Smith's wallet. She handed it to me and then sat back down on the bed.

"I haven't touched a thing," she said.

I pulled out the driver's license, looking at his address.

"And you have the phone?"

"I do, but I've been afraid to turn it on. Plus, it had gone to locked mode after Valentine's call, so I couldn't access it anyway."

"Alright, we'll keep the phone here for now. What did you do with the gun?"

"I hid it in the desert."

"With his body?"

"No. I didn't want anyone finding it if they somehow dug up his body."

"I hate to say this, Emmy, but just in case something happens, why don't you tell me where it is."

"We were very close to it recently."

'What?"

"I left it by Victor Smith's truck. I was afraid to leave it near the body, so I waited until I ditched the truck. If you're facing his car from the road, it's buried a few feet from the base of the tree on the left."

"Thanks. I hate asking, but it's better I know."

"No problem. Is there anything else?"

"I think that's it for now. I'm going to have a busy rest of the day."

"Please be careful," Emmy said. "After all, if we are meeting my parents tomorrow, this wouldn't be the best time to get made."

She was right, but I couldn't just stand pat. I, actually we, were making too much progress to slow down now.

"I'll be careful," I said.

Emmy sensed that I was about to leave. She rose from the bed as I stood up from the chair.

"Thanks for all you're doing for me," Emmy said.

"To you as well. I'd still be interviewing Nia or Kenneth Croy if you hadn't put me in the game."

"You can do some investigating that I'm not able to."

"You're right. And I plan on commencing that shortly."

She didn't bother repeating her request to be careful, but I could tell she wanted to. Instead, she gave me a hug and I hugged her back. I had begun seeing Emmy as a younger sister, or even, a daughter. I just wanted to protect her.

I couldn't imagine anything horrible happening to her from here on in. It would be my fault at this point.

"I'll see you at nine tomorrow, Emmy," I said.

"I can't wait to see the expressions on my parents' faces."

"That makes two of us."

I left a minute later, avoiding two people in the parking lot who were exchanging things and obviously up to no good.

CHAPTER 26

"That's fucking it!"
     I yelled, just as I exited Flamingo Road on my way back to The Cosmo.

When I arrived, I quickly valeted my car and hustled up to my hotel room. I took out the copy of Emmy's police reports, hoping it would have the information I sought.

My F-bomb occurred because I had a guess as to why the two pages were ripped out of Emmy's journal.

I went back over my logic as I thumbed through the different reports.

If someone had gone to Emmy's house looking for evidence against themselves, for example a journal, and found it, they'd just take the whole thing.

Emmy said there was a few minutes between Victor Smith throwing her in the back of his van and the time they drove off. If he had time to quickly search for a journal, he's certainly not thumbing through it and ripping out a few pages. He's just grabbing it and taking it with him.

So, I asked myself, in what scenario would someone just tear out a few pages?

The only time that would make sense is if you couldn't take the whole journal.

And when would that be?

It was then that I had come to my conclusion and dropped the F-bomb.

My theory was that the pages were ripped out by one of the police officers who arrived at Emmy's house when she was first reported missing. This likely would have been under the instruction of Bo Valentine or Junior Remington. They would have told the officer to be on the lookout for a diary or journal.

The original plan may well have been to grab the whole journal, but I'd seen it, and it was too big to fit into a pocket or police uniform. Furthermore, the officer couldn't just put it by his side and risk someone else seeing what he was doing.

The officer either had been told ahead of time, or maybe came to a quick decision, to just rip out a few of the pages. And he had likely been told the incriminating entry would be amongst the most recent.

My guess is that the officer in question went straight to Emmy's bedroom, found said journal, and when he realized it was too big to walk out with, he ripped the last few pages out. Then, when it was inevitably tagged as evidence, the incriminating section was already gone.

And thus, returned to Emmy's parents along with other non-vital information.

It made perfect sense. Or so I thought.

I finally found the police report in question.

Three officers responded to Emmy's house on the initial visit.

Ryan Mallory. Howard Kloss. Samuel Waddle.

I had more than a sneaking suspicion one of them was involved in this.

I'd finished my meeting with Trent less than three hours previous, but I needed to talk to him again. Time was moving fast and if I could take some shortcuts to save some time, I needed to jump at the chance.

I called Duncan.

"Hello?"

"Hey, Duncan. It's Quint."

"You really can't get enough of me, can you?"

"I'm making progress, but I need a big favor."

"What is it?"

"Can I get Trent Ebbing's phone number?"

It's like I could hear Duncan pondering from the other end.

"I feel like you owe me some information. How about you drop by this evening after you talk to Trent?"

"I'd be fine with that. Does that mean you're giving me his number?"

"It does. It's 702-555-5820. Got it?"

I wrote it down on my computer and would save it to my cell phone when I hung up. I was terrible at navigating my phone while talking on it.

"I got it, Duncan. Thank you."

"You're welcome. I feel like I'm in the dark."

"It's not intentional, I'm just learning new information by the minute. I'll tell you about it tonight. How about six p.m.? I'll bring a pizza with me."

"That sounds nice. Be safe, Quint. You've got me a little worried."

"I'll fill you in tonight on all I've learned."

"See you then."

And Duncan hung up on his end. I looked down at my phone. It was 12:47 p.m.

I debated the pluses and minuses of calling Trent Ebbing and decided it was worth it. He'd made it clear he was no fan of Bo Valentine, so it's not like he'd go squealing to the Chief of Police.

I started dialing his number.

"Hello, this is Officer Ebbing."

"Trent, this is Quint Adler. We met this morning."

"Yeah, I remember," he said sarcastically.

"Are you by yourself?" I asked.

"No, I'm in my precinct."

"Is there any way you could walk outside? I've got an important question and I'd rather your fellow officers don't hear your answer."

"You're a pain in the fucking ass."

I thought he was going to say my name at the end, but he didn't. Smart, considering he was surrounded by his fellow officers.

"Please, it's important to me."

"Alright," Trent said and I didn't hear anything for about a minute. And then, "I'm outside. This better be important."

I could sugarcoat it, but what was the point? I just asked my question.

"Three officers responded to Emmy Peters' house when she was first reported missing. Ryan Mallory. Howard Kloss. And Samuel Waddle. Of those three officers, who is the closest with Chief Valentine?"

I thought he'd ponder this for a few seconds. I was wrong.

"Sam is. No one calls him Samuel. He's in his late twenties and has been on the force about five years. He's got loftier aspirations and has kissed Chief Valentine's ass since day one. He thinks it might give him some pull around the different precincts. Ryan and Howard aren't exactly my favorites, but they are better than Sam. Are you sure it's just one?"

In my mind it had been just one rogue cop ripping the pages out, but there certainly could have been someone else on it.

"I don't know, to be honest," I said.

"That's alright, but don't assume things are correct just because they fit into your narrative. Investigate first."

It was part lecture, part advice. He was right, though.

"Thanks, Trent."

"Are you going to tell me what's going on?"

I thought about it.

"What time are you off work?" I finally asked.

"Around six."

"Can you be at Duncan's house by 6:30?"

"Yes."

"I'll tell you everything I know."

"See you tonight."

I hung up the phone and called Duncan back.

"Like I said, you can't get enough of me," he said.

"I'll be there at 6:30 now and Trent Ebbing will be coming too."

"There's a lot going on isn't there?"

"Yes."

"Okay, I can wait for the rest."

"Thanks."

"And pick up the pizza from Verrazano. It's the best there is around here."

"I will. Bye, Duncan."

"Goodbye, Quint."

CHAPTER 27

I sprawled out on my bed, hoping to get a few minutes of sleep. It didn't come.

I started going back over the police report from the officers' first visit to Emmy's house.

My focus was now on Sam Waddle, with Ryan Mallory and Howard Kloss not above suspicion. Waddle may have been a small domino in the grand scheme of things, but if I could prove he ripped the pages from Emmy's journal that would go a long way.

It would likely lead to the Chief of Police Bo Valentine having instructed him to do so. All because Junior Remington told Emmy Peters too much and had to be eliminated. Then, when Emmy turned up 'missing', Valentine knew they couldn't have anything mentioning Junior Remington become evidence, and that meant disposing of any journal entries they might find.

Those were the conclusions I had reached. Sure, there were probably some minor discrepancies along the way, but I felt my logic was sound. After all, this had all started because Junior Remington had drunkenly told Emmy too much.

At least I thought so.

What if, I asked myself, Victor Smith was just some complete and utter sadist who kidnapped young women for fun, and none of this was related?

That didn't seem likely and it certainly wouldn't explain the phone call from Bo Valentine during Emmy's abduction. That was a coincidence I could not overlook. It's what tied it all together.

Assuming my suspicions were, for the most part, correct, how did I get close to Sam Waddle?

I couldn't just confront him, could I? Not unless I wanted to turn this whole case on its head. Maybe in the near future, but I couldn't do that yet, not with the meeting of Emmy and her parents less than twenty-four hours away. If I confronted Sam Waddle, I'd in turn draw attention to myself. That would put Emmy in harm's way. I couldn't do that, not after all she'd been through.

Sam Waddle would have to wait a day.

My investigation would not be put on pause, however. There were other things to explore.

Since I wasn't exactly sure what to do next, I went where any PI in 2021 would go.

The internet.

I spent the next hour investigating the case via Google, *The Las Vegas Daily*, and the police reports.

I tried to start from the beginning, which wasn't with the abduction of Emmy. This case had its roots well before then. I decided to start by reading about the downfall of The Gambler's Gambit.

A few things stuck out.

First off, I was surprised how much interest *The Las Vegas Daily* took in the casino. And it came about very suddenly.

From the beginning of 2019 until August of 2020, The Gambler's Gambit was never the primary reason for a story. It was mentioned in the occasional article, but was never the feature of it. Then, starting in August of last year, every week or two an article was written about the casino. And it was always shown in a bad light.

On August 26th of 2020, *The Daily* published an article titled "People up to no good at The Gambler's Gambit."

On September 1st, the title was "More crime at The Gambit."

On September 12th, "Drugs, Gangs, and Crime. Welcome to The Gambler's Gambit."

On September 22nd, "Deepening troubles at a Las Vegas Casino" was published.

And then on October 6th, there was a four page exposè titled, "Going downhill fast: The sad story of The Gambler's Gambit."

It laid out all the problems that The Gambler's Gambit was going through. Drugs, gangs, fights, unconfirmed reports of rigged slot machines were all mentioned. One of the quotes from the author was, "Of every Vegas casino, and I've been to them all many times, The Gambler's Gambit is the only one that I don't feel safe at. I wish the Nevada Gaming Control Board would do something about it."

Maybe The Gambler's Gambit really did have all those problems, but this article felt like a hit piece.

I looked at who wrote it. The reporter's name was Lyle Banks. There was a picture at the end of the article. Lyle wore glasses and looked to be on the wrong side of forty by a few years. He had long, curly, red hair.

I went back and looked at all the other articles about The Gambler's Gambit. They were all written by Lyle Banks.

It's possible these types of articles were his specialty at the newspaper, but I was suspicious nonetheless.

I checked for later articles on The Gambler's Gambit, but there weren't many. There were a few brief mentions of more crime, but no more exposés.

Then, on December 16th, there was a final article.

"The Gambit comes to a close," it was titled.

"The Gambler's Gambit, a Las Vegas casino built in 1991, and well regarded at one point, has gone under. There had been reports of crime and drug dealing taking place in recent months. There must have been something else going on as well, because the Nevada Gaming Control Board has taken their gambling license away. We will keep you updated on what happens with The Gambit, but let's be honest. It was an eye-sore and not many people will miss it."

A little personal jab at the end from Lyle Banks. As had become par for the course, something fishy was going on.

If Banks was indeed involved, that means they had hotel big wigs (Junior Remington), law enforcement (Bo Valentine/Victor Smith), and the media (Lyle Banks) involved.

Some people might think I was in over my head, that I should stand down.

But not me. That's not my style.

I was looking forward to going after these assholes.

CHAPTER 28

"This better be good, Quint!"

It came from Duncan Hobbes' mouth and Trent Ebbing nodded in agreement.

"Do you mean the pizza?" I asked.

They both laughed.

"No, smart guy. The information you have."

We were sitting in Duncan's kitchen and I'd just walked in holding the pizza. It had taken longer than I expected and Trent beat me there.

I set the pizza on the island in the kitchen, the first thing I'd seen on the granite in the many times I'd visited. To say Duncan kept things clean would be an understatement.

"You guys want to sit inside or out?" Duncan asked.

"I'm fine with either," I said.

"Let's sit outside," Trent said.

"Outside it is," Duncan said.

He grabbed some paper plates and we each dished ourselves a few slices of pizza. I'd got half pepperoni, half combination, figuring if you don't like one of those choices, you didn't like pizza.

We arrived at the table we always sat at, the canopy positioned to block the sun, which was still shining bright at 6:30. The ubiquitous pitcher of lemon flavored ice water was there. Duncan was nothing if not consistent.

We took our seats and each had a bite of the pizza. Duncan was right, it was delicious.

"This is great stuff," I said.

"I told you. The best in Vegas."

We sat mostly in silence over the next few minutes, devouring the pizza in front of us. I had certainly not eaten well on my trip to Vegas, grabbing random things on the go and the occasional fast food. I'm not saying Verrazano's pizza was five-star dining, but damn if it didn't hit the spot.

Trent was the last to finish and we all knew it was time to get down to business. I wasn't going to tell them that Emmy was alive, but I was going to throw everything else on the table. Both of these men deserved that. They'd helped me immensely.

"Are we ready?" Duncan asked.

Trent nodded.

"Alright, I'll first start off with why I think Emmy was abducted," I said, knowing I had to tread lightly to not give away my one big secret. "I believe she either had a meeting or overheard something from Junior Remington that set this in motion. She was working at The Remington and apparently Junior would come and talk to the showgirls after practice from time to time. Maybe Emmy asked to talk about her debut novel or maybe it just happened organically. Shit, maybe Junior asked her out on a date."

I hated lying to these two men, but sometimes it's unavoidable.

I continued.

"Regardless of how, I believe Junior Remington said too much to Emmy, which put her in harm's way. Someone then put out a hit on Emmy. And considering that Victor Smith, the man I believe was commissioned to kill Emmy, was friends with Bo Valentine, that puts him at the top of my suspects list."

"You'd asked about Victor Smith before. How do you know he was the one hired to kill Emmy?"

The question came from Trent, but my eyes moved to Duncan. He stared at me, and the slightest of smiles started to form. To most anyone else it would be unrecognizable, but I'd come to know Duncan fairly well, and I noticed it. My guess was that he wondered how I knew all of this. That maybe, just maybe, I'd learned it all from Emmy herself.

I couldn't give anything away, so my eyes darted away from Duncan and back to Trent.

"I've got an inside source that I can't divulge. I hope you understand, Trent."

"I'll give you a one time pass. I know how important they can be."

I looked back at Duncan. The corners of his lips had curled up slightly higher. It wasn't a full-fledged smile, but it was trending that way.

"Thanks, Trent. This source told me that he thinks this all started with the demise of The Gambler's Gambit."

I used the word 'he' intentionally, hoping it would give Duncan second thoughts.

"What about The Gambit?" Trent asked.

"I think that Junior Remington and Bo Valentine conspired to bring The Gambler's Gambit down. With those two casinos having a pretty good section of the Strip to themselves, if one of them was gone, it would probably mean millions to the other casino."

"Maybe tens of millions," Duncan said, his face having returned to normal.

"Maybe," I admitted. "And I think there might be a third party involved."

"Who?" Trent asked.

He was usually so stoic, but I could tell I had his full attention. He was probably imagining himself taking Bo Valentine into a precinct, handcuffed.

"Have you guys heard of Lyle Banks?"

They both nodded.

"Yeah, any Vegas local knows him," Trent said. "He's a blowhard, but a pretty good writer. And he gets all the best scoops."

"Well, I went back and read his articles. *The Las Vegas Daily* had numerous articles about The Gambler's Gambit and they were always critical of the casino. Drug deals. Fights. Customers complaining. And every single one of these articles was written by Banks. And I'll be honest, they seemed to get a little too much attention."

"What do you mean?"

"They would be the lead story of that day's online edition. I mean, does a guy getting busted for selling coke at a casino really warrant being a lead story? I'm sure it happens many, many times a day in Vegas. And yet, the only time Lyle Banks ever wrote about it was when it happened at The Gambler's Gambit."

"That's pretty darn suspicious," Trent said, confirming my thoughts.

"It must have worked," I said. "As you guys know, The Gambler's Gambit went under last December, surely, making Junior Remington millions of dollars. That's more than enough to pay off Bo Valentine and Lyle Banks. And obviously, Victor Smith as well."

I saw Trent drop his head.

"Fuck Victor Smith. What a poor excuse for a cop if what your source says is true."

"You might have some corruption in that force of yours," Duncan said.

"Starting to sound like it. I pray your niece is still alive somehow, Duncan. She's your niece, right?"

"By marriage. She was my wife's niece. So yeah, mine as well. But thanks, I hope so too."

Duncan looked at me as he said it, trying to get a reaction from me, but I remained stone-faced.

"So what's next?" Trent asked.

"I should be free around eleven a.m. tomorrow," I said. "I'd love to give Lyle Banks a shakedown. I imagine he's not as deeply involved as the other two and he'd be the easiest to crack."

"If you're right about everything and we accuse Lyle Banks, it will get back to Junior and Bo in a New York minute."

"I know," I said.

"And you're still ready to go forward with this?"

"100 percent," I said. "If not, all we have is a circumstantial case and it's not even all that strong."

"That's if your source is willing to talk. Testifying against Bo Valentine might give someone second thoughts."

"Yup," I said succinctly.

Whenever my "source" came up, I tried to steer the conversation towards a different path.

"One more thing," Trent said. "By the end of the day, can you send me all the evidence you've collected?"

"Sure," I said.

"If we're going to shake down Lyle Banks, I don't want to be caught with my dick in my hand without any corroboration. Bo Valentine would chop it off, if you catch my drift."

It was hard not to.

"I understand. I can assure you there is enough evidence."

"Then fuck it, let's do it!" Trent said. "I never liked reporters anyway."

He had a child-like smile as he said it.

I didn't mention that yours truly used to be a reporter.

"Would we surprise Lyle Banks at *The Las Vegas Daily*?" I asked.

"Tomorrow is Saturday. I'll find out if he's working, but I'd guess he is. It will be nice to see his co-workers' reaction. Shit, I'd rather do this at eight or nine. Why do we have to wait until eleven a.m.?"

"I'm meeting with that source of mine."

"Alright," he said.

I didn't bother looking over at Duncan.

"Is there anything else?" Trent asked.

"I think that's it for now. I'll be sending you my findings later tonight."

"Great. It's about time I get home then," Trent said. "I've got a few sources of my own and I'm going to dig into this friendship between Junior and Bo."

He rose from the table, exchanging handshakes with both of us.

"Can I walk you out?"

"C'mon, Duncan, how many times have I been here?"

"Fair enough."

With that, Trent walked toward the house.

Duncan and I sat in silence for about a minute, making sure Trent was gone.

"I heard Chance and Liz are flying in early tomorrow morning."

I knew where this was going.

"They are."

"God, I hope I'm right with what I'm about to say."

He paused and I saw his eyes get moist.

"You're bringing them to Emmy, aren't you?"

I had no doubt that my eyes would have given me away. Not that it mattered. I couldn't lie to Duncan anymore. Not when he asked me point blank.

"Yes," I said.

Duncan started sobbing.

I couldn't blame him, finding out that his beloved niece, who he'd been really close to, was alive after all.

I was ready to give him as much time as he needed, but he stopped about thirty seconds later.

"I'm sorry," he said.

"Don't be."

"I'm not sure the last time I've shed tears of joy. Maybe never."

Duncan wiped his nose with a handkerchief from his pocket.

"How did you know?" I asked.

"I noticed a slight difference when I saw you yesterday, but I didn't know what to attribute it to. I started getting my hopes up when you told Trent that you had a source. I didn't know who else could have been so close to the investigation. Obviously, it was possible I was mistaken, but when you brought up Emmy having had a meeting with Junior Remington, I started dreaming it as possible. That sounded like inside information if you know what I mean."

"I noticed. You had a slight little smirk."

Duncan laughed. "Yeah, I did. Maybe you know me better than I thought."

"I'd like to think so," I said.

"I wasn't going to bring it up with Trent here, obviously. But I figured if I brought it up once he left, you wouldn't lie to me."

"I couldn't. And it's not like I wanted to in the first place. I had to respect Emmy's wishes though. She wanted her parents to find out first."

"Rightfully so. And I don't even care about all that. I'm just glad she's alive. Where has she been staying?"

"A horrendous motel."

"Is she still there?"

"If things go right, this will be her last night."

"And Chance and Liz don't know the truth yet?"

"No. Emmy is afraid they'd act differently and someone would notice. Or, it would somehow get to Bo Valentine."

Duncan laughed out loud.

"What is so funny?" I asked.

"You think I produced the water works? Wait until Chance and Liz find out that their Emmy is alive."

I smiled. Ever since I'd started conducting the investigation, in the back of my mind I was always hoping that might be the end result.

"It will be a fantastic moment," I said.

"Enjoy it, because this case isn't over," Duncan said, ending the sentimental portion of our conversation.

"I realize that."

"You've done great work, Quint. Fantastic, really."

"Thanks."

"How did you find Emmy?"

"She kind of found me, but it was because of my probing into Carrie Granger."

"So you were right about her?"

"Yes. However, she didn't know Emmy was alive when you first met with her, so you weren't wrong, either."

"Where did you and Emmy meet?"

"In the desert, where they had intended to kill her. Victor Smith abducted her and…"

Duncan raised his arms as if to say he'd heard enough.

"There's probably some things I'd be better off not knowing," he said.

"I understand."

He stared at me intently.

"Don't think this is some Christmas present you are just putting a bow on. These are major Las Vegas players you're talking about. And if you and Trent go accuse Lyle Banks tomorrow, shit is going to hit the fan. So don't think you're just wrapping this case up. You are all still very much in danger, myself included, if I get too close."

"I understand."

"Okay, good, because the hard part may just well be starting. These guys aren't going to go down without a fight. And if a lengthy jail sentence is staring them in the face, I have no doubt they'd kill to protect themselves. Shit, they've tried already."

Duncan was right and I had to ask myself if I was getting complacent. I didn't think so, but it was important to heed his words. We were likely entering a very dangerous phase of the investigation.

"As usual, it's good advice. Thanks, Duncan."

"I don't expect to be included in the reunion tomorrow, but please let me know how it goes. And obviously, I'd like to meet Emmy whenever you find it to be safe. I'll trust your judgement."

"Let's get her situated at a new hotel and then I'll broach the subject with her. You should know that she's mentioned you several times and looks up to you very much."

"Thanks for that, Quint."

"You're welcome. It's true."

"Why don't you head back to The Cosmo. I think some extra sleep might do you some good."

"Thanks, Duncan."

"No, thank you, Quint. You've done an amazing service to this family."

CHAPTER 29

P er Duncan's suggestion, I wanted to get a good night's sleep, but there were still some things I needed to go over.

It was after seven by the time I arrived back at The Cosmo and I was shooting to fall asleep by 9:30. After the exhausting last few days I'd had, I assumed sleep would come easy. On the other hand, my mind was a busy mess.

I guess we'd see.

I went back to my trusted friend Google and looked to see what I could learn about Lyle Banks.

Turns out, a lot.

Lyle Lance Banks was forty-two years old and grew up in Las Vegas. Like Emmy, he'd graduated from UNLV, majoring in journalism in 2002. He'd spent the last almost twenty years working for newspapers, magazines, or blogs. He worked for *The Denver Post*, *The Register-Guard* in Eugene, and *The Arizona Republic*, along with some small magazines.

In 2012, he'd come home, being hired as one of the lead writers for *The Las Vegas Daily*, where he remained to this day.

Most of his articles seemed to paint the city in a good light. There were many stories of how quickly the city was expanding, ribbon-cutting ceremonies for new casinos, and reports on how the unemployment in Las Vegas had hit an all-time low.

Which made his depressing articles about The Gambler's Gambit stand out even more. He was a champion of the city, always stressing what a great place it was to live. And here he was, badmouthing, and more to the point, trashing, one of the Strip's casinos.

It didn't make sense, unless you had suspicions like me.

I decided to hit up a more unsavory section of the internet.

I googled 'Lyle Banks Bo Valentine', Lyle Banks Junior Remington', 'Lyle Banks criminal record', 'and since we were in Las Vegas, 'Lyle Banks gambling problem.'

I went through the Lyle Banks and Bo Valentine matches first. There were a few of Banks' articles in which he praised the job Bo Valentine was doing as Chief of Police. I found three examples of it. It could be nothing, but for a newspaper columnist, siding with a public official seemed like bad form, at the very least. I had a feeling it was more sinister.

Banks had written a few articles about The Remington and several that mentioned Sidney Remington, but I couldn't find any connection, nor any articles, mentioning Junior Remington. Not that they necessarily had to have been acquaintances. Bo Valentine could have been the conduit to Banks with Junior, not knowing Banks personally.

Lyle Banks didn't have a criminal history. I shelled out the money for a website that supplied that information, knowing it's something I'd be using frequently in my new profession. Banks was clean, however.

My last Google search turned out to be the most interesting of all.

It appeared that Lyle Banks did like to gamble.

Some of the stories were fun to read. He was written up in Gambler's Daily, a Vegas blog, for having hit a nine game parlay for $13,800 back in 2016. Another story in the same blog referenced a horse racing Pick 6 that Banks and three friends hit for $46,000.

Now, most people reading these two stories might think Banks was a great gambler, or had plenty of money, but I thought the opposite. When someone has big wins like that, they almost always have big losses on their ledger as well. Those just don't get written up by websites like Gambler's Daily.

After several more minutes, I found something. It confirmed the feeling that had been building.

It was from a gambling forum named *"Bad Beats Build Character."*

The subset of this forum was *"Celebrities who lose in Vegas."*

The post that got my attention said the following:

"I don't know if he is a celebrity, but there's a writer for The Las Vegas Daily who is a total scumbag with a serious gambling problem. He owes half of the regulars at The Westgate Sportsbook a few grand. Always saying he'll get you back next time. And then pretends he's some big wig when all he does is write some bullshit leisure articles about Vegas. Let's just say this guy doesn't have much money in the Banks."

The last sentence was what got me. It had to be a reference to Lyle Banks! A writer for the Daily and a 'Banks' reference? There was no question.

Would Bo Valentine or Junior Remington know that Banks had a gambling problem? They very easily could.

And could they have used that to bribe him into writing articles meant to damage The Gambler's Gambit?

I'd bet on it!

CHAPTER 30

SATURDAY

I had another rough night of sleep.

A nightmare, my second in a week, felt all too real.

I had brought Emmy up to her parents' suite at The Wynn. As they hugged and her parents celebrated, the curtains surrounding the room were all raised in unison. It was revealed that we were actually just in a gigantic fish bowl, with people looking down on us.

On the outside of the bowl were Bo Valentine, Junior Remington, Lyle Banks, and a police officer with a huge name tag saying Sam Waddle. They all had automatic rifles pointed at myself and the Peters family.

Lying on the ground next to them was the decomposed body of Victor Smith, whose deformed mouth started counting down from ten.

"Ten.

Nine.

Eight.

Seven.

Six.

Five."

At five, the other men readied their assault rifles and aimed them at the four or us.

"Four.

Three.

Two.

One."

There was a pause that seemed like it took forever.

"Fire!" The corpse of Victor Smith yelled.

Our little fishbowl exploded with gunfire, the four of us taking hundreds of bullets and receiving a quick death.

And yet, despite being dead, I could hear Chief Valentine say something to the others.

"Let's sweep this under the rug. I'm ready to be done with this. We'll blame it all on Victor Smith."

Everyone started laughing, even the decomposed body of Victor Smith.

~

The nightmare had set my sleep back and by the time I got out of bed it was 7:45 a.m., very late for me. The last two days had obviously taken their toll.

I took a shower and changed into some tan shorts and a white polo shirt. It was going to be north of a hundred degrees yet again, but instead of wearing flip-flops, I ominously chose some Nike running shoes.

Just in case fleeing from bad guys was on the docket.

~

I waffled between getting an Uber or taking my rental car.

I decided to drive myself, in case Emmy needed a ride to a new motel.

Being seen in public with Emmy was risky, but so was her taking Ubers around town. If I brought my car, at least, we'd have the option.

At 8:20, I went downstairs to retrieve my car.

I'd told Chance and Liz Peters that I'd be at the Wynn waiting downstairs at 8:45. I was then going to have to make an excuse to go back downstairs and let Emmy up.

While there were some nerve wracking moments to come, the utter exaltation that Emmy's parents would feel made it all worth it.

The valet got me my car at 8:27 and I set off down the Strip.

~

I self-parked at the Wynn. If I did indeed have to drive Emmy around, I'd rather have us meet in the parking garage where it's dark and no one is paying attention. The valet at the Wynn was a little too out in the open for me.

The parking structure elevator took me to the casino floor and I started walking through the Wynn. I texted Chance Peters telling him he could come down and let me in.

A minute later, I arrived at the elevators. As usual, there was an employee on duty checking room keys in order to let you in. Without one of those, I had to wait until Chance showed up, which he did soon thereafter.

"How are you, Quint?"

"I've been very busy," I said.

"That's good to hear. We'll talk when we get upstairs."

"Of course."

We rode the elevator in silence, there being two other people on it. Talking about your missing daughter probably didn't seem like good fodder to Chance Peters.

Little did he know, she was no longer missing.

Liz Peters was waiting for us outside of their hotel room. She led me in.

While they were still on the top floor, the suite wasn't quite as fancy as their last one. Not that I cared. That's not what I was there for.

Chance and Liz both seemed very business-like, but I could tell they were quite nervous. There was no tour of the suite this time, nor was there a breakfast feast waiting for me.

"So, what have you discovered, Quint? From your call, this feels like something important."

I looked down at my phone. It was 8:55 already. I figured it was better to be there when Emmy arrived. The less time she was out in public, the better.

"I've turned up some very interesting evidence," I said.

And I hated what I had to do next, but it was necessary.

"Oh shit," I said. "I left it in my car."

"Really? Jeez, Quint," Chance said.

"I'm so sorry. Can I borrow your key for one second? It will save you a trip downstairs to let me in."

"I guess," he said.

Liz looked on at me, disapprovingly.

"I'll be back in a few minutes," I said.

I headed to the elevator and took it down to the lobby.

Sure enough, Emmy was standing right next to the employee who verifies you are staying at the Wynn. She'd bleached or re-bleached her hair since I'd seen her the day before. It was now a shiny platinum.

Emmy wasn't wearing her standard jean shorts and a t-shirt. Instead, she had on some lightweight white pants and a yellow blouse. She looked beautiful. It must have been the nicest clothes she had and was obviously trying to look presentable to her parents. Even her bangs looked straighter.

She had also brought a backpack, meaning Emmy had checked out of The Bored Cactus forever.

"She's with me," I said to the Wynn employee, flashing Chance's room key.

We walked to the elevator. Emmy looked extremely nervous and how could you blame her?

A few other people joined us on the elevator, so like Chance and I, neither of us said a word until the others got off.

When we were the last two remaining, I asked, "How are you?"

"Take a guess," she said, trying to muster a slight smile.

"When we get to the door, stay outside for one second. I'm going to try and warn your parents against making too much noise. Just in case."

"Good luck with that," she said.

The elevator made its way to the top floor and we headed down the hall.

"Stay here, I'll be out in thirty seconds," I said, once we arrived.

"Okay," Emmy meekly said.

I gave her a quick hug.

"Thanks," she said.

I let myself into the room. Chance and Liz looked surprised.

"That was quick," she said. "How the hell did you get to your car that quickly?"

I didn't answer her question.

"I'm going to show you guys what I've discovered, but promise me you won't yell too much."

Chance looked at me, not sure what to think.

"What exactly are you saying?"

"Just please," I said. "Try to keep it down."

I looked back in their direction and they looked as nervous as Emmy. They knew something monumental was about to happen, but I couldn't tell if they expected the miracle they'd been praying for; seeing Emmy in the flesh.

I walked to the door and opened it.

"Come on in," I said to Emmy.

Emmy walked in and I let her glide past me. I shut the door behind me and remained by the front of the room.

This was their moment.

CHAPTER 31

The first thing I heard, before a word was said, was Liz Peters start crying. Both Emmy and Duncan had cried in my presence over the last few days, but I'd never quite heard tears like this. While most versions of tears are sad, this was possibly the most joyful sound I'd heard in my life.

Unadulterated jubilation. Exhilaration. And any other similar word.

My heart swelled.

"Oh, Emmy," Chance said, his voice shaking. "I'd always hoped."

I heard them hugging each other and a few kisses.

I remained by the front door as the tears of joy continued. It could have taken fifteen minutes for all I cared.

I heard Emmy say her first words.

"I've been waiting for this moment for four months," she said. "I'm sorry it couldn't happen earlier."

"I'm sure you did what you had to do, Emmy. This is the greatest moment of my life," Chance said.

"Thanks, Dad. I love you both so much."

I could have easily broken down and cried as well, but I had to remain strong for the family.

As the tears subsided, Chance told Emmy he liked the new look.

"You can even make a platinum blonde with bangs look good."

"Thanks, Dad."

"Where did Quint go?" I heard Liz Peters ask, barely being able to get the words out.

"I think he's giving us a few moments," Emmy said.

Despite only knowing each other for two days, I felt like she understood me quite well. It was the same feeling I shared with Duncan.

Chance walked around the corner and gave me the biggest bearhug of my life.

"Oh, Quint. You'll never know just how much you've done for this family," he said.

"Thanks, Chance."

"Please, come join us."

I walked around the corner and Liz Peters came and hugged me. It was the exact opposite of Chance's. I could barely feel Liz's arms enveloping me.

"Thank you, Quint. Thank you. Thank you. Thank you," she said.

"You're welcome, Liz."

Chance kept looking at Emmy as if to verify this was all real.

"Did you know what was coming, Dad? When Quint came down to get me?"

"I had no idea. After he got back up here and told me he was going to show me something, that's when I allowed myself to consider the impossible. And here you are."

"How about you, Mom?"

"I thought the opposite. That he was going to say he had proof you were dead."

Liz's tears continued to flow and who knows what emotion they were representing at this point.

"Oh, Mom. I'm so sorry I had to put you through all this," Emmy said and brought Liz in for another in the long line of hugs.

"I'm sure you had your reasons, Em," Chance said for a second time. "We're just grateful you're alive!"

"Are you hungry, Emmy? We could order something from room service."

I thought she would turn down the offer. I was wrong.

"I'm starving," she said. "Do they have any banana pancakes?"

"If they didn't, they will now," Chance said. "Anything for my Em."

Chance Peters was a little smug and a lot rich, but he loved his daughter as much as any father could. I liked Chance and was so happy I'd played a small part in this moment.

"Quint, what would you like?"

"Those Eggs Benedict were good last time."

"And how about a mimosa?"

"I've got more work to do."

"Alright, we'll cut you off after two."

Chance picked up the phone and ordered for everybody. He was like a kid in a candy store.

"They said it will be forty-five minutes," he said.

"Time suddenly doesn't seem so important when you've got your daughter back," Liz said.

It might have been sappy, but I knew there was a lot of truth to it. The last four months for Chance and Liz probably felt like four years.

Emmy looked at everyone.

"Mom, Dad, I know this is a time to rejoice. But I'm not out of the woods yet. I think we need to talk about everything that has happened."

Liz somberly nodded.

"Well then, Em, you've got forty-five minutes. Because once that champagne arrives, we are doing nothing but celebrating!"

~

The tears of joy gave way to concern as Emmy started telling her parents the story of her abduction and escape, having to kill Victor Smith, the incoming call from Bo Valentine, deciding she couldn't turn herself in, and her times at The Bored Cactus. And finally, she relayed Carrie Granger's involvement and that I was getting suspicious of her, so Emmy created the plan to lure me to the desert.

Chance and Liz were mesmerized and rarely interrupted.

Emmy told them I was still working the case, with the help of Duncan and a Las Vegas police officer. I didn't mention that I'd told Duncan she was alive. It was better if Chance and Liz thought they were the first to find out. And I knew Duncan wouldn't spill the beans.

Emmy pointed towards her backpack and said she'd moved out of The Bored Cactus this morning.

"You can stay with us if you want," Chance said.

I hadn't said a word, but felt it was time to chime in.

"My worry is that Bo Valentine might have other police officers looking for Emmy. If he doesn't yet, he will after I confront Lyle Banks later this morning. I don't think Emmy should be at the Wynn, or anywhere near the Strip in general. Actually, I told Emmy she should be back in LA, but she didn't like that suggestion. Chance, your daughter is like you in many ways," I said.

I saw Emmy let out a slight smile.

"I'm not leaving Las Vegas until this is over. Not after what I've been through," she said.

"I know not to argue with my daughter when her mind is made up. So, what do you suggest, Quint?" Chance asked.

"Something off the Strip, but hopefully nicer than The Bored Cactus."

"Just let me know. I'll give you a card."

"I don't think that's the best idea," I said. "Some people in Vegas know who you are. Bo Valentine certainly does. If they were alerted to the fact that Chance Peters booked a hotel off the Strip, they'd start asking questions."

"So you think we're being followed?"

"That's very possible. And it's a certainty they are paying attention to you. As Emmy said earlier, if you guys knew she was alive and had stopped coming to Vegas, Bo Valentine would have known something was up."

"So what do you propose? Find a motel that takes cash?"

"Yes, I think that would be best," I said.

At that moment, there was a knock at the door.

"Emmy, I think you should go hide in the bathroom," I quietly suggested. "It's possible someone on the Wynn staff may know that Chance has a missing daughter. No need to risk having the room service guy see you."

"Smart thinking," Chance said.

"That's why you pay him the big bucks, Dad," Emmy whispered, and walked to the bathroom and locked the door.

Chance let the guy in and he set the food down on one of the tables. He had pimples on his face and looked like he could still be in high school.

Chance gave him a $20 bill.

"Thanks so much," the young man said eagerly.

Once he left, I walked back to the door and made sure it locked behind him. I then knocked on the bathroom door and told Emmy she could come out. I was definitely starting to behave like a PI, watchful of everything, suspicious of most things.

We each grabbed a chair and sat around the table.

"Alright, we are done talking about this case while we eat," Liz said.

Before we had a chance to eat our food, Chance had poured four mimosas.

"Raise your glasses," he said. "To the greatest day of my life. To the return of our beautiful, talented daughter Emmy. And to Quint, the man who made it happen."

We all clinked our glasses and took a sip.

There were smiles all around from Chance and Liz. Emmy and I, who knew this case was far from over, smiled, but with far less aplomb.

Thirty minutes later, I'd eaten two Eggs Benedict, one piece of toast, and half a mimosa. There was a lot of work to do and even one or two drinks wasn't advisable.

We'd managed not to talk about the reason we were all there throughout breakfast. Most of our time was spent with Emmy asking questions about some of their old friends in LA. I was happy not being the center of attention.

I just ate and bided my time. Once we got Emmy situated, I was going to confront Lyle Banks and blow this whole case up. There would be no more hiding in the shadows for Banks, Waddle, Junior, or Valentine.

"I can't allow that, Quint."

"I'm sorry," I said, caught daydreaming, and not sure what Chance was talking about.

Emmy realized I'd zoned out from the conversation.

"He's not going to allow me to stay at another motel," she said.

I tried to get things together.

"I hate thinking of her staying at some dump off the Strip near creepy guys with drug addictions."

He didn't realize it, but he'd just described The Bored Cactus.

"You're making a mistake, Chance," I said. "As I said earlier, I think Bo Valentine keeps his eyes on you. It's likely he knows you flew into town this morning. He might follow you. Having Emmy around, even if she's just in your hotel room, is too risky."

"And I think having her by herself in some dingy motel is far riskier."

We were at a standstill.

"I understand. You feel helpless with Emmy somewhere else. But trust me, you'll feel way more helpless if some rotten officers of the LVPD showed up with some guns, looking for Emmy."

Chance thought it over.

"I don't know what to think anymore," Chance said. "I wish I could just go to the police."

"That's the last thing we want to do, Dad. I'd probably be killed if I ended up in jail."

I saw Liz wince.

"Don't say things like that, baby," she said.

"Sorry, Mom."

"Why don't you just come back to LA?" Liz asked.

"They'd go after me there as well, Mom. And I meant what I said earlier. I'm not leaving Las Vegas until this is over."

Emmy had proven again and again how tough she was, and it was obvious there would be no changing her mind on this matter.

Chance spoke next.

"If we think it's dangerous to go through the Las Vegas police, I'll go to the F.B.I. instead. I'm sure Duncan has some connections."

"Give me twenty-four hours, Chance," I said. "I think a lot is going to change in that time. If I've got nothing at that point, you can call the F.B.I. or anyone else you want. But keep in mind, we still have no concrete evidence. Just what Emmy heard Junior Remington say and the fact that Bo Valentine called Victor Smith. No court is indicting for that limited amount of circumstantial evidence. It's also why they will do anything to get rid of Emmy. They know she's the only person that can tie this all together. So if they have any inkling that she's alive, they will come after her. I just don't want them to find her because they were tracking you."

This was becoming too much for Liz. She looked away when I said "to get rid of Emmy."

Chance took a long break before he answered.

"Alright, you can put Emmy up in a motel for one more day. That's it, though. At noon tomorrow, I'm going to the F.B.I. or some other entity. So get your evidence while you can."

"Thank you," I said. "I know how painful it is letting Emmy go again, but it's the right decision."

"I want to meet you tonight and again tomorrow morning. And we will facilitate how to get Emmy back here."

"That's fine, Chance." I said. "I will call around to a few motels now and find one that accepts cash. I'll check in and leave Emmy in the car. Then, when I'm sure no one is watching I'll get Emmy in the room. No one will know she is there. And she'll stay in for that night, won't you, Emmy?"

"I've done it for four months. I can do it one more night."

Chance and Liz nodded, but what Liz said next hurt.

"We get reunited and then we have to separate again. The greatest moment of my life has given way to more apprehension."

We all looked at each other, but no one spoke.

"It's only for twenty-four hours," I finally said.

"Bring our baby back to us," Chance said.

"I'm right here, Dad," Emmy said. "Like I just said, I've done this since January. One more day is no biggie."

Chance and Liz didn't look convinced.

As joyous as the reunion had been, it ended on a somewhat sour note.

CHAPTER 32

The Dry Heat Motel was a slight improvement over The Bored Cactus. That's the one nice thing you could say about it.

It was still a dump with a similarly cheesy name.

The orange and green colors may have once been vibrant, but those days were long gone. The parking lot was a sea of broken rubble. The lines marking the parking spots were barely visible.

I was glad that Chase and Liz let Emmy and me do this alone. I'd called ahead and they said paying cash was fine, so I hoped this was going to be quick.

It took us twenty minutes to arrive from the Wynn. It was a good fifteen miles south of the Strip and relatively close to The Bored Cactus.

We arrived after 11:00 a.m. I hadn't expected to be ordering room service and now my timetable was all screwed up.

I texted Trent that I'd let him know when I was on my way to *The Las Vegas Daily*. I told myself to concentrate on Emmy and getting her safely into the motel. Lyle Banks could wait.

I parked at a neighboring motel and walked over to pay for the room, asking Emmy to recline her seat and keep her head down.

∽

Ten minutes later, I gave Emmy a quick hug and watched as she entered Room #112 at The Dry Heat Motel.

Little did I know, she wouldn't last twenty-four hours there.

Everything, and I mean everything, was about to change.

CHAPTER 33

The *Las Vegas Daily* was only five minutes north of the Wynn.

Unfortunately, I was no longer leaving from the Wynn and my GPS said I was twenty-five minutes away.

I texted Trent, apologized, and was able to give him an exact time of arrival.

The address was 1111 West Carey Avenue in North Las Vegas. Victor's body, Victor's car, The Bored Cactus, and The Dry Heat Motel, had all been south of the Strip. Duncan's house in Summerlin was west of the Strip. I was now making my first trip north.

1111 West Carey. Some people think that a series of 1s is good luck. But for who? I wasn't exactly feeling lucky at the moment, more like anxious.

Yes, it had been my idea for Emmy not to stay with her parents, but I had a bad feeling when I'd left her at the motel.

Liz Peters had been right. They had been reunited with their daughter and then I yanked her away an hour later.

As I made my way to *The Las Vegas Daily*, I tried not to think about that decision. Emmy was separated from her parents and that was that. I still thought my decision was correct and being near her parents was too risky.

~

Trent Ebbing was waiting for me when I arrived outside the offices of *The Daily*, as most people called it. He was dressed in civilian clothes and I assumed I knew why. If Lyle Banks' co-workers saw a cop show up to interrogate him, they would start talking.

And, although Trent and I had agreed to shake things up a bit, we wanted to keep a modicum of subtlety. If Trent showed up in his blues, Banks might just refer us to his lawyer. If we approached as friends, or at least, the illusion of that, maybe he'd talk to us.

"You ready for this, Quint?" Trent said.

"Ready as I'll ever be."

"Remember, we don't exactly have him dead to rights, so let's try to tip-toe our way to information."

Trent hardly seemed the tip-toeing type, but I appreciated his goal of not blowing this whole thing up just yet.

"I'm all for being understated," I said, "until we no longer have to be."

We walked towards the building.

We were greeted by a giant rock with jagged edges into which the words *The Daily* had been carved. The building itself was red brick, with glass columns that rose from the bottom of the structure and were rounded at the top. It was modern and old school all at once.

A receptionist was waiting for us when we opened the door. She was in her thirties, quite skinny, and had orange glasses on.

"How can I help you guys?" she asked.

"We had a tip we wanted to share with Lyle Banks," Trent said.

"Does he know that you are coming?"

"No, we just found out about this tip. It could be a huge find for him."

I could tell she was conflicted. Protocol probably said that you're supposed to call ahead and tell the reporter. On the other hand, we were telling her that this could be a game-changer for Lyle Banks.

"Well, alright, let me go find him for you."

We had won out. She started walking towards the individual offices.

Soon thereafter, she headed back with Lyle Banks in tow. He looked oddly identical to the picture they posted of him at the end of his articles. Having been a reporter, I usually thought those pictures looked like some odd retro version of the person in question. Lyle Banks' picture was spot on.

His long, red, curly hair would have looked more appropriate on a twenty-one year old frat boy, not someone in their 40s. But hey, as someone who recently turned forty, I get the idea of wanting to relive your youth. I wasn't going to crucify him for his hair. I had enough other reasons.

"I'm Lyle Banks," he said and extended his hand.

"Trent Ebbing."

"Quint Adler."

I looked at Banks when Trent introduced himself. As I always reminded myself, I had to trust my instincts. That's part of the reason I'd become a PI.

And my instincts were telling me that Banks knew who Trent was. He tensed up just a little bit.

While it's unlikely he'd know the name of every cop in town, he might have heard Trent's name in passing.

"Good to meet you guys," Banks said. "Shall we go to my office?"

"Sure," I said.

And we followed him towards the back of the building.

Once we arrived, he let us in and shut the door behind him. The office was all glass and we could see out and everyone else could see in. It had a very open feel, obviously.

There was an average sized desk with an executive chair behind it and two small foldable chairs in the corner.

"I'm sorry, this office is a little cramped for three people."

Banks unfolded the chairs and set them down in front of his desk. He sat down himself.

"So, what's the tip you guys had? And thanks for thinking of me."

Trent looked at me. I'd sent him some of what I knew, but I still knew it better. His nod meant he was deferring to me.

At this point, it was going to be hard to be subtle. Banks would likely know pretty soon who I was talking about.

Fuck it, I told myself. He was either directly or indirectly involved in almost getting Emmy killed. There was no reason to worry about offending the man in front of me.

"You're going to write a redemption story," I said.

Banks looked on, thoroughly confused.

"I don't understand."

"It's the story of a guy who got in over his head," I said.

Banks' facial muscles tightened.

"I'm listening."

I continued.

"The guy may be a good person who just made a few mistakes. I'm not really sure. You see, this guy has a gambling problem. And it got him into trouble with the wrong people, which included the Chief of Police of his town."

Banks tried to remain stone-faced, but it wasn't working. His expression started to give him away.

"Now, I don't know all the details," I continued. "For example, I don't know if this guy owed the Chief directly or whether the Chief just used his gambling addiction against him. It doesn't really matter in the end, because this guy scrapped all his morals to do the dirty work for him. He wrote salacious stories with the intention of bringing down a casino, all to help out the Chief and the son of a Las Vegas real estate magnate. I don't know exactly why those two were in cahoots, but I'll find out soon. There's no stopping this investigation now. It's like a snowball that's caught steam and is going downhill fast. It's getting bigger and bigger and anyone who tries to stop it will get run over."

Lyle Banks looked like he wanted to say something, but held his tongue, so I continued.

"Making matters worse, this conspiracy led to the abduction of a young woman," I said, making sure not to mention I knew Emmy was alive. "I don't know if the guy knew what was going to happen to the woman, but I don't really care. He was immersed in this, so in my opinion he's as much to blame for her death as anyone else. That is, assuming she is dead, which everyone believes."

Once again, Banks looked close to spilling the beans. I just needed to give him one more push.

"There's no way out of this, Mr. Banks. I'll be contacting some national media once I walk out of here. And I'll tell them just how unhelpful you've been. Here, I'll start by calling CNN. I know some people there," I said as I grabbed my phone from my pocket.

My plan had worked.

He couldn't hold back any longer.

"I had no idea they were going to kill the girl!" Banks yelled.

He realized he'd said it way too loud, so he spoke in a more measured tone as he continued.

"You're right, I have a gambling problem. And I owe a lot of people money, especially at the Westgate Casino. People were starting to talk and I knew if word got out, I'd lose my job. That's when Bo Valentine came to me. I knew him a little bit, having been a reporter in Las Vegas for almost ten years. He's ubiquitous in this town, him and that stupid mustache of his. So, he showed up at my home one day, and told me all of my financial problems would go away if I'd write 5-10 articles that chastised The Gambler's Gambit. I'm sure you don't want to hear any defense for my actions, so I won't give them to you. Just know that I was between a rock and a hard place. I was either going to lose my job and have people after me financially, or my money problems would go away and I'd keep my job. The Gambler's Gambit was a shithole anyway and probably would have gone under regardless. I just gave it a push in the right direction."

"You had that power?" I asked.

Trent had been silent. He was learning some of this for the first time.

"*The Las Vegas Daily* is well read in this town. If your casino is routinely featured on the front page in an unflattering way, the Gaming Review Board will take notice. And they did. The Gambler's Gambit lost their license in December, which brings me back to my point. That girl went missing in January. I was already done with Valentine by then."

Banks' story was believable. And yet, I didn't believe it. I knew he was lying about Emmy.

I stared at him, feeling my anger rising.

"You're sticking to that story?"

"Of course. It's the truth," Banks said.

I no longer had any empathy for Lyle Banks. And I was ready to prove him a liar.

"Last night, I spent a lot of time reviewing old articles from *The Daily*. There was one article about Emmy Peters and it appeared on page five."

"If you say so."

"Do you know who Dakota Jones is?"

Several days back, at The Cosmo's coffee shop, I'd started reading an article about a fourteen-year-old girl who'd gone missing in Vegas. At the time, I was fearful it was related to Emmy. Although the two disappearances proved to be unrelated, the articles about Dakota Jones led me to what I was asking now.

"Yes."

"Do you know how many articles your paper wrote about her disappearance?"

"Several."

"Eight to be exact. And six were written by you."

"So?"

Banks was hopelessly trying not to be swept up by the gathering snowball, but it was too late.

"Why did your paper write so many articles about Dakota Jones and so few about Emmy Peters?"

Lyle Banks just stared at me and wouldn't answer. So I talked for him.

"When we are done here, I can ask around the office if you'd like. See if old Lyle Banks gave reasons not to focus on the Emmy Peters disappearance."

"Stop!" he yelled. "You shouldn't have come here. This will get back to Bo Valentine."

"A twenty-two-year old girl is likely dead. I'm sorry if making this comfortable for you wasn't my goal."

"I'll talk to you guys anywhere else. Just not here."

I looked over at Trent who finally spoke.

"Where and when?"

"I don't know. Anywhere, just not here. How about tomorrow?"

"No," I said. "This thing is moving too fast. We either talk later today or we finish this here."

"Alright. Later today."

"Before I agree to this, you have to answer my question."

Banks bowed his head.

"Yes. He told me to keep the woman's disappearance out of the papers as much as I could."

I quickly thought of something.

"Did that go for Victor Smith as well?" I asked, assuming I'd get a quick denial. I was wrong.

"Yes. No one else seemed to know he was missing, so that was easy. Emmy Peters was tougher, but I used my pull around the office."

"You're in a lot shit, Lyle."

Although I was only on my second case as a PI, using people's first names when they were in trouble had become an MO of mine.

"I knew after the fact," he said. "I had no idea they were going to hire someone to kill that girl. I don't even know what she did. Valentine came to me and told me we had to keep it out of the papers or everything I'd done regarding The Gambler's Gambit would come to light."

I stared at Trent. We'd hit a treasure trove with this interview.

"One last question and then we'll leave."

"What?" Banks asked, sounding like a broken man.

"Did Junior Remington ever contact you?"

"No, but I'm not a dummy. I knew who had the most to gain if The Gambler's Gambit went under. So I kind of assumed Junior or the old man was involved."

"What's your cell phone number?" I asked.

"702-555-9275," Banks said, not raising his eyes to look at me.

I entered it into my phone.

Trent and I stood up from our chairs.

"Am I going to jail for a long time?" he asked, looking at Trent as he did, all but confirming he knew he was a cop.

"You're in a load of shit, Mr. Banks. If you want to look at the bright side, you've got more maneuverability than Valentine or Junior Remington."

"But I'm going to jail?" he asked.

"You better hire a good attorney," Trent said.

"I'll be a dead man in jail," he said.

"I guess you should have thought about that," Trent said.

With that, we walked out of the office of Lyle Banks.

We took a right and made our way towards the front entrance.

The receptionist gave us a funny look. I wonder if people in the office heard a few of Banks' loud exclamations.

We were about two feet from the door, when we heard a loud popping sound.

Trent realized what it was before I did.

He started sprinting back in the direction of Lyle Banks' office. I followed behind him.

My heart was pounding.

Please, please, please don't be what I think this is.

The shrieks in the office would have confirmed my biggest fears. If only I'd been able to process the sounds I was hearing. Instead, I was in my own little world.

We arrived at the outside of Banks' office and peered in through the glass.

I turned quickly away, as if that would somehow change what I'd just seen.

Lyle Banks had killed himself.

I forced myself to look back at his body.

Lyle Banks was seated in his chair with his head face down on the table. A single gunshot had been fired in the right side of his brain. Blood was coming from it. The gun, a small pistol, had fallen on the table and sat flush against his neck.

I finally took stock of my surroundings and noticed everyone yelling throughout the office. It was mayhem. A few people approached Banks' office, and then abruptly turned away.

I looked at Trent Ebbing and he looked at me.

"Holy fuck!" I said.

"So much for our star witness," he said.

I hated that Trent voiced it.

I hated it more that I'd been thinking the same thing.

CHAPTER 34

"Somebody call the cops!" a voice yelled in the panicked offices of *The Las Vegas Daily*.

A complicated situation was about to get a lot more problematic.

It's not like Trent and I could just leave the premises.

We were the last two people to talk to Lyle Banks and then he'd blown his brains out. While neither Trent nor I had pulled the trigger, we'd most certainly been the ones who pushed him in that direction.

At least, that's what people would think.

People were milling around us, but I had to know what Trent thought before the police showed up.

"What do we do? We're surely going to be taken in for questioning," I whispered amongst the people around us.

"Don't say a fucking thing. Ask for a lawyer. You can't let Valentine find out what you know."

"He's going to find out I'm a PI if he doesn't know already."

"Yes, that part is inevitable. It's the other things I worry about. We can't have him suspecting that Emmy is still alive."

My heart rate increased.

"What will he do?"

"Anything and everything to stay out of jail. He just got one 'Get out of Jail Free' card with Banks killing himself."

I looked back at his body. More blood was oozing from his head.

Somebody yelled that the police were on their way. Great.

"What's going to happen to you?" I said.

"I'm probably fucked. I'll try to think on the fly and come up with something to explain it all. That will only work if you don't contradict me. So I can't have you saying anything. Will it make you look guilty of something? Yes. So be it. It's better than the alternative."

Just then, the first two Las Vegas police officers entered *The Las Vegas Daily*. It had been less than five minutes since Lyle Banks had killed himself.

They made their way directly towards us.

We needed to get away from Banks' office, and from the officers that were sure to assemble there.

"Clear out," one of the officers said. "Make your way back toward the front of the building."

I happily did as instructed. I looked for Trent, but he was already a few strides ahead of me with his back turned to the cops. I assumed he didn't want them to recognize him.

As I approached him, he leaned in and whispered.

"I've changed my mind. If you have the chance, try to get out of here before the police question you."

"Really?"

"Yes, but don't go back to your hotel. You'll have to investigate while on the run. I'll get a burner and text you when my fellow officers are done with me. If they ever are."

"You sure about this?"

"Yes. If we're both sitting in jail or an interrogation room, Valentine will have several hours to tie up his other loose ends. He'd get all the GPS information on your cell phone and who knows where that would lead him."

His meaning was obvious. My GPS would show that I was just at The Dry Heat Motel. Trent was right, I needed to avoid getting taken in by the cops. At all costs.

"Why don't you leave with me?" I asked.

"I'm a cop. There's nowhere I can hide."

"Alright, I'll go it alone."

"Good. Hopefully, I'll be in touch soon."

"You're scaring me, Trent. They can't just kill a cop in jail."

"You wouldn't think so," he said, a non-answer if there ever was one.

We arrived at the entrance of the building. Three new cop cars pulled up right at that moment.

"Everyone please come outside and wait out here to be interviewed."

And then, from a good twenty feet away, I heard an officer say, "Trent! What are you doing here in your civvies?"

As he walked towards us, Trent whispered.

"Go outside. And duck around the corner when you're given the chance."

"Be safe, Trent."

"You too, Quint."

The officer who called Trent's name was ten feet from us now.

"Go!" Trent said softly, but firmly.

I walked to the door, and turned around, watching as the officer approached Trent.

I hope he had a plan.

"Wait outside," an officer said to me.

I did so.

Once I made my way out of the offices, I realized I had one thing working to my advantage. It was a disorganized mess. New officers were arriving and no one seemed to know who was in charge.

"Line up against this wall," an officer said to everyone congregated outside.

There were probably twenty of us outside at this point.

I intentionally made my way down to the far end of the wall. It would be the closest escape route.

The arriving police were parking in front of *The Daily,* so I assumed if I could duck around the end of the wall, I wouldn't have any officers waiting for me.

This was a suicide, after all. It's not like this was an active murder scene, where they were looking for other suspects. If that had been the case, there's almost no chance I would have been able to escape. They'd have set up a perimeter.

There were two people within a few feet of me up against the far side of the wall. Luckily, it wasn't the receptionist or someone who knew I'd been one of the two people talking to Lyle Banks. If that were the case, they'd likely have pointed me out to one of the officers.

I thought of a plan.

I started fake sneezing, making a loud noise into my cupped hands. The two people next to me gave me a look, as if to say, '*Don't get any closer.*'

"Excuse me for a second," I said.

I walked around the corner and as I suspected, no cops were there waiting for me. I had to seize the opportunity. I picked up my pace, hoping to get as far away as possible.

I made the mistake of turning around. No one was following behind me, however.

I kept walking briskly. About a minute later, I'd made it to West Carey Avenue.

I saw two LVPD cars coming up the road towards me. Being out on the main road, they'd just assume I was some random pedestrian. At least, that's what I told myself.

The first car passed me and didn't look in my direction. I kept walking.

The second car was right behind it, and I had that sense you get when someone is looking at you.

I took a brief glance to my right and my suspicions were proved correct.

The driver of the police car was looking directly at me.

And it was none other than Bo Valentine.

PART 3: ON THE RUN

CHAPTER 35

I was ready to break out in a full sprint, but Bo Valentine kept driving and followed the other police car into the parking lot of *The Las Vegas Daily*.

There was a very good chance that Valentine had no idea who I was. Or, in his rush to get to the crime scene, my face didn't register.

Whichever the case, he hadn't pulled a U-turn, and the further I got down West Carey Avenue, the safer I felt.

At least, for the moment.

But, what now?

Trent had told me not to go back to my motel. Was I supposed to live off the grid, like Emmy had done?

Furthermore, what was my next point of action?

There had been five people involved in this conspiracy that I knew of. Two of them, Victor Smith and Lyle Banks, were already dead. Bo Valentine was unapproachable, obviously. The same was true of Junior Remington.

The only cog left that I thought might potentially turn was Sam Waddle. And even that was a longshot. What did I have to offer that Bo Valentine couldn't trump? It's not like I had the district attorney's ear and could offer him a sweet deal. I didn't even have a cop on my side anymore, with Trent being taken in for questioning soon, if he hadn't already.

I assumed Trent would be released at some point today. After all, this was a suicide. And while they'd want to know everything that Trent had talked about with Lyle Banks, it's not like they could hold him for murder.

Still, I had a bad feeling. Valentine would realize what Trent had been up to. No, I didn't think it was easy to kill a cop while questioning him, but I also didn't see any way that Valentine could let him go.

Shit! I really wish Trent had tried to flee with me.

I kept walking on West Carey, unsure of my next move.

There was no way they had an APB out on me yet, so I decided to order an Uber. I knew I'd have to ditch my phone at some point, but I wasn't there yet.

~

The Uber arrived.

I'd put The Cosmo as my destination, but decided to change it mid trip.

"Is there a place around here where I can pick up a cheap throwaway phone?" I asked.

"Sure. Sal's Phones has what you're looking for."

"Thanks. I'm going to put that as a stop before my final destination."

"Whatever suits you, pal."

The New York accent was unmistakable.

I wished I was in the Big Apple. Or New Orleans. Or Paris.

Anywhere but Sin City.

Here the cops would be after me soon. Here my friend Trent was in serious trouble. And here, Emmy might not be safe any more.

I was scared and had to formulate a plan.

There was something I had to do first, knowing I was going to be powering my phone down soon.

I took screenshots of the phone numbers of Emmy's burner phone, Chance's cell phone, Duncan's phone, and Trent's phone, even though I probably wouldn't be hearing from him for a while.

I emailed the screenshots to myself, knowing I could log onto my email from one of these burner phones.

Despite having a pit in my stomach, my mind was sharp.

"We're pulling up to Sal's," the Uber driver said.

"Thanks. I'll be out in a minute."

"I ain't going nowhere, pal."

At any other time, I probably would have enjoyed this Uber driver and his frequent use of the word pal.

But not now.

~

Seven minutes later, I had a prepaid burner phone with internet access.

Trent had warned me not to go back to The Cosmo, but part of me wanted to risk it.

The Uber driver could tell I was thinking about something.

"Are we still going to The Cosmo?"

"Give me just a second," I said.

"No problem, pal."

I thought it over. I wanted to get the police reports from my room, but I'm not sure it was worth it. I still thought it unlikely the LVPD was after me yet, but the cameras at *The Daily* had my face. My rental car was in their parking lot. It wouldn't be long.

"You know what, I'm going to change my destination on the app. Take me to The Bored Cactus."

"From The Cosmo to a shithole. Interesting choice."

"You know The Bored Cactus?" I asked.

"Hey, it's not all high-rollers I pick up, pal. We get the dirt balls too."

"Fair enough."

And off we went.

I'd considered going to The Dry Heat Motel where Emmy was staying, but I couldn't risk the police finding me there and then discovering Emmy because of my stupidity. So, I chose The Bored Cactus which I also knew wouldn't be asking for a credit card.

Which made me think of something else.

"Can I do one more stop?"

"What now?"

"Just a quick stop off at an ATM. Any one will do."

"Sure. You don't have to change your destination."

"Thanks," I said.

"You got it, pal."

On our way to an ATM, I powered down my cell phone. Better now than when I arrived at the motel and they could trace it there. If the Las Vegas police found me, it wasn't going to be by a foolish mistake of my own.

We arrived at The Bored Cactus fifteen minutes later. I'd taken out $400 from my checking account and knew I had to make it last. My credit cards were off limits from here on in.

I thanked the Uber driver and was hoping to get one more "pal" out of him, but all I got was a "Take care of yourself."

I went to the front desk and paid for two nights, telling him I'd lost my driver's license and giving him a fake name. The young man at the desk couldn't have cared less. I imagine he'd heard and seen it all at The Bored Cactus. It was $120 after tax for the two nights.

I kept my head down as I walked across the motel parking lot and to my room. It was on the first floor and only a few doors from where Emmy had stayed.

I laid down on the uncomfortable bed and looked at the time on my new burner phone.

It was only 12:47.

And I'd thought the last two days had taken forever.

Silly me.

CHAPTER 36

As much as I wanted to, I couldn't fall asleep.

Time was too important. I was going to be on the radar of the Las Vegas police very soon, so if I had to do some things in public, I best do them immediately.

I had an idea. It was kind of crazy, but I liked it.

And by kind of crazy, I mean full blown, I'd lost my mind, crazy.

Which made me like it even more.

I looked around the room for something to write on. There was the small little pad that every motel supplied, but it wasn't big enough for what I needed.

Against my better judgement, I walked back to the front desk.

"Can I help you?" asked the young, indifferent employee I'd just dealt with.

"Do you have a piece of paper to write on?"

"There's a little pad in your room."

"I need an eight and a half by eleven."

He didn't look too clear on the concept.

"The size a printer uses," I said.

"Do you just want a piece of printer paper?"

"That would be great, thanks."

He walked back into their office and returned a few seconds later with two sheets of paper.

"Thanks so much," I said.

"You're welcome."

～

I arrived back at my room and started writing.

I didn't like what I'd written on the first sheet of paper so I crumpled it up and threw it away.

And I wasn't all that impressed with what I wrote on the second, either. It seemed too condensed, too rushed. In my defense, my plan necessitated that I get everything on one sheet of paper while writing longhand. I decided it was going to have to do.

I read it again.

"Emmy Peters was told by Junior Remington that he'd helped bring down The Gambler's Gambit. One day later, Victor Smith tried to kill Emmy. After Emmy rightfully defended herself, Smith got a phone call from Bo Valentine. This was not a coincidence.

Bo Valentine and Junior Remington had worked with Lyle Banks of the Las Vegas Daily to bring down The Gambler's Gambit in order for The Remington to become relevant again. Banks had a gambling problem and Valentine held this over his head. Banks told me exactly this before he killed himself.

When Junior had told Emmy too much, Valentine knew their entire scheme was at risk of being exposed, so he hired Victor Smith to kill Emmy. Valentine also had something on Victor Smith. Apparently he'd prevented him from getting fired over an excessive force case.

Officer Sam Waddle is involved too. He ripped out a few pages from Emmy's journal that would have incriminated Junior Remington.

Officer Trent Ebbing is being held by Valentine right now and Trent knows the truth. Get him out!

Don't let Valentine and the rest of them sweep this under the rug.

Every single word of this is true!"

Although likely, I wasn't positive that Waddle had ripped the pages from the journal. And it's possible Trent wasn't being held by Valentine just yet. Besides that, it was the truth, or at least, what I believed the truth to be.

It was going to have to do.

Knowing my phone was going to stay powered down and I couldn't call an Uber, I walked back to the front desk.

"Can you call me a cab?" I asked.

"Sure," he said. "It'll be a yellow cab. Usually about ten minutes."

There weren't many places left where asking for a cab wasn't weird. I could tell it was still commonplace at The Bored Cactus.

I went back to my room and grabbed the piece of paper.

The yellow cab arrived.

The driver was a man in his sixties of Indian descent.

"Where to?" he asked.

"The closest Kinko's or similar copy shop," I said.

"I know a place. It's about ten minutes away, though."

"That's fine."

I arrived at the UPS type store.

The cashier asked if I needed any help, but I turned him down, not wanting him to read what I'd written.

Soon, I'd want everyone in Vegas to read it. Just not yet.

I made 500 copies and paid the man in cash.

I hadn't narrowed down exactly where I was going to distribute the "flyers", so I had the cab driver take me back to The Bored Cactus.

I needed a little more time to think.

As I sat, debating what to do, I threw on the old school T.V. I wanted to see if there was any information on Lyle Banks' suicide.

I found a local news channel and didn't have to wait long.

A middle aged woman read from a teleprompter:

"Lyle Banks, a well-known writer for *The Las Vegas Daily*, committed suicide in front of his co-workers today. Apparently, he had a meeting with two men in his office, and pulled out a gun seconds later. Police arrived at the scene within minutes, but they believe the two men fled by time they arrived. People are looking for the men in question. The Chief of Police, Bo Valentine, spoke from outside the offices of *The Daily*."

The feed cut to a statement being read by Valentine. He was dressed in his police uniform with his handlebar mustache making him stand out. He looked heartbroken, like someone had killed his dog. It was a convincing act.

"Hello to my fellow Las Vegas citizens. We had a tragedy here today at *The Las Vegas Daily*. Lyle Banks, whose writing we have all loved over the years, took his own life in front of his colleagues. This was only seconds after a meeting with two men. You have to wonder what would drive someone to kill themselves. We have to assume the meeting is what led him to commit this regrettable act. Now, I'm not going to call the two men suspects. Banks did kill himself after all, but it wouldn't surprise me one bit if these two people were up to no good. We'll have more as the day progresses. Thank you."

Holy shit!

Valentine was trying to paint Trent and me as the bad guys.

The reason was obvious. If I was killed in the course of them trying to locate or arrest me, they could lie and say I was mixed up in something illegal.

It's much easier to frame someone if the public already thinks you may be guilty of something.

What about Trent? Valentine didn't mention one word about him. Surely, he knows it was him. Trent was talking to an officer a few minutes before I saw Valentine pulling into the lot of *The Las Vegas Daily*.

I wasn't sure exactly what was going on, but I knew it was sinister.

My guess was that Valentine had Trent either in a holding cell or in an interrogation room.

Trent hadn't committed a crime, obviously, but if Valentine was spreading the rumor that he was involved somehow with Banks' death, then maybe they'd treat him as a suspect.

I was scared for Trent and my statement to him came flooding back to me.

"They can't just kill a cop."

And his response: *"You wouldn't think so."*

Killing a cop is obviously something that would almost never happen, but this wasn't some ordinary situation. Bo Valentine surely felt the walls caving in. He'd probably do anything, and I mean anything, to prevent himself from being caught.

How would they harm Trent, though?

It's unlikely the Chief of Police would be the one questioning him in jail. He's out answering questions and giving press conferences.

And then I was consumed by a horrible thought.

He'd use Sam Waddle.

CHAPTER 37

I had to call Duncan. I knew it was risky, but there was just too much going on, and I didn't know how to proceed. Duncan had been there from the beginning with his sage advice and I needed it now more than ever.

I pulled up my email and found the screenshot of Duncan's cell phone number.

I dialed it from my burner phone. It went to voicemail.

This didn't shock me, what with Duncan not knowing this number.

I left a voicemail asking him to call me back at my new number.

And I waited.

～

Thirty minutes later, I still hadn't received a call back from Duncan.

I tried not to panic.

My thoughts turned to Emmy's parents.

If they'd seen the news about Lyle Banks, they inevitably would have called me. And my phone would go straight to voicemail.

I'm sure at the moment they were cursing me for allowing Emmy to leave their sights. With all that was going on, I can't say I blamed them.

～

My phone rang a few minutes later. I recognized it as the number I'd recently called.

"Duncan?"

"Yeah, it's me."

"You scared me half to death. Why didn't you call back sooner?"

"Because I've been dealing with Chance Peters."

"I'm sorry."

"I'm assuming you were at *The Las Vegas Daily* when Banks killed himself."

"Yes."

"And Trent was with you?"

"Yes."

"Where is he now?"

"I don't know. He had me leave before the cops took everyone in for questioning."

"And he stayed back?"

"Yeah. An officer recognized him. He said a cop couldn't just go on the lam."

"The shit has really hit the fan, Quint. Valentine made a statement where he's subtly accusing you and Trent of Banks' murder."

"Yeah, I saw it. What do you think they're doing with Trent?"

"I don't want to think about it."

"Is there any chance they just let him go?" I asked, afraid of the answer.

"Not if Valentine wants to stay out of jail."

"We need to get him out of there," I said.

"How, Quint?"

"Shit, I don't know. I thought you would."

Duncan didn't respond.

"What other cop was Trent close to?" I asked.

"Are you sure dragging another cop into this is the right thing to do?"

"If there's any way it helps Trent, then yes."

"There's a guy named Heath Bennett. I've worked with the two of them together a few times. They joined the force at the same time and have remained close over the years."

"I'll reach out to him. I'm starting to worry that Valentine has a lot more cops on his side than just Sam Waddle."

"I've been having the same feeling. You cannot turn yourself in, Quint."

"I have no plans to."

"And that includes Emmy, obviously. You can't let the police get her. I made that abundantly clear to Chance."

"They must be pissed at me right now."

"That's an understatement," Duncan said.

"This case has become so fucked up in the last several hours. Lyle Banks killing himself has thrown this case on its head."

"You and Trent said that's what you wanted."

"I didn't want this," I said.

Duncan took it rhetorically and didn't answer.

"So, what's next?" I asked.

"Shit!" Duncan exclaimed.

"What is it?"

"You're not going to like what you're about to hear, Quint."

"What is it, Duncan? You're scaring me."

"The Las Vegas PD are pulling up to my place right now."

"Oh, no," I said, unable to muster anything else at the moment.

"Listen to me closely. There's a McDonalds on the north end of the strip, just past The Stratosphere. Meet me in the parking lot at 7:00 p.m. Don't get out of your car. I'll find you."

"I'll be there," I said.

"If I'm not there, you can assume that Valentine got me."

"Got you in jail or got you, got you?"

Before Duncan could answer, I heard a loud knock in the background.

"I have to go, Quint. I'll see you at 7:00. Hopefully."

And his line went dead.

While I was consumed with worry about Duncan, I tried not to harp on it for too long or I'd become catatonic.

I just hoped that he had an old bag of tricks that would help him in dealing with Bo Valentine or any other corrupt LVPD officers.

I used the internet on my burner, trying to find a number for Heath Bennett. Nothing.

I guess I shouldn't have been surprised. Cops were probably the last people on earth who wanted the public to have their phone numbers.

Calling the dispatcher for The Las Vegas PD was hardly ideal, but I was running out of options. I decided to go with it.

"Hello, Las Vegas PD," came the voice.

"Hi, I'm looking for Officer Heath Bennett."

"And what is this regarding?"

"I've got a tip for him," I said, choosing the route that Trent had gone with Lyle Banks.

Odd choice by me, considering how that ended up.

"I'm connecting you now."

If Heath Bennet wasn't on Trent's side, and by default, my side, then I was fucked.

He could tell Valentine and they could try to find out where the phone call came from.

Could you retroactively trace a call after it's already over? I wasn't sure.

I sounded like a novice. Which, being that this was my second case as a PI, I was.

Being a novice in most fields won't get you killed, though. Mine was the exception.

The connection went through, but there was no answer, so I was connected to Heath Bennett's voicemail.

I had to decide quickly. Was it worth the risk?

Without a friend on the force, I had no chance of helping Trent. Or, of fighting against Bo Valentine.

It was worth the risk.

"Officer Bennett, my name is Quint Adler. I'm friends with Trent Ebbing and I know you are too. I think he's in big trouble. He has evidence that Bo Valentine paid someone to commit a murder. Do anything you can to keep Valentine away from Trent. Sam Waddle as well. He's working for Valentine. I fear that they will try to silence him. I can tell you everything I know if you call me back. Just don't tell anybody else at the Las Vegas Police Department. My number is 702-555-1802. Thank you."

I hung up the phone, not knowing if I'd made the right decision.

With all my attention drawn towards Bo Valentine, I felt like Junior Remington had gone largely under the radar.

It was, after all, Junior who had blabbed to Emmy and got this entire mess started. He'd also likely told Valentine what happened, which led to every-thing that followed.

And that's where it got fuzzy. Who had ordered the hit on Emmy? Valen-tine seemed the most likely candidate, considering he was friends with Victor Smith. Maybe Junior gave Valentine the order and then Valentine went to Smith.

I guess it didn't really matter. If they decided together that Emmy had to be taken out, then they both deserved to rot in prison. Truthfully, they probably deserved worse.

Was there any way to get to Junior? Emmy had mentioned an ex-wife, but I was sure she wouldn't know anything. Most people don't talk to their ex-wife, much less tell them about a conspiracy to kill a twenty-two-year-old showgirl.

And it's not like I could show up at The Remington casino with everything that was going on.

Bo Valentine remained my best bet.

CHAPTER 38

The time was 3:15.

I'd thought about Trent, Duncan, Chance, and Liz.

There was one person that was conspicuously missing.

Emmy.

The reason was obvious. I couldn't handle the fact she was very much in the line of fire again. Things had gone off the rails and my decision to confront Lyle Banks had led to it.

I'd argue it was necessary in trying to take down Bo Valentine, but the fact remains that my decision led to the shit show this case had become.

If something happened to Emmy, I don't know if I'd ever be the same private investigator going forward. Honestly, I wouldn't be the same person.

∾

The more I thought about Emmy, the more fearful I became.

These were all 'what ifs', but they all seemed very plausible to me.

What if the LVPD, and Valentine specifically, finds out who I am? Once they figure out that I'm in Vegas investigating on behalf of Chance Peters, they will try to figure out the last time I was in touch with Chance.

Once they do, what if they ask for video footage from the Wynn and see me taking a platinum blonde up to their room? It wouldn't take Valentine long to guess who that woman was.

The video would also follow us out of the room, down to the casino floor, and out to the parking garage. I didn't know whether they had video in their parking garage, but I'd assume they do. So, they would eventually see Emmy and I get in my rental car together.

That's when I hoped their tracking would go dead.

Valentine was the Chief of Police, however. He had availability to things that your average citizen does not.

Are there cameras covering the freeways of Vegas? What if Valentine could see where my vehicle was headed, or worst case scenario, know which exit I got off the freeway?

And if he'd seen that, he'd surely have footage of me pulling into The Dry Heat Motel and getting a room for Emmy.

If this were all true, and honestly, I thought it was all in play, Valentine would be sending someone to Emmy's motel with plans on silencing her forever.

"Fuck!" I yelled aloud.

I took out my new burner phone and went to the internet. I logged into my email and downloaded the screenshots I'd taken.

I looked at the phone number for Emmy's burner phone and dialed from my own burner.

The phone rang three times and wouldn't allow me to leave a message.

I quickly realized my mistake. She wouldn't know my burner phone number, and thus, it would be blocked.

Maybe my brain wasn't working as well as I'd thought.

I had two options. Take a cab to The Dry Heat Motel and tell Emmy herself. Or, take a cab to get away from my motel so I could use my real phone to call her.

I mulled it over.

And as I did, the television brought up a picture of Trent Ebbing. My greatest fears were being realized.

CHAPTER 39

"There's been a shooting at the Las Vegas Police Department. The victim's name is Trent Ebbing and early reports are that he is a police officer. Details are sketchy at this time, but we've also heard rumors that Ebbing was one of the men who confronted Lyle Banks before his suicide earlier today. We have no idea how or why he was shot, nor do we know his condition at this time. Stay tuned and we will share any information we receive."

I wanted to scream. I wanted to cry. I wanted to punch the T.V. I wanted to go back in time and not question Lyle Banks. I wanted to tell Trent that I was sorry.

There were a lot of things I wanted to do.

None of them would change what happened.

Trent had been shot. And there was zero question as to who had ordered it.

I put my face in my hands and said a quick prayer for Trent. I didn't expect it to change anything, it just felt right in the moment.

Please, still be alive, I thought to myself.

Now what?

I had to do something. I couldn't just keep hanging out in this motel room, watching bad news come across the TV screen.

It may have been too late for Trent, but there was still Emmy to think about. And Duncan.

If the LVPD took Duncan in, was he looking at the same fate as Trent?

Everything was so screwed.

~

With no callback from Heath Bennett, I had zero influence within the LVPD. And I needed some. If not, Valentine would just go unchecked until everyone was dead. Me. Emmy. Duncan. Trent, who already could be.

I decided I had to leave the motel.

I'd rather die out there trying to bring down Valentine, than sit and watch the T.V. as my friends got taken out one by one.

I was going to be on the move for the foreseeable future and ordering cabs at every step left me too exposed.

So I decided to take a risk of my own.

It had been almost four hours since Lyle Banks had killed himself. Would the LVPD be done there? I couldn't be sure, but I thought it was likely. I needed a car, so it was worth a gamble.

And let's be honest, everything was going to be a gamble from this point forward.

I grabbed my bag that contained the 500 copies. It's the only thing I had with me besides the keys to the rental car, my wallet, and my two cell phones.

I still hoped the copies would come in useful at some point.

I left a few scattered around the motel room.

If the LVPD found out where I'd been staying and raided the room, maybe some officers would find the flyers and ask a few questions.

Assuming there were still some cops not under Valentine's rule.

~

I went to the front desk of The Bored Cactus for the final time.

It was 4:15.

"Can I get another Yellow Cab?" I asked.

The clerk dialed a number.

There was a television on in the room behind the front desk. It was hard to hear, but it sounded like the news was on. It made me think of Trent once again. Please be alive!

"He's on his way."

"Thanks."

I didn't bother telling him that I wouldn't be coming back.

I went to my room and looked outside, waiting for the Yellow Cab to arrive. No need to sit out in the parking lot and have somebody remember my face. I still feared that my name and face would be plastered all over the T.V. as the other guy who confronted Lyle Banks. I was sure it was coming at some point.

The cab arrived and I walked out of my motel room and headed in its direction.

It was the same Indian guy as before. Unlike Uber, this Yellow Cab company probably only had a few employees.

"Hello, again. Where to?"

"Nice to see you again. I'm going to 1111 West Carey Avenue."

I intentionally didn't mention that it was the location of *The Las Vegas Daily*. That had been all over the news today and might arouse his suspicions. And let's be honest, this guy probably already thought I was a little odd. I'd taken a ride to get 500 printouts of something, back to The Bored Cactus, and now a ride past the strip and into North Las Vegas.

He made his way out of the parking lot and we set off towards the offices of *The Las Vegas Daily*.

"When we arrive, can you drive around the block one time before you drop me off?" I asked when we got close.

If he hadn't thought I was weird already, he surely did now.

But I had to do it.

"Whatever you want," he said, not sounding overly suspicious. There was some music playing in the cab and my hope was that he hadn't been listening to any news.

If there was any police presence still out front, I'd just have him drive me somewhere else.

As we passed the entrance and then took a right on the nearest side street, I didn't see any cop cars.

We took four straight rights and ended at the entrance once again.

"Do you want to get out this time?" he asked.

"Yes. Thanks."

I was low on money, but I gave him a $20 tip. Somewhere, in the deep recesses of my mind, I believed he'd be less likely to report me if I'd been generous.

I got out of the Yellow Cab and the man drove away. I did one more look around, but didn't see any LVPD presence.

I made my way to my rental car, the gray Subaru Legacy.

I got in the car quickly, reversed, and drove out of the parking lot. Part of me was expecting a roadblock in those first few blocks, the LVPD waiting to arrest me.

It wasn't to be, though. I lived to fight another day. Or an hour. Who knew at this point.

I looked down at my burner phone. It was 4:58. I still had two hours until I had to meet Duncan.

What should I do in the meantime?

CHAPTER 40

I wasn't going to be back in North Las Vegas any time soon, so I figured now was the time to use my regular phone.

Even if it was being traced, I'd be gone in a few minutes.

Plus, I had to talk to Emmy.

I couldn't avoid it any longer.

I pulled over, grabbed my phone, and called Emmy.

"Quint, is this you?"

"Yeah, it's me."

With all that was going on, I couldn't blame her for asking.

"Everything has gone to shit," Emmy said.

She wasn't wrong.

"I know and I'm sorry."

"It's not your fault."

"Are we sure about that? It was my idea to confront Lyle Banks. And now Trent may be dead."

"You were just trying to get evidence on Bo Valentine, something we need. You made the right decision. Don't beat yourself up about Trent."

"What's the latest on him?" I asked, realizing I should throw on the local radio station. "I've been busy for the last forty-five minutes or so."

"They said he was shot, but I haven't heard anything else."

"Let's hope he's still alive."

"Of course," Emmy said.

"Have your parents got ahold of you somehow?" I asked.

"I never gave them my burner number."

"I know. I just thought maybe through Duncan or something."

"He knows I'm alive?"

"Yes," I said.

And then I debated whether to tell her that the LVPD was at his house. I was tired of telling white lies and half-truths.

"He could be in a little trouble as well."

"Oh, no. What?"

"The cops were knocking at his door when I last talked to him. I'll know more at seven."

"What's at seven?"

"I'm meeting up with him."

"Where?"

"Emmy, I think it's better if you don't know."

"Really? You can't possibly keep me out of the loop now."

"You're right. It's a McDonald's past The Stratosphere. And by the way, I have a new burner number. Take this down."

"702-555-1593."

"Alright, I've got it. So, what's next?"

A well-seasoned PI would have this mapped out a lot better. I was flying by the seat of my pants and didn't know if I was making the right decisions.

Was it better if I was with Emmy? If we could assemble a "team" would that make us more formidable? Or would having some of us together just make it easy to eliminate us in one fell swoop?

I didn't have the answers and it was eating me up.

I'd thought I'd handled the case well when it was slow moving and I was spending my time interviewing people. Now that it had become frantic, I was like a chicken with my head cut off.

If I didn't formulate a plan, and quickly, it might just be me with the proverbial head cut off.

"Emmy, I'm powering this phone off. I'll call you back in five minutes from the other number."

"You better."

"I will."

I sat on the side of the road for ten minutes.

I tried to rack my brain for a plan that might work.

I'd come up with others during the course of this case. Some had worked, others not so much.

But this was the most important yet.

I was going all-in with whatever I came up with.

I thought of our advantages, which were few. Emmy, and what she knew, being the most important.

And our disadvantages, which were several.

I looked over at the 500 copies I'd made. A good start, but how do I get those words to the masses?

We had to magnify our advantage. Literally. Magnify its voice. Her voice. Emmy's.

It was at that moment that I formulated my plan.

I couldn't be sure it would work, but I thought it was our best chance. And we had to do something. We could no longer sit back and just let Valentine be the aggressor.

∾

I started my car and headed back towards the Strip. I'd be bypassing it, however.

I called Emmy.

"Hey."

"Get ready. I'm coming to you."

"What do you have in mind?"

"I'll tell you when I get there."

∾

I had to make a few phone calls on my way there.

I started with Tom Butler, my former boss at *The Walnut Creek Times*.

CHAPTER 41

After parking a half-mile away, and making sure no one followed me, I quickly entered Emmy's room at The Dry Heat Motel.

I arrived full of piss and vinegar and ready to take on the world.

It didn't last long.

Just as I was telling her about the particulars of Lyle Banks' suicide at *The Las Vegas Daily*, Emmy pointed towards the T.V.

"We at Channel 7 news have confirmed the other person who was in the meeting with Lyle Banks before he died. He's a private investigator named Quint Adler. Police currently have little information about the man, only that he fled as opposed to staying and talking to the police."

They weren't wrong.

"Please alert authorities if you know where Mr. Adler is," the newscaster continued. "The other man in the meeting with Banks was Trent Ebbing, a Las Vegas police officer, who was shot in custody a few hours ago. Details are still murky and we haven't received an update on his condition. We will continue to keep you posted throughout the day."

"Not quite the welcome I was hoping for," I said.

Emmy managed a half-hearted smile.

She'd changed from her pants and blouse from this morning and was now wearing some tan shorts and a dark blue t-shirt.

"You realize how serious this is, don't you?"

"Of course I do, Emmy. It's like you said, I need my sense of humor now more than ever."

I'm not even sure I believed what I'd just said. I was now a wanted man. This was getting more dire by the minute.

"Now what?" she asked.

"I came up with an idea, and honestly, I think it's our best chance."

"I'm listening."

"Alright, here it goes," I said. "We have no leg to stand on right now. We can't go to the police. I'm persona non-grata at *The Las Vegas Daily*. And the TV stations of Vegas think I'm a felon on the run. But, we need to get our version of events out there. Your version of events, Emmy. Basically, the truth. We need to turn the tide against Valentine. Otherwise, we are sitting ducks."

I paused.

Emmy said, "So…"

"So, we are going to go live."

"What do you mean?"

"I mean, you are going to tell your story live on the air. I have some connections in the media from my time as a reporter in the Bay Area. I talked to Tom Butler, who owns the newspaper I used to work for. In the twenty minutes it took me to get here, he was calling all of his media friends. And trust me, he knows a lot more than me. And they are going to help amplify what you say."

"How, exactly?"

"I'm going to record you on Facebook live. I'll post stories on Instagram and whatever other social media sites let you go live. I'll need your help on a few of these. You're surely more tapped into social media than I am."

"Not for the last four months," Emmy said.

The joy in meeting her parents this morning had likely given way to a return of the anxiety she'd felt for the last four months.

It bothered me to no end.

I had to stay on point, though.

"So, Tom and his friends are going to magnify your message. He's going to post links to wherever we are streaming from. He's going to have every employee of *The Walnut Creek Times* tweet about it. Keep in mind, they are all friends with other people in the media, so this is going to get out there to the right people. Tom even said he'll try and call a few TV stations in Vegas and see if they might run it live. They would never have listened to me, but they might listen to Tom Butler. Like I said, he knows a lot of people in the business."

"This all sounds great. But what, exactly, will happen?"

"It's hard to know. If our video goes viral, which I expect it to, people within the LVPD will start hearing about it. And I mean while it's going on. So will the local media. Viral videos spread like wildfires these days. And when you're talking about your meeting with Junior Remington, what happened with Victor Smith, and how Bo Valentine fits in, this thing will get people talking, I hope. And from there, we can turn the tide of public opinion against Bo Valentine. Maybe he'll be asked some awkward questions at his next press conference, whatever will take the focus off of us. And most of all, make it safe for us to turn ourselves in."

"I think I like it, Quint."

"Thanks. And it's not like we have many great options, Emmy. Bo Valentine is looking for us, rest assured. This is when we fight back. Maybe your video will be seen by Junior Remington. Or Sam Waddle. Or any other cop that Valentine has under his thumb. And maybe they'll realize their time is up and it's time to turn on Bo Valentine. We can't just sit around and wait for him to find us. That wouldn't end well."

"I'll just have to trust you that this will go viral."

"It will. Imagine once your friends start seeing you go live on social media. They assumed you were dead. They'll call their friends who will call their friends and so on down the line. I promise you, this will get to the masses in a short amount of time. And I think it just might turn the tide in our favor."

"I'm starting to believe you."

"Good. This is our best chance."

"Do I need to prepare?"

"Maybe just go over everything again in your head."

"Trust me, it's all there. It probably won't ever leave," Emmy said, and I believed her.

"Of course. Sorry."

"Are we going to film from here?"

"I'm still debating that. For optics sake, I'd thought about driving out to the desert and having you broadcast with the body of Victor Smith in the background. You explaining how you'd almost lost your life on that exact spot would have made great theater. The internet access is too spotty out there, though. We can't risk it."

"That would have packed an emotional wallop. For the viewer, at least."

Her meaning was obvious. It would be painful for her, but the masses sure would enjoy it.

"Listen, Emmy, I'm not trying to use you. I'm literally trying to save our lives."

"I know, Quint. I just hate being front and center in doing so."

"Once this is over, you can stay out of the limelight forever."

"That would be nice, even though we both know that's impossible."

"We'll cross that bridge when we get to it. For now, let's try to stay alive."

Emmy nodded.

～

We started getting ready on our end.

Emmy had to download Facebook, Instagram, and Twitter on her burner phone, and log in using passwords she hadn't used in months. She was doing a lot of emailing back and forth to reset her passwords.

At the same time, I was talking to Tom Butler and letting him know the URLs of Emmy's accounts and where the live feed would be coming from.

We decided that it would be best to have me filming Emmy as she filmed herself, thus giving us two live feeds going at once.

I didn't want to get ahead of myself, but I was starting to believe this just might work.

CHAPTER 42

When I was close to finishing the work on my end, I thought of Cara and my mother.

I imagined they'd heard by now. My name was tied up in the death of a journalist. And it looked like I was on the run.

No, they didn't live in Vegas, but like I'd told Emmy earlier, news spreads like wildfire these days.

Cara had friends in Las Vegas. It's inevitable that one of them had seen it, especially since it was dominating the news here.

I felt terrible. I couldn't imagine what they were thinking at the moment. My poor Mom.

My mind had to stay focused, however. I couldn't let something beyond my control affect what Emmy and I were working on. I'd have all the time in the world to spend with Cara and my mother, but I had to get out alive first.

I took the remote and tried three different Las Vegas channels. They all were covering this breaking story in one way or another.

One channel mentioned me. Another was talking about Lyle Banks. And a third was discussing Trent Ebbing.

None were talking about Bo Valentine, Junior Remington, Sam Waddle, or Victor Smith.

The bad guys weren't the center of attention.

That's what I was hoping our live video would change. Put the focus on the assholes who started all of this.

Emmy hadn't been mentioned. Not once.

For her own sanity, it was probably for the best, but I found it odd.

My guess was that Bo Valentine hadn't told the media why I was in town.

That would get people asking questions about who Emmy Peters was. That's the last thing Valentine would want.

He wanted to kill me before Emmy Peters' name became public knowledge. He'd say that Trent Ebbing and I had been caught up in something illegal, maybe with Lyle Banks. Which would be why Banks killed himself. And it was why Ebbing had "allegedly" attacked a fellow officer.

I'm sure Valentine had a plan to prevent this from ever doubling back to him.

He always seemed to be a step ahead.

But now, I had a plan too.

~

After a few more minutes, I could tell Emmy was getting close.

"Just a few more things," she said. "I have to activate Twitter and post a tweet linking to my Facebook page. And I need to post a story on Instagram to check out my Facebook."

I probably understood social media better than most forty-year-olds, but I was still a novice compared to a twenty-two-year-old.

"Sounds good," I said. "I'll post one minute before we are going to go live. And I'm going to list the phone number to the Las Vegas Police Department, *The Las Vegas Daily*, the local news...anything else?"

"Maybe a local F.B.I. office. I definitely don't trust the LVPD right now."

"Good point. I'll add that."

"I'll be ready in five minutes," Emmy said.

~

Before we got there, another bombshell dropped.

CHAPTER 43

"We've got some breaking news in to Channel 7," the middle-aged Hispanic man said. "Sidney Remington II, son of the real estate magnate Sidney Remington, has been found dead in his office at The Remington casino. Junior, as he was affectionately known, had taken over day-to-day operations of The Remington a few years back. Early reports are that Junior took his own life, but we have not confirmed that yet. We also don't know if this has anything to do with the previous incidents today. Stay tuned and we'll get you more information as soon as we can. Junior was a well known man about town and will be greatly missed."

Before I had a chance to say anything, Emmy covered her head in her hands.

She wasn't crying, but this was just one more thing that had been dumped on her.

"This is all too much," she said.

I looked to see if she needed some calming words, but she shooed me away.

"I'll be okay," she said.

"They are dropping like flies," I said.

"You don't think Junior killed himself?"

"It's possible. I'm sure he saw the walls closing in. But I also think it's possible that Bo Valentine is eliminating everyone in his wake. He's taking them out one by one. If I were Sam Waddle, I'd be worried I was next."

"Us too," Emmy said.

"Yeah. Us too."

~

After going through each of the local news channels to see if they had anything to add, Emmy turned to me.

"Does this change our plan at all?" she asked.

The cramped motel room seemed to be getting stuffier by the moment. We had to get our live video up, and leaving the room at this point was dangerous.

"Not one bit," I said. "If anything, it makes it more urgent."

"I agree. If Junior didn't kill himself, it just proves that if Valentine gets ahold of us, we are dead."

I nodded in agreement.

Just then, my phone rang.

It was a local 702 number, but I didn't recognize it.

I decided there was more upside than downside to answering it.

"Hello."

"Is this Quint Adler?"

"Yes, it is."

"This is Heath Bennett. You called me earlier."

I was suddenly glad I'd picked up.

"Heath, thanks for calling back. Duncan Hobbes told me that you are friendly with Trent Ebbing."

"I am. I tried to go see him at the hospital, but they aren't letting anyone in."

"On whose order?" I asked.

"I don't know, probably the Chief of Police."

"Did you listen to my voicemail?"

"Yes. You don't really think Valentine is part of this, do you?"

"I know he is. And so did Trent. That's what got him shot."

"That's not what they are saying. Apparently, Trent got aggressive under questioning and attacked the officer interrogating him. Trent grabbed the other officer's gun and the guy had no choice."

"And there were witnesses to this?"

"That's the rumor. One officer was interrogating and one was watching as it went down."

"Let me guess, Sam Waddle was one of the two cops."

"No, he wasn't."

Emmy was looking at me and could tell I didn't like what I'd heard.

"You're sure?"

"I can only go by what I've heard."

I tried to think. There was another possibility. Maybe it wasn't Sam Waddle who was the officer who tore out Emmy's journal.

What was the name of those other two officers?

It came to me.

Ryan Mallory and Howard Kloss.

"Was it Ryan Mallory?" I asked.

"How did you know that?" Heath sounded shocked. "He was the guy with Trent in the interrogation room."

"And let me guess who the witness was. Howard Kloss?"

"My God. How the hell did you guess that?"

"So it was?"

"Yes, it was. What the hell is going on?" Heath Bennett asked.

"It's just like I told you. This is all Bo Valentine covering up a murder for hire."

"What murder for hire?"

"Are you still at your headquarters?"

"Yes."

"Is Bo Valentine there?"

"No."

"You're sure?"

"Yeah, he's been out most of the day, at *The Las Vegas Daily* and then a few press conferences. He came back about a half hour ago and left a few minutes later."

"Do you know who with?"

"I can't be sure, but since you mentioned his name, Sam Waddle did leave about the same time."

"Son of a bitch," I yelled and Emmy looked over at me.

It looked like all three officers who responded to the call to Emmy's house had been under Bo Valentine's rule.

And now, two of them were lying about the shooting of Trent. And the other one, Sam Waddle, was likely riding around with Bo Valentine, trying to find Emmy or me.

"What's next?" Heath asked.

"Do you believe me?"

"I don't know how else you are pulling Ryan Mallory and Howard Kloss out of your ass. I guess I do."

"I'm telling you the truth. Okay, so here's how you can help," I said.

"No guarantees, but I'm listening."

"Are you calling from the precinct or your cell phone?"

"The precinct."

I didn't have time to worry if my phone was getting tapped.

"What's your cell number?" I asked.

"702-555-7721."

"When we get off the phone, I'm going to send you a link to a Facebook account. It's a woman named Emmy Peters, who was supposed to be the victim of the murder-for-hire."

"I know the name. We dealt with her father a few times early on."

"And then the case kind of just vanished, didn't it?" I asked.

"Yeah it did, now that you mention it."

"I'll bet you can guess why."

"Valentine."

I paused to let his own answer sink in.

"Bingo," I said.

"Okay, so what's going to be on Facebook?"

"A live video in which Emmy will lay out everything that happened," I said.

"Alright."

"And please, play it loud around the office. Or, put it on a projector if you've got one. I need everyone in the LVPD to see this. It might be my only chance."

"You know this will be my badge."

"Not if I'm correct. You'll be a hero."

"I don't know."

"Ask yourself this. Do you trust Trent and Duncan, or Bo Valentine? Those are your two choices."

After there was no response, I had to make him understand.

"I'm telling you the fucking truth!"

I rarely yelled, but it seemed necessary at the moment.

"Alright, I believe you."

"I'll send you the link to the Facebook account right now. Get it set up to go. We'll probably be going live in about three minutes."

"Alright. Be safe."

"You too. Thanks for this. It will all become clear very soon."

"I sure hope so," Heath said.

And the line went dead.

I asked Emmy for her Facebook URL and I texted it to Heath Bennett.

We spent the next two minutes getting ready to go live.

"I'm ready," Emmy said.

"I think I am too. Give me thirty seconds. I've got one last call to make."

I dialed Tom Butler and told him we would be live in about one minute.

"Roger that," he said.

I hung up the phone and looked at Emmy. There wasn't much room in The Dry Heat Motel.

"Let's have you talk up against the bathroom door. If you're up against the window or the front door, the glare might prevent us from seeing you."

"Alright."

I went to tighten the blinds and as I did, I saw a LVPD police car pull up and park right outside of our door.

"Start the video, Emmy! NOW!!"

CHAPTER 44

"Are the cops here?" Emmy asked me.

"Yes. Please start!"

I looked through the blinds and they hadn't opened their car doors just yet, but they were parked in the parking spot directly in front of our room.

"Should we run?" Emmy asked.

There was no way to escape out of the back of the motel room. The only exit was the front door and the cop car was positioned right there.

"Emmy, start the damn video! We have less than a minute. If we run, it would just give them a reason to shoot us."

"Okay."

And ten seconds later, she said, "Alright, I'm live."

I went live as well.

"Start talking," I said.

We needed to get this out there. Even if the worst happened to us.

"My name is Emmy Peters. On January 16th of this year, I met with Junior Remington who told me that he and some other people helped tank The Gambler's Gambit."

I looked out the window. The officers were getting out of the car.

"Speak faster," I said.

I was trying to film her, while simultaneously looking out the blinds.

"The next day I was kidnapped and almost murdered in the desert by a former cop named Victor Smith. Right around the time I was supposed to be killed, Smith's phone rang and the call was from Bo Valentine."

I looked out.

The officer from the driver's seat stepped out and I recognized the mustache immediately. It was Bo Valentine.

The officer who exited the passenger side I assumed had to be Sam Waddle.

"Emmy, they are going to be here in five seconds. Keep your Facebook live going. No matter what! Put it in your pocket, but make sure it's still running. It might be our one chance."

I looked out and the officers were a few feet away.

"Put your phone in your pocket," I whispered, doing the same with mine.

While I knew we couldn't run, giving ourselves up was still better done outside.

I opened the door, intent on making a scene.

"We surrender!" I yelled as loud as I could.

The reason was twofold. I wanted to make sure our respective phones picked up whatever I said. I was also hoping that some neighbors would hear the commotion and step out of their motel rooms. Bo Valentine wasn't just going to shoot us with witnesses looking on.

My plan didn't work, however. No one stepped out of their motel rooms. They probably just assumed it was a drug bust and didn't want their faces to be seen.

"We surrender," I yelled again and sat on the ground.

Emmy walked out the door right after me and yelled "I surrender" just as loudly as I had.

I looked up at Bo Valentine who had pure hatred in his eyes. If looks could kill, we'd be dead three times over.

"We finally meet," I said.

And his eyes narrowed even more as he looked down at me.

"Emmy Peters is being arrested by Bo Valentine," Emmy said aloud.

Still, no one emerged from their motels.

"Get them in the car. Now!" Valentine yelled at his fellow officer. As he approached, I was proven correct. Waddle was on his name tag.

"Get to your feet," he said to me.

I stood up and he handcuffed me.

Right before he stuffed me into the back of the cop car, I yelled.

"My name is Quint Adler. If I end up dead, it was Bo Valentine and Sam Waddle."

But still, no one was to be seen. I imagined there weren't many people who wanted to deal with the police in motels like this.

Waddle shoved my head against the top of the door as he pushed me into the car. It was no coincidence.

Emmy would not go quietly either.

As I heard her shouting, I came up with an idea on the fly.

It was based on a few factors.

One, they'd never take us to the precinct. Not after what happened to Trent.

Another two witnesses being shot in custody would be too suspicious, even for Valentine.

Two, I thought I could convince Valentine to drive to the desert. I'd tell him that Victor Smith was buried there. More than that, I could say his phone was there as well. And it had incriminating evidence of Valentine's phone calls on it. That would be hard for Valentine to ignore, knowing it to be true.

I looked out and Emmy was like a wet noodle, refusing to get to her feet. Despite the fear I felt, I'd never been prouder of her.

And she gave me the time to implement my plan.

I leaned down and spoke towards my shorts pocket, praying my phone would pick it up.

"If you are facing The Bored Cactus motel, take a right and follow that road for two miles until you see a van parked behind the only two visible trees. I'll lead Valentine and Waddle there. Please, be there. If not, Emmy and I are dead."

I couldn't say any more as Sam Waddle was opening the door to throw Emmy in.

Valentine and Waddle quickly got in the car and reversed at a high speed out of the parking lot. I understand that people at a shitty motel don't want to deal with the police, but I was still shocked no one had come out of their room.

That might have given us a fighting chance. Now all we had was my crazy plan.

A few seconds later, we were driving on a main road, our lives undoubtedly in peril.

CHAPTER 45

"You think you're a pretty smart guy, don't you, Quint?"

Bo Valentine spoke, his voice the same baritone as it sounded on T.V. I despised the fact that he called me by my first name.

"I guess it doesn't really matter anymore," I said.

"You know, maybe you're not that bright. You did end up in the back of my cop car after all."

He laughed, quite loudly.

"Do you know how I found you?" he asked.

The last thing I wanted to play was a guessing game with Bo Valentine, but sadly, I was curious.

"Traced my burner phone?"

"No. Guess again."

"You followed Emmy?"

"No. Guess again."

I was done with this crap.

"You'll tell me if you want to."

"Ah, we were just starting to have fun," he said.

I didn't respond. Emmy and I both had our wrists handcuffed behind our backs. It was the most defenseless feeling imaginable.

"As you may have guessed," Valentine said. "I have some friends around town. And when you came to my attention this afternoon, I put those friends to use. And one of them reached out to some hotels and less savory motels. Much to my surprise, my guy got a call about thirty minutes ago from the clerk at The Dry Heat Motel. Said you'd checked into a room earlier today. Little did I know, you were going to have the lovely Emmy with you as well. Thanks for bringing her to me."

I was crushed. This was all my fault.

Why hadn't I just let Emmy stay with her parents? Why did I have to override Chance and say they shouldn't stay together?

I had led Valentine to Emmy, as well as to me.

And it was going to cost us our lives.

"Is there anything we can do to get out of this?" I asked.

"I don't know that you have anything to offer me, besides your silence. And you'll forgive me if I don't believe that's in the cards."

"Emmy has kept her mouth shut this long. And I see no reason to rock the boat."

Valentine quickly turned around and creepily ogled Emmy.

"Ah, Emmy. We finally meet. I never had the pleasure. I received a phone call from Remington to eliminate you, but that's all. I would love to know how you escaped? A very impressive feat, I must say."

Emmy and I looked at each other. Valentine had just admitted on tape, for the world to hear, that he'd gotten a phone call from Junior Remington to eliminate her.

Assuming our live feeds were still active, which was a very big if. Also, Valentine's voice would have to be audible through our clothes and down to our phones. I had my doubts, but his baritone voice might just make that possible.

"Your guy Victor Smith got a little sloppy. Was that the best you had to hire?" Emmy said.

I knew why she'd asked it. She was looking for confirmation from Bo Valentine that he'd hired Smith, whom Valentine hadn't mentioned by name.

"Victor was the best I could do in a pinch. He owed me and I knew he'd do what I asked. And it's not like I had much time to be choosy. Fucking Remington. So, how did you escape?"

He did have something on Victor Smith, just like I'd thought.

"I maced him," Emmy said.

"He hadn't handcuffed your hands?"

"He'd handcuffed my legs."

"I guess that makes sense."

"And I escaped from the duct tape he'd used to wrap my arms with."

I couldn't tell where Valentine was headed. He appeared to just be driving around aimlessly. We were on some back side streets, surely intentional, keeping the odds that people saw us in the back to a minimum.

The fact he hadn't put on his sirens told me we weren't going back to the precinct. No surprise there, but it did reinforce just how dire our situation was.

"I assume you killed Victor?" Valentine asked.

Emmy hadn't lied yet and I couldn't really blame her. There was no reason to.

"Yes. With the gun he'd brought to kill me."

"Well, that's pretty impressive, Emmy. I'm sorry that you won't be escaping this time."

Waddle hadn't said a word. I wanted to scream out for his help, but I knew he was too far entrenched in this.

I decided to take my chance. Who knew how much longer before they just pulled over and killed us?

"You can't kill us yet, Valentine. There's still something out there that you need."

"Nice try, Quint. What could I possibly need from you guys?"

"Victor Smith's phone and his van."

Valentine didn't respond for a few moments and I knew I'd connected.

I continued.

"Unless, at some point in the future, you care to explain why you were calling Smith while he was in the process of trying to kill Emmy. I'm no police officer, but I think that would be a tough one to explain anyway."

"You'd have made a good cop," Valentine said.

I didn't give him the satisfaction of a response.

"And where is all of this?" he asked.

I was drawing him in, but I couldn't be too obvious. I took too long to answer.

"Or, we could just kill you now and get it over with," he said.

"It's in the desert," I said, my answer sounding like it came because of his threat.

"Big desert out there."

"That's all I'm going to tell you until I get something."

"What could you possibly want?"

"For you to release Emmy. She'll disappear a second time and you'll never hear from her again."

We both knew there was no way he would let either one of us go.

But I had to keep pretending I had an incentive to move forward.

"I'm not releasing her. If you take me to the van, though, I'll give her a fighting chance."

"How?"

"I'll give her a two minute head start in the desert. And then, we come after her."

"I'm not going to get a better offer, am I?"

"No," Valentine said.

"I'll take it. Do you swear on your life you'll extend her that chance?"

"Sure, Quint. I promise. She's still a dead woman," he said and started laughing.

The man was pure evil.

"Alright, let's go to the van," I said. "Get back on Interstate-15 and head south for a few miles."

Once we got near The Bored Cactus, I knew I'd have to give a few wrong directions first to try to extend the time until we arrived.

And hopefully, give people time to show up.

That was assuming someone had heard me talk into my phone.

If not, this was all just a charade that was delaying our inevitable death.

CHAPTER 46

Valentine took a U-turn and found the nearest entrance to Interstate-15 and started heading south.

Emmy looked over at me at one point and I gave her the slightest of nods.

I was trying to tell her to trust me, but I'm sure she wondered why I was leading us to Victor's car.

"Is Trent alive?" I asked.

I'd been so concentrated on trying to give ourselves a shot at surviving, I'd forgotten to ask about my friend.

"For now," Valentine said.

Sam Waddle still hadn't said a word.

"What does that mean?"

"It means he's alive at this moment. But last I was told, he wasn't doing all that well."

"You had Ryan Mallory shoot him, didn't you?"

I was behind Valentine and couldn't see his face, but I thought I detected a slight flinch.

"Looks like you know more than I gave you credit for."

"And Howard Kloss will back up his bullshit story of Trent reaching for his gun?"

"Ding ding ding!"

"I've got another question. If Waddle, Mallory, and Kloss were the officers to show up at Emmy's apartment, why didn't you just take the whole journal?"

"Wow. You know about that? I'm truly impressed by your investigative skills."

"That's not an answer."

"If a friend or family member said Emmy had a journal, and then it went missing, the officers at the scene would have to answer a few questions. If just the incriminating pages were torn out, and then the journal was turned in, we were above reproach."

"And you knew the part talking about Junior Remington would be at the end of the journal."

"Very good, Quint. You do realize I can never let you go now."

"You weren't going to anyway. You're the biggest coward of all. Always making someone else do your dirty work. Victor Smith. Ryan Mallory. Howard Kloss. The mute in the front seat."

"Not this time, Quint. I'll pull the trigger myself."

"How do you possibly think you'll get away with this?"

"I'll figure something out," Valentine said. "The only thing I know for sure is that I wouldn't get away with this if I allowed you two to go free."

"Let the courts decide. Explain to them that Junior Remington made you do it."

Valentine let out a loud cackle.

"Junior. Now that's funny. I might see the inside of a courthouse, but I won't be seeing the inside of a jail cell."

How was he so confident?

"You have a judge on your payroll, don't you?"

"You're so close and yet, so far away."

"Why don't you explain it to me then?"

"No, I don't think I will. When is the exit? I'm growing tired of our conversation. And do you know what I think? I think Victor's phone has been powered down for months and nobody is ever going to find it. So if we don't arrive at our destination soon, I think we'll just go find our own plot of land in the desert and dig a couple of ditches."

I couldn't delay any longer. There would be no point in giving Heath Bennett or someone else more time if we were going to be killed in the meantime.

"It's the next exit," I said.

There were four people in the car, but only three had spoken.

"How about you, Samuel?" I said. "No chance of pulling out your gun and turning it on Valentine?"

I saw him shrug.

"Fat chance. I just wish I'd been given the job of doing away with that little piece of pie in the backseat. I'd have made some alone time with her first."

I looked at Emmy who was so thoroughly disgusted she couldn't muster anything to say.

I couldn't let it stand.

"You're a poor excuse for a human," I said. "You take orders from this asshole and then try to act like you're some tough guy to a young woman."

I expected a response from Sam Waddle, but Valentine spoke instead.

"Careful, Quint. I might just tell him to blow your heads off right here and now."

Sam Waddle took out his gun and twirled it around on his fingers. He then aimed it at Emmy's head for several seconds.

It was petrifying.

And yet, seeing Emmy wince, I was more furious than scared. I wanted to rip the heart out of both men in the front seat.

"Alright, Sam, you can put your gun back in your holster for now. Don't worry, I'll let you use it soon."

Sam Waddle blew on the top of his gun as he lowered it.

"To be continued," he said.

Bo Valentine took the next exit.

"Take a right off the freeway," I said.

Valentine turned around.

"Enjoy these last few minutes, you two," he said, laughing as he did.

CHAPTER 47

I couldn't risk delaying any longer.

Sam Waddle pointing the gun at Emmy had ended that. He was a maniac and might just shoot us before we got to Victor Smith's van.

"Take another right," I said.

"Aren't we doubling back the way we came?" Valentine asked.

"You're getting what you want," I said. "We're only a few miles away."

We rode in silence for the next minute.

"Up ahead is a place called The Bored Cactus motel. Take a left and go past it."

I panicked for an instant, trying to remember what I'd said into my phone.

'If you are facing the hotel, go to your right.'

That was correct, but coming from a different freeway exit had thrown me off. If I'd given the wrong directions, we stood no chance.

"Keep going?" Valentine asked.

"Yes. We're going to follow this road for a few miles."

"You know, now that I think about it, I don't think I'm even going to see the inside of a courthouse. Who can possibly rat on me? Victor Smith? He's dead. Lyle Banks? He did me a big favor by blasting a hole in his head. Sam, here? He won't say a damn thing. That leaves Trent, who is on death's doorstep and you two, who are even closer."

Valentine laughed loudly.

I almost mentioned Emmy's parents or Duncan, but didn't want to give Valentine any ideas. The madman might go after them after he finished with us.

"All that's left would be circumstantial," Valentine continued. "Lyle Banks could have tied it all together. I really do owe you and Trent a big thank you for that, Quint. Actually, why don't you thank Trent yourself, seeing as the two of you will be reunited in death sometime very soon."

I wanted to scream. I couldn't take any more of Bo Valentine. A true sociopath.

I wasn't a very religious man, but I prayed with all my heart that someone was waiting at Victor Smith's van. Ready to save us.

"I've got a feeling Trent is going to pull through this," I said. "And you're going to be fucked when that happens."

"Once I dispose of you two, I think I'll double back to the hospital. I might just put Sam here on Trent's door detail. Maybe tell him to smother Trent with a pillow when he gets the chance. No, I don't think Trent will be making some late inning comeback. Plus, you two will be dead. What do you care?"

Valentine's horrendous laugh permeated the cop car.

"I originally thought this might have just been one terrible plan gone wrong," I said. "I no longer think that. I think you've been a corrupt criminal for a long time."

"Bingo," he said. "This won't be the first ditch I've dug."

Had I been over my head from the very beginning? It was looking that way.

I glanced over at Emmy who was turning ashen white. I nodded at her, trying to keep my mind focused.

Had we made a mistake in not trying to run for it at the motel? I still didn't think so. There was no back exit from Emmy's room and the cop car was parked right in front. We'd have been apprehended - or shot - in seconds and wouldn't have been able to get Emmy's live version of events, even though it was way shorter than what I'd planned.

At the very least, if we were shot and buried in the desert, I hoped Emmy's words had gotten out to the public.

I reprimanded myself.

Stop thinking like that! This isn't over!

I had to believe our escape was still possible.

We were less than a minute from reaching Victor Smith's van.

I'd let Valentine pass it by a hundred yards or so. It would give us a longer walk and give people more time, if there were any.

But as I looked around, I didn't see any cars or signs of human life.

It looked like my plan had failed. Emmy and I were going to be killed out in the desert and it would be all my fault.

"How close are we?" Valentine asked.

"Up about a hundred yards," I said.

"I can't wait," Waddle said.

I ignored him.

We drove by the two trees and I waited a good twenty seconds.

I couldn't stall any longer.

"Park here," I said.

"Plenty of good spots available," Valentine said, alluding to how desolate it was. "This will be a nice final resting spot for you two."

Valentine kept the police car parked in the middle of the road. He exited the car at the same time as Waddle.

I turned to Emmy and whispered.

"There might be people here. Be alert."

She stared at me intensely, letting me know she was ready to fight.

Valentine opened my door. There's no way he could have heard me, but he did see me whisper in her ear.

"You trying to say a sweet goodbye to Emmy here? Shame this beautiful girl with these long legs will be exiting this world shortly. Hope you got a chance to tap that, Quint."

I wanted to say *"Fuck you"* with all my heart, but I thought he might just kill me then and there.

"Let's just get this over with," I said.

Valentine had me turn around and then grabbed me by the back of the handcuffs, yanking me out of the police car.

Sam Waddle did the same with Emmy on her side of the car.

"Alright, you two, let's get walking."

And we started heading toward the van.

CHAPTER 48

My eyes darted around, hoping to spot something I'd missed on the drive in.

No such luck. My heart continued to sink.

Both Valentine and Waddle had their guns pointed at us. Trying to run would have been pointless.

Our wrists remained handcuffed and we were truly no threat to them at all.

Victor Smith's gun was buried by the tree on the left hand side. Not much good that was going to do us.

I tried to walk as slowly as I could, which didn't seem to piss off Valentine. It's like he was enjoying holding the moment over my head.

We were about halfway there, when Valentine spoke.

"Ah, I think I see the van. Poor Victor."

We walked closer.

"What a brilliant hiding spot. There's no way you could see the van from the road. Was this your idea, Emmy?"

"None of this was my idea," she said, ignoring the actual question at hand.

"I'm going to assume it was. Quint was nowhere near Vegas when this happened back in January. Funny, how some stranger Quint had never met, sits down with a drunken Junior, and it leads to a series of events which will end in Quint's death as well. By killing Victor Smith, you have ostensibly caused Quint's death, Emmy. Hope you'll think about that in these last few minutes."

Emmy looked sick.

Bo Valentine was despicable on every level.

We arrived at the van.

What now? I had no wallet to give him.

I could tell him it was in the van, but how much time would that give us? Sam Waddle would just break a window and within seconds, realize there was no wallet.

I stared at Emmy. I hadn't done my job. She'd been alive when I arrived, but through a series of bad decisions, her life was going to end because of me.

Don't give up, I told myself.

I realized we were all within inches of each other and hiding between a series of trees and the van. We were too hidden. If there was, by some small miracle, a police officer with their gun on us, he couldn't risk shooting. We needed to be further out in the open.

I thought of something. Emmy had told me she'd put the shovel, hoe, etc. in the back of Smith's van after she buried him.

"The phone is buried next to his body," I said. "You're going to need the shovel in the back of Smith's car."

Valentine looked at me.

I couldn't read his expression, but I knew he wouldn't turn down the chance to see where Victor Smith was buried. Plus, he undoubtedly wanted to get ahold of that phone.

Little did he know we were a good fifteen miles from Smith's actual final resting place, not that it did us any good.

"Sure. Let's see old Victor's bones." Valentine said. "Sam, break that window and get the stuff from the back of the van."

Sam Waddle covered his wrist with the blue of his police uniform and smashed the window. It shattered in one fell swoop.

Waddle opened the van door, hopped in the back, and emerged with a shovel and a hoe.

"Follow me," I said.

I'd delayed long enough to where someone coming from the Strip should be close. Maybe it was all a pipe dream, but I had to cling to it. It's all I had.

I was going to walk straight from the trees into the desert. If we stayed in the line of the trees, it's likely that Valentine and Waddle's vision would be blocked and wouldn't see another car arriving.

I led the way. Emmy was behind me. Valentine next. And finally, Sam Waddle.

I hoped to hear a gunshot ring out, but no such luck.

Once we'd walked around fifty yards, I stopped.

If we went any further, we'd be too far removed from the trees and we'd see the main road once again.

"This is the spot?" Valentine asked.

"Yes."

"How the hell do you know? Did Emmy show you?"

"She did. And I know it's fifty yards from the trees, on the left of this little cactus right here."

I pointed to some random cactus on the ground.

"Victor's body is buried here?"

"That's what I just said."

Valentine glared at me and then pointed at Sam.

"Get to work," he said.

Sam Waddle made quick work of the Las Vegas dirt. When I was digging up Victor Smith's body, all I had was a shovel. The hoe that Waddle worked with was loosening up the ground much quicker.

It meant we didn't have much time.

Within a few minutes, he was already a foot deep.

After about five minutes, he was three feet deep.

"Where's the body, Quint?" Valentine asked.

"Just a few more feet," I said, afraid to admit I'd finally run out of options.

"You know, Quint, I can tell you've been trying to prolong the inevitable, but your time has arrived. If Sam doesn't hit bone in the next two minutes, I'm going to kill you both."

Two minutes passed.

It felt like the hourglass to my life was on the last few grains of sand.

"You can stop, Sam. Victor's body isn't out here."

"It might have been a few feet further up," I said.

"Just stop, Quint. This is over. Just like your life."

Sam Waddle slowly stepped out of the now four foot hole.

I looked at Emmy.

"I'm so sorry, Emmy."

"I am too, Quint. Without me, you never would have been involved."

"Don't say that," I said. "This isn't your fault."

As Sam Waddle went to go pick up his gun and belt, which he'd left just outside of the hole he'd dug, Bo Valentine walked towards him.

In what felt like slow motion, Valentine took the gun from his holster, raised it to the back of Waddle's head, and pulled the trigger. Waddle never saw it coming.

I heard Emmy let out a gasp.

Sam Waddle's lifeless body tumbled over and slumped down into the hole he'd just dug.

Bo Valentine turned to us.

"Leave no loose ends," he said.

"That's some way you treat friends," I said.

"If it's any consolation, I'm about to treat my enemies the same way."

And then he raised his gun towards us and I knew my life was ending.

CHAPTER 49

I was too far from Bo Valentine. Charging him would be pointless.
And honestly, what was I going to do with my wrists handcuffed behind my back?

"Run, Emmy!" I yelled.

And threw my body in front of hers.

I closed my eyes and waited for the end, hoping by some miracle that Valentine's gun would jam and Emmy could escape.

It was a pipe dream and I knew that.

And then, I heard the sound of the gunshot.

∼

But I didn't feel anything. Valentine must have shot past me and killed Emmy. I didn't think I could bear seeing Emmy's lifeless body.

Afraid of what was waiting for me, but unable to stop myself, I opened my eyes.

And to my shock, Bo Valentine was no longer standing in front of me.

In fact, he was on the ground, gasping for air.

I felt Emmy's arms on my shoulders. I turned around and made sure she wasn't hit.

"I'm o-okay," she struggled to get out.

Emmy looked like she was in shock. That made two of us.

The gunshot I'd heard had not been fired by Bo Valentine. It had been fired at him.

I looked back down at Valentine. He had fallen on his back and was only a foot from the hole where Sam Waddle lay dead.

Valentine's gun had fallen about two feet from his hand. While he didn't appear to be in any shape to grab and fire it, I couldn't chance it. I walked over and kicked the gun several feet away.

I looked down at Valentine, feeling not one iota of pity. He'd been seconds, if not milliseconds, from killing both of us.

He tried to take in a small breath, but couldn't complete it. He didn't have much longer.

Emmy came over and looked down at Valentine, but quickly turned away.

This was all too much for her.

We both heard a noise coming from behind us.

Two uniformed police officers were running from the trees in our direction, already within yards of us.

They arrived by our side a few seconds later.

A tall, dark haired man spoke first.

"I'm Heath Bennett."

"You saved our lives," Emmy said.

"I'm not sure any words would be sufficient right now," I said. "I owe you everything."

"It's a good thing I called you back," he said.

"Sure was."

Heath took out a key from his belt buckle.

"Turn around, you two."

He unlocked our handcuffs and that's when everything hit home. Against all odds, we were going to live

Emmy went and hugged Heath.

His partner had gone to the side of Bo Valentine.

Valentine's breathing had become even more labored.

The second officer tried to make a call, surely for an ambulance, but he couldn't get any service.

Not that it mattered. As we looked down, we realized Bo Valentine was on borrowed time.

He was trying to say something, but nothing would come out.

And then in an instant, it was all over.

There was no doubt.

His eyes were unmoving and his body sat motionless.

Bo Valentine was dead.

CHAPTER 50

The sun disappeared behind the two trees as we waited for an ambulance, many more police officers, and undoubtedly, the media.

The officer whose name I hadn't picked up had left us to get better reception and call it in.

Emmy was coming out of her shock, but still had an almost quizzical look about her.

"Can I go wait under the trees?" she asked Heath Bennett.

"No, let's wait here," he said. "This crime scene is going to be picked apart with a fine-toothed comb. Let's just wait here until the cavalry arrives."

"Can I sit down at least?"

"Sure."

I joined her. Emmy had been tougher than you could have expected any young woman to be, but she looked like she might break.

"We'll get out of here soon," I said.

"I know. Thanks, Quint."

"We'll get you a suite at the Wynn."

"You know what I'll do?"

"What's that?"

"Take a two hour bath. I've been stuck taking gross showers in shitty motels for four months now."

"You've earned it," I said.

"Yeah, I have," she said.

And she started crying.

∽

After I'd consoled Emmy for a few minutes, I walked over to Heath Bennett.

"You saved our lives, Officer Bennett. I'll never be able to thank you enough. Thanks for believing in me."

"Call me Heath. I think we can be on a first name basis after what just happened."

I smiled.

"Of course."

"And you're welcome. You deserve a lot of the credit."

"I'm assuming you heard me say this location."

"I did. And it's a good thing you did. Your live feed cut out a few seconds later."

"How about Emmy's?"

"The last thing we heard her say was 'I surrender.' Then hers cut out."

I looked over at Emmy. It's amazing how lucky we were to be alive.

"And then you drove this way?"

"It took a minute to convince Officer Scala to join. I thought I might well need a second officer."

"All the other officers stayed at the precinct?"

"They didn't know about it. I couldn't risk playing it for the entire office, Quint. I listened on my own computer."

"It doesn't matter. You came and that's all that matters. You saved our lives in the process."

"You're welcome."

"You really did wait for the last second."

"We had been here less than a minute. When we arrived, Valentine was standing between you and Emmy. Keep in mind, all I'd heard from the recording was you turn yourself in. I couldn't just shoot the Chief of Police on that alone."

Emmy had gotten off the ground and joined our conversation.

"And then you saw him shoot Sam Waddle?" she asked.

"That's right. And he turned the gun in your direction. I certainly had probable cause at that point."

"You fired the shot?" I asked. "Or Officer Scala?"

"I did."

"Thank you," I said for what felt like the fifth time.

"You're a hero," Emmy said.

"I've got a million questions for you two, but it can wait."

"Thanks," Emmy said. "I'm not sure I'm up for them right now."

"I understand, but they will be coming soon."

It was then that we heard the first ambulance. And a few seconds later, the sounds of multiple police cars.

My eyes drifted to Bo Valentine. I'd be amazed for the rest of my life that we'd escaped with our lives. He was literally a split second from killing us.

And there was a trail of dead in his wake.

And likely there would be a long investigation into all that happened.

But I decided to focus on the positive.

I grabbed both Heath Bennett and Emmy Peters by their shoulders, bringing them in for a group hug.

CHAPTER 51

The next several hours were a blur.

I remember the paramedics arriving and being shocked at how many cop cars followed. It felt like there were twenty of them. Maybe more.

I answered questions for a good thirty minutes until the sun was starting to set. Then I was taken to the main LVPD precinct on the Strip.

That's when it all started to run together. I could only answer so many questions on Bo Valentine and the rest of the people involved before it felt like I was watching a rerun.

Emmy had ridden in a different police car. I assumed because they didn't want the possibility of us getting our "stories straight." I'm sure that's standard police tactic, but we had nothing to hide. They'd know that soon enough.

I imagine we both had aspects of the investigation that the LVPD was interested in. Obviously, Emmy could fully describe what happened with Victor Smith in the desert and her subsequent four months on the run.

For me, they'd be more interested where Trent Ebbing fit in and what exactly Lyle Banks told us before he shot himself.

They touched on everything, every person I talked to, every suspicion I had, every piece of evidence I'd gathered.

There was a thirty minute span where they only wanted to know what Lyle Banks had said.

And yet, I never complained. I understood how necessary and important this all was.

I sat there, patiently answering their questions for hour upon hour, and only interrupted twice.

Early on, I asked if Trent Ebbing was still alive. They said he had come to and was likely to live. I was overjoyed.

While I was obviously grateful that Emmy and I had lived, it would have been very tough on me if Trent had died. I thanked my lucky stars.

My guess was that Trent's career as a police officer was likely over, but seeing what I had from the LVPD, maybe that was a blessing. Although, the world could use more good cops like Trent.

A few hours later, I asked if I could call my girlfriend - I didn't mention we were broken up - and my mother. Much to my surprise, they said that both of them had arrived at the LVPD in the last thirty minutes.

I was floored.

They must have heard I was on the news and when they couldn't get ahold of me, decided to fly out to Vegas. Knowing both of their personalities, I shouldn't have been surprised. I asked if I could see them and one of the officers interviewing me said that would have to wait. I understood.

Mercifully, my interviews ended around midnight. The rotating officers who interviewed me seemed to believe everything I said. I'm sure they'd follow up and verify all I'd said. I was fine with that.

I'd spoken nothing but the truth.

CHAPTER 52

SUNDAY

At 12:19 a.m. on Sunday morning, I walked out of the main precinct of the Las Vegas Police Department.

The first two faces I saw were Cara and my mother.

They came and hugged me at the same time, reminding me of my other three-way hug hours earlier with Emmy and Heath Bennett.

There'd been entirely too much hugging lately, yet oddly, none had felt out of place.

Cara spoke first.

"I'm sure you've got quite the tale to tell."

"I do. Can we wait though? I just spent hours telling and re-telling it."

"Of course. I'm just glad you're alright."

"Does this mean you two are back together?" my mother asked.

"Jeez, Mom, not a *I'm glad you're okay, Quint* first?"

She laughed.

"Sorry. Of course, I'm glad you're okay, Quint!"

"Thanks, Mom."

I spoke to them both.

"We'll have a lot of time to talk when we get back to the Bay Area. Which I'd like to do as soon as possible."

"Do you have a follow up with the police?"

"Yeah, tomorrow morning. After that, I'll hopefully be free to go."

"Should I set up a flight back for tomorrow afternoon?" Cara asked.

"Why don't you hold off. I need to meet up with Emmy and her family. I'll call them tomorrow morning and find out what time and then we can set up a flight."

"Alright. We're staying at Caesars. Do you want to come stay with us for the night?"

What I wanted to do was go see Trent Ebbing at the hospital, but the officers had told me it was too.late to see visitors. That would have to wait until the morning.

"Don't take this the wrong way, but not tonight. I'll come by tomorrow morning."

"We understand," Cara said.

And I believed her. My mother, on the other hand, probably couldn't understand why I wanted to be alone. Once she heard all I'd been through, she might understand why I needed a good night's sleep.

And it's not like that would be some cure-all. I was going to carry the brunt of what happened for a very long time.

"We got a rental car. At least let us drop you off at your hotel," my mother said.

"That would be great. I'm staying at The Cosmo."

As we started walking toward their car, my mother walked ahead of us and I knew why. She wanted to let Cara and me talk through our problems.

"I'm sorry the way we ended," Cara said.

"I am too."

"Can't believe that was only last Friday," she said. "It feels like a month ago."

"Well, nine days in Vegas kind of feels like a month if you know what I mean."

"Now that we're past midnight, isn't it ten days?" Cara asked.

"I finished the case in nine days. I'm now on vacation."

"You're a weird guy, Quint," Cara said and hugged me.

"Shhh, don't tell anyone."

CHAPTER 53

I was woken up the next morning by a phone call from Chance Peters.
"Hello?"

"I told you Emmy should have stayed with us," he said.

It took me longer than it should have to realize he was joking.

In my defense, the phone call had jolted me awake.

"I'm kidding, Quint! You're a literal life-saver. You've brought our daughter back to us and we'll never, ever forget it."

"You're welcome, Chance. I was only doing what I was paid to do. No, that doesn't sound right. I was only doing what was right by you, Liz, and Emmy."

"Well, thank you, from the bottom of my heart."

"Of course."

"Listen, we're going to do a sort of welcome back party for Emmy at 1:00 today. I know it's kind of all of a sudden..."

"Are you sure about this? A lot happened yesterday, and I'll leave it at that."

"It was her idea. We're taking her back to Los Angeles tonight for a while, and she wanted to say goodbye to everyone."

"Alright, as long as she's fine with it. I'm flying back tonight as well."

"So you'll come to the gathering today?"

"There's no way I'd miss it," I said. "Can I bring two people?"

"Of course. Who?"

"My mother and my girlfriend," I said, finding it easier than explaining we were broken up.

"I can't wait to meet them. Call me when you're downstairs and I'll come let you up."

"Just like old times," I joked.

"Indeed. Thanks for everything, Quint."

~

Yesterday had been such an ordeal that I didn't feel like driving. I didn't trust my reaction times.

So I went downstairs and sat in the cab line.

"Where to?" the man asked.

I gave him my customary dollar.

"Sunrise Hospital on Maryland Parkway," I said.

He reiterated what I said to the cab driver. A true middleman.

We arrived at the hospital a short ride later.

Sunrise Hospital was brown and white and had several buildings, each looking to be four or five stories. The design was forgettable, but my guess was that most hospitals tried not to stand out aesthetically.

I found out Trent was in Room #205 and I took the elevator to the second floor. There was no police officer watching his door. Bo Valentine likely could have sent Sam Waddle in there to suffocate Trent.

Think pleasant thoughts!

I had to stop focusing on the past. It was over and all my friends were alive. That's what mattered.

There was a woman in the room when I peered in, so I sat outside and waited.

I realized that I knew very little about Trent Ebbing. Was that his wife? His girlfriend? Did he have kids?

I guess none of that really mattered. He'd been there for me when I needed him. That's what made him a friend, not how much I knew about him.

She left a few minutes later and apparently didn't recognize me. Good. I was hoping my name wasn't plastered all over the T.V.s. I'd already dealt with that after the Bay Area Butcher case.

I walked in and the first thing I saw was a big smile from Trent. Unfortunately, the second thing I saw was him wince.

"Damn," he said. "Smiling isn't supposed to hurt."

"How are you, Trent?"

"I feel like I've been shot," he said and tried to laugh, which elicited another wince.

"Maybe wait until you're out of the hospital to work on your stand up comedy act," I said. "And don't laugh at that."

Trent let out a sly smile.

"I think," he said, "if I live to be a hundred years old, I will never forget yesterday."

"That goes for Emmy and myself as well," I said.

"I have no doubt. Once I came to, I asked about you guys. I heard you were pretty close to joining me in the hospital."

"Actually, we were pretty close to being in the morgue."

"I'm sorry."

"Don't be. You did all you could and more. I'm just glad you're going to be alright."

"It will be a long process, but I'll get through it. And then I'll start thinking about my new line of work."

"I'm sure you'll be great at it," I said.

"Thanks, Quint."

"Listen, I'm flying back later tonight, but I imagine I'll be back in the coming days. Another interview with the LVPD or something else will pop up. Can I take you out to dinner? You can invite a loved one."

"You sure you want to meet my wife? She might blame you for having me stuck at home for the next several months."

I laughed.

"I'll take my chances."

"Dinner it is then. Once I get my phone back, I'll call you and we'll set something up when you return."

"Call me if there is anything you need, Trent. You really went beyond the call of duty for Emmy and myself."

A doctor came in and told me I had to leave soon. I almost complained I'd only been there a few minutes, but Trent's health was obviously more important.

"Emmy's father called the hospital today," Trent said. "Asked if there was any way I could make it to her get together today."

"I'm guessing not."

"Doctor said no. Actually, she said, '*Not a chance in hell!*'"

"Probably for the best."

"Certainly. Emmy's father also offered to pay for all of my medical bills, but I told him that's covered by the LVPD."

"Nice of him to offer."

"Sure was."

The doctor came back in to check if I was gone yet.

"I should go," I said. "I'm hoping for a quick recovery."

"I'll get better, Quint. Don't you worry about me."

I was afraid to hug him, so I just extended my hand. He shook it and even that seemed to cause some pain.

"Thanks for everything, Trent."

"You're welcome, Quint. Take care of yourself."

"No, you take care of yourself."

We both smiled and I left a few seconds later.

～

I called Duncan on my cab ride back from the hospital.

I thanked him for all he'd done and apologized for not meeting him at McDonalds like we planned.

"None of that matters. You got Emmy home safe, and that's all that I care about. Although, once you didn't show at McDonald's, I was a scared old man."

"Everything happened so fast yesterday. I couldn't keep all of my commitments."

I heard Duncan laugh.

"You're a funny guy, Quint."

"What happened with the cops that showed up at your house?" I asked.

"Old Duncan outfoxed them. There was no way I was going into their precinct. They might have done to me what they did to Trent."

"I just left the hospital. He's going to be okay."

"I heard and I'm utterly grateful. Remember, I'm the one who put him in touch with you. It would have been hard for me to forgive myself if he'd ended up dead."

"Will I see you at the Wynn today?"

"I wouldn't miss it for the world. And I genuinely mean that. To get to hug my niece again, when for so long I'd thought she was dead, will be one of the great moments of my life."

"That's beautiful to hear," I said.

"You played a big part in it."

"Thanks."

"See you later today."

"See you, Duncan."

~

My next stop was to the LVPD for another set of questions. Round two went much quicker and I was out of there in an hour. I told them that Valentine said it wasn't the first ditch he'd dug. They said they'd be investigating everything about the man.

I found out some information myself. Ryan Mallory and Howard Kloss had been arrested for their parts. And Mallory was going to be charged with attempted murder for shooting Trent.

While the investigation would go on for weeks, I assumed all the "bad guys" had been caught or were dead.

Bo Valentine. Sam Waddle. Victor Smith. Junior Remington and Lyle Banks, both by their own hands. Ryan Mallory and Howard Kloss had been arrested.

I walked out of the precinct with a promise to keep in touch. I told the officer that I had plans on coming back to visit Trent Ebbing and we could do another interview then if they'd like.

He said that would be fine.

~

By the time I got back to The Cosmo and texted back some friends who'd reached out, it was time to get ready for the get together at the Wynn.

I called Cara and told her that Caesars was close to the Wynn and I'd just meet them there.

I took a shower and grabbed my last clean shirt from my closet. It was a little flashy, a green button up dress shirt with some sort of flower on the side of it. It wasn't a Tommy Bahama, but might as well be, and was certainly something that Duncan would wear.

I would happily wear it.

CHAPTER 54

E mmy's "party" was a riotous affair.

It started with Chance Peters coming down to let me, Cara, and my mother up.

He gave my mother a bear hug that hopefully didn't have my Dad rolling over in his grave. Cara got the same treatment.

I guess I couldn't blame the man.

Having Emmy back in his life would make it worthwhile again. It had surely been a horrific four months.

Once we arrived on the top floor, Chance told the women the room number, and asked me to hold back.

He took a check from his pocket and handed it over.

It was $20,000. Sure, the man was rich, but it was still extremely generous.

"Thanks so much, Chance."

"I could give you a million and it still wouldn't be enough."

"In that case…"

Chance laughed.

"You're going to be a great private detective. If I gave you a million dollars, you'd never become that. This is me doing you a favor."

"You suck at giving favors," I said.

Chance laughed even louder this time.

We made our way towards the party.

And as we did, I came to a decision. I was going to give Trent Ebbing half of the money. Sure, he'd have his medical bills paid for, and surely get a full pension after being shot on duty, but it was still the right thing to do.

The man had almost died while helping me out. Now it was my turn to help him.

We entered the suite and Liz Peters was smiling at my mother.

"Your son forever changed the course of our lives," she said.

My mother blushed as if I'd just won the Nobel Peace Prize.

"Thank you," she said. "I haven't always loved his decision to become a PI, but hearing something like this makes it all worthwhile."

It was a nice moment.

There were streamers zig-zagging through the suite and it did have a festive atmosphere.

I saw Emmy across the room and waved. I imagined this would be one of her last days as a platinum blonde.

She was talking to someone I didn't recognize and I could say hello later.

I saw many familiar faces at the party, several of which I knew to be Emmy's friends.

I apologized to Carrie Granger and told her I was only doing my job.

"You don't have to apologize," she said. "It worked out for the best."

We talked for several minutes and she seemed like a new girl, much more carefree. She no longer had the burden of being the only person who knew Emmy was alive.

I asked her if *Old School Vegas* would continue even with Junior Remington dead.

My question caught her by surprise.

"I hope so," she said.

Kenneth Croy was there and I was happy to see it.

I saw Chance Peters, who was a little drunk at this point, lift Kenneth up in the air. Considering he'd labeled Kenneth a suspect early on, it was a sight to behold.

Kenneth and I talked for a bit and got along well, but he felt like a fish out of water at the party. Maybe it was because Emmy was moving back to Los Angeles for the time being. Or, maybe it was that he finally realized she was a bit too young for him.

Whatever the case, he looked like a lost soul, and I didn't expect their relationship to continue.

I cornered Duncan and tried to get a few final pointers about the PI business. I'd be a better PI going forward because of Duncan's help. There was no doubt about that.

"I'm always a phone call away," he said.

"Ask and you shall receive," I said. "Boy, are you going to regret saying that."

Duncan laughed.

"On the contrary, it will be nice to see you grow as a PI. And let's be honest, you've already worked the case of a lifetime and came out smelling like roses."

"Not sure that's the smell I'd go with, but thanks."

I told him that I might be taking Trent and his wife out for dinner when I returned.

"I accept," he said.

"I hadn't even invited you yet."

"But you were going to."

As usual, Duncan was right.

~

One person who was missing was Heath Bennett. He was undoubtedly still working on our case, but this party would not have been possible if it weren't for him and his partner, Officer Scala.

I'd talked to Tom Butler and my live feed had cut out early on for him as well. I wasn't going to get any help on that end. Without Bennett, both Emmy and I would be dead.

On my return to Vegas, I vowed to spend more time thanking Bennett. Maybe invite him to the dinner with Trent and Duncan.

~

As the reunion progressed, I kept an eye on the two women crashing the party, Cara and my mother. They seemed to be smiling the whole time and just happy to be a part of it. I have no doubt my mother was soaking in the good vibes that came with telling people that I was her son.

I watched from afar as Emmy and Cara talked. I wondered if Cara introduced herself as my girlfriend or not.

Was there a small part of Cara that was jealous? Maybe. Obviously, Emmy and my relationship was always going to be platonic, but we were also inextricably linked forever.

Not many people go through what we did. I hoped we would remain friends through the years. But if at some point, she preferred to not focus on all that happened and pushed me away, I'd understand.

~

After Cara stopped talking to her, I approached Emmy.

She was looking out on the Strip pensively.

"I saw you met Cara," I said.

"She's delightful. What were you doing breaking up with her?" Emmy said and smiled.

Cara was the logical guess, but it was probably my mother who'd told her.

"I'll make it all better when we get back to the Bay Area."

"You better. She's way too good for you."

"If I had a penny for everyone who told me that."

"I heard my Dad gave you a few pennies."

"He was very generous."

"For what you did for this family, it was nothing."

"I know. He basically said the same."

"Are we going to stay friends when this is all over?"

"I'd like to. But if you just want to forget everything and move on, I'll understand."

I'd said almost verbatim what I'd been thinking minutes earlier.

"That will not be the case. We'll always be friends."

"Glad to hear it."

She looked towards Kenneth Croy.

"I don't think that will be true of everyone. Think I'm going to start dating a guy my own age."

Another thing I was right about.

"I'd say that's probably a good call. But Kenneth is alright."

"Yeah, he is. I'll let him down lightly."

I smiled.

"What time are you guys leaving tonight?" I asked.

"Eight. You?"

"8:30. I might see you at the airport."

"You've been told this a million times by now, but thank you for everything, Quint. You not only saved my life, but in a different way, saved my Mom's and Dad's too."

We looked over at Chance who was doing some primitive form of dancing.

"Wish I hadn't saved those dance moves."

Emmy laughed.

"Why don't you go join him?" I asked.

And I watched as Emmy walked over and began cutting up a rug with her father.

∾

As the party was wrapping up, I went and talked to Cara.

She'd been great, allowing me to make my rounds, knowing I had a lot of people to talk to.

"How are you holding up?" she asked.

"It's been nice to see everyone again. I spent the early part of my trip asking a lot of these people some tough questions. I guess I'm forgiven since Emmy got home safe."

"She's a great person, Quint. I had a nice talk with her."

"I saw. She told me I was an idiot for breaking up with you."

Cara looked genuinely puzzled.

"I didn't tell her."

"My Mom," I said.

And we both laughed.

"Listen, Cara, I shouldn't have to tell you this, but I will. Nothing ever happened with Emmy and me. It was strictly a job."

"I never, ever suspected that. You're wrong about one thing, though."

"What's that?"

"This was more than just a job. You gave this family more joy than you'll ever realize."

"Did you see Chance's dance moves?"

Cara laughed. "Is that what you call them?"

"Liz looked mortified. In a good way," I said.

Cara turned serious.

"Quint, I want to tell you something as well. I was wrong about trying to get you not to take this case. Look at what you accomplished. If we get back together, I'll be proud of the fact that I'm dating a PI. You're going to be a great one."

And then, in front of the entire party to see, I kissed Cara long and hard on the lips.

CHAPTER 55

W e arrived at McCarran International Airport around 7:00 p.m.
Sure enough, once we got to our gate, Emmy, Chance, and Liz were waiting at the one right next to us.

I guess it couldn't end any other way.

We all exchanged pleasantries. I could tell that they really enjoyed the company of my mother and Cara. Maybe Emmy and I wouldn't be the only friendship that lasted.

"And guess what?" Chance said.

"What?" my mother eagerly asked.

"Liz hit a junior jackpot. That's what it's called, right?"

"A mini-jackpot," Liz said. "On the quarter slots. Paid $500 dollars."

I could have been a party pooper and thought 'the rich get richer', but I was happy for Liz. I had come to really like this family.

I sat down next to Cara. I was exhausted and couldn't wait to sleep in my own bed tonight.

I decided that my brief one night stand with the woman named Heather would forever stay a secret. We were broken up, after all.

I couldn't wait to make love to Cara tonight. We hadn't made it official, but me kissing her in front of everyone had all but confirmed we were back together.

Chance kept talking about the junior jackpot as he repeatedly called it.

It made me think of Junior Remington.

Who, even though he was at the core of this case, I'd never interacted with. And he'd taken the cowardly way out, just like Lyle Banks.

I thought back to the conversation when Bo Valentine had mentioned that Junior ordered him to kill Emmy. Eliminate was the verb he used.

Only, he hadn't mentioned Junior.

I went back over the conversation again. He had never said Junior.

I started to panic.

"Emmy, can I talk to you?" I said.

"Of course."

"I'll be right back, Cara."

"No problem."

I walked over to the slot machines that were ubiquitous at McCarron airport. Emmy followed me. We found a little area where no one else was sitting.

"What is it, Quint?"

"When I first met you, you told me that no one calls Junior Remington anything other than Junior."

"Yeah, that's right."

"You're positive?"

"Yeah."

"Not Remington or Sidney the second or anything like that?"

"No. His father was either Sidney or just Remington. But when you were talking about his son, you said Junior."

I took a deep breath.

"What is it, Quint?" Emmy asked.

"Valentine told us he got the order from Remington. He did not say Junior."

"You're sure?" Emmy asked.

"I'm positive. Could that be a mistake on his part?"

"Jesus. No, I don't think so. Everyone knows that Junior is Junior, even someone who just met him. He introduces himself as Junior and corrects someone if they call him Sidney or Remington. For someone like Bo Valentine, who's likely known him for years, he would absolutely be Junior."

"Fuck," I said.

"Are you saying what I think you're saying?"

"Is it that crazy to think the call to kill you came from Sidney Remington? He was the boss after all. Even if Junior had the job title of running The Remington, we know who was in charge. Maybe he had a recording of Junior's office or maybe Junior told him what he'd divulged to you. What I do know is that Valentine said Remington ordered him to do it."

"This is insane."

I saw Chance Peters walking in our direction.

"Don't say anything," I whispered.

"Is everything alright, you guys?"

"Fine, Dad. Just saying goodbye to Quint."

"We're boarding now honey, so come back over. We'll make sure we see Quint soon, his mother and Cara as well."

"Alright, I'm coming, Dad."

Chance Peters walked back to the gate.

"I've got to go," Emmy said.

"I understand. Let me keep recreating the conversation with Valentine. Maybe I'm just not in my right mind."

"Let's hope so."

I said it to appease Emmy, but I knew I was thinking straight.

"Bye, Emmy. Safe travels."

She turned to go and then swiveled back around.

"You know what? I don't want to hear any more about this. I think I'm fine with letting it be."

"You're sure?"

"I'm positive. I've been through enough."

She was certainly right about that.

"Alright. I'll never mention it again."

"Thanks for everything, Quint."

"You're welcome. Take care, Emmy."

And she walked back towards the gate.

~

The Peters boarded a few minutes later and neither Cara nor my mother seemed to notice I was on edge.

I continued going back over our conversation with Bo Valentine.

I kept remembering him saying to Emmy something along the lines of '*I got a phone call from Remington to eliminate you.*' It was indisputable that he'd said Remington and not Junior. A few seconds later, he'd said, '*Fucking Remington.*' He still had yet to use the name Junior.

At that point, I said something to Valentine, basically suggesting that he should turn himself in, that maybe Junior Remington had forced Valentine's hand. He laughed and said, '*Junior. Now that's funny.*'

It didn't register at the time. Was Valentine laughing at the idea of Junior ordering him around?

Was Junior, the one that Emmy described as buffoonish, going to give orders to the Las Vegas Chief of Police?

It seemed unlikely.

But he might take orders from a real estate magnate who owned half the city...

~

My mind began wandering to a really dark place. Could Sidney Remington have killed his own son and made it look like a suicide? He would have known that Junior was a liability and everything would be coming back to him unless he took matters into his own hand.

If that crazy, morbid idea were in fact true, everything had worked out perfectly for Sidney Remington.

His son was gone. Bo Valentine was gone. Everyone else was gone.

And no one would suspect him.

My head was spinning.

A few minutes later, our plane started boarding.

"So what's next?" Cara asked as we stood in line, my mother right next to us.

"As far as what?"

Although trying to carry on a conversation, my mind was still focused on Sidney Remington.

"As far as your next PI case. It's going to be hard to top this one," Cara said.

"I'll probably take a case in the Bay Area. Hopefully something small," I said, my mind still elsewhere.

"I know you well, Quint. You're still thinking about what happened here. Are you done with this case? " she asked.

The whole trip flashed before my eyes. It felt like ages since meeting Kenneth Croy on that first night. Duncan. Chance and Liz. The all-time shock of seeing Emmy alive. Trent. Lyle Banks and going on the run. Valentine and being close to death. Heath Bennett saving our lives.

And finally, with my suspicions of Sidney Remington, everything came full circle.

It was quite the whirlwind.

Three questions quickly popped into my mind.

Did I have any real evidence that Sidney Remington was involved? Was Bo Valentine saying "*Remington*" instead of "*Junior*" enough to get a detective to re-investigate the case? Would the LVPD prefer this investigation be wrapped up quickly?

I feared the first two questions were a no. And the last one was almost definitively a yes.

Cara nudged me in the shoulder.

"Quint, I asked if you were done with this case."

"I think so," I said. "But never say never."

THE END

ALSO BY BRIAN O'SULLIVAN

Thanks so much for reading *NINE DAYS IN VEGAS*!

Being a self-published author, your support is crucial to my success. Give yourself a pat on the back and I hope you'll tell a friend or eight about my novels :)

Quint Adler, P.I., the 5th Quint novel will be out later this year and is available for pre-order on Kindle.

If you have not read the first three in the Quint series, what are you waiting for?

They are:

Book 1: *Revenge at Sea*

Book 2: *The Bay Area Butcher*

Book 3: *Hollywood Murder Mystery*

My other novels include a personal favorite, *The Bartender*! It's exciting as hell and hope you'll pick up a copy :)

And if you like political thrillers, make sure to check out my two-part series, *The Puppeteer* and *The Patsy.*

Finally, I'd be honored if you left a review for *NINE DAYS IN VEGAS* on Amazon for me. Cheers!

Thanks for your continued support! Means more than you will ever know.

Sincerely,

Brian O'Sullivan

ABOUT THE AUTHOR

Brian O'Sullivan is the author of seven novels and one short story. *NINE DAYS IN VEGAS* is the fourth novel of the Quint Adler Series, with *QUINT ADLER, P.I.* set to be released later this year.

Brian lives and writes in the Bay Area and usually heads to Los Angeles or Las Vegas when he wants to let loose.

Follow him on social media by clicking here:

instagram.com/osullivanauthor

Made in the USA
Coppell, TX
31 August 2021